Carolyn Beasley is an award-winning fiction writer.

The Fingerprint Thief

Also by Carolyn Beasley

The Memory of Marble (short stories)

THE FINGERPRINT THIEF

Carolyn Beasley

SNIPER BOOKS

Sniper Books

Typeset in Garamond

Cover design & photography
© 2018 Sniper Books

Sniper Books

The Fingerprint Thief

1

The killer had removed her fingerprints.

My task was to get them back.

To the practitioners of forensic science, I was insignificant. Not a medical examiner who revived the secrets of a corpse's last moment, never the hard bitten detective who read body language to trick a suspect into confession. Merely the 'dabs girl' who saw only the latent loop and the smudged whorl. My colleagues thought that in my technician's world, dry as the ink I left behind, I had no need for observations like entry and exit wounds, the stain of DNA sweated through skin, the scars of a bite on flesh.

But they were wrong.

These could hold the memory of a sinister touch.

I kept these thoughts tightly coiled from the other technicians moving around the crime scene. While they were distracted by litter on the ground or the flicker of the spotlights, I memorised the details of the body in front of me.

A young woman.

Shot in the chest with a small calibre handgun.

A bloodless wound the size of snake bite.

Her body was in a sitting position on the sand, her back against the low bluestone wall that stretched for the kilometre of Williamstown's beach.

She wore a black mohair jumper over black flared pants. Her Mary Jane shoes were the same style as my favourite pair back at university.

She could have been me at nineteen.

I swallowed a lungful of cold air to steady myself, then knelt on a plastic sheet in front of her as I prepared to do my job. I closed my eyes for a few seconds and listened. The ocean sighed as it began and ended against the shore a few metres away. In the distance, a train's wheels clack-clacked over sleepers. I tried to ignore the people moving around us. When I work, I pretend I'm alone. A futile effort. Someone yelled as sand was kicked up and seized by the wind. It whipped past and scratched a trail across my face. Voices complained about the air too cold even for this arctic July. The woollen turtleneck I've worn under my white overalls scratched at my skin.

On my paperwork I marked that it was 1.04 a.m.

Her fingerprints were not all that was stolen. The killer had taken her nails as well. Yet the first technician on the scene hadn't fitted the clear plastic bags designed to preserve contract traces on the woman's hands. He should have.

The dermal layer had been cut away and the epidermis left to weep. At last, there was blood. It had been quick to dry and covered her fingers like skin. My stomach clenched—only a beating heart can pump blood. She had been alive when he'd sliced off the ridges.

The puzzle of this girl's death had just grown more complicated. Her gunshot wound was bloodless, but the fingers had bled.

She was alive when her fingers were tampered with.

But dead by the time the bullet reached the heart.

2

Night pressed on. So did I.

A plastic marker was at her feet. Evidence had been found and removed for examination.

With soapy water, I gently swabbed the blood from the girl's fingers and examined what the water revealed. Flaps of skin with smooth edges hung over the epidermal pulp. Beneath these flaps her flesh was soft. I squeezed her fingertip. Liquid cells seeped out. Oxygen had begun to eat at the clotting proteins that are the blood's armour.

Fingerprints exist on both the dermal and epidermal layers of the skin, but it's only on the outside layer that they can be seen by the naked eye. Her epidermis had never been exposed to air, so was therefore too soft to form definite ridges. I'd be able to print her patterns from the skin that remained, but I could easily misclassify them. What I saw as the curve of a loop might really be the outer circle of a whorl.

I had little choice but to enhance the epidermis. With a pair of metal tweezers, I manipulated the liquid beneath the pulp of her fingerpads. This process enlarged the tiny peaks of skin that made the lines of a fingerprint. A higher peak meant a stronger impression in ink.

Science did not approve of this method. Like reading age from marks left inside a glove or profiling personality from impressions left on a glass, our training said it couldn't be done. Yet I'd used these techniques. My colleagues said I was a good guesser. Mum said I'd inherited her gift of feeling what people left behind. I simply believed that emotions could be transferred through skin, that they defy the laws of biology and physics. My hypothesis was like a pointing finger. It showed me where to look before I applied the tests and procedures required by law. It could give a body a name but could not be used in court.

I spent five minutes on each finger to recreate the girl's prints, but seven for each thumb. The thumbs are always more resistant. Their thickness and broader surface area mean more fluid must be manipulated. They are the most independent of all the digits and—like all things strong—respond best to gentleness.

In just under an hour I finished.

Police officers were fewer now, their dark trousers and thick overcoats replaced by twenty or so men and women in white overalls. Seven technicians walked a line search that began at the first grains of sand a half kilometre away to the west. The rest searched the naturestrip that stood between the footpath and the road.

I turned around.

Alex was squatting at the edge of the light's perimeter, examining a section of sand by the low stone wall.

My case slipped from my hand and fell open on the sand with a thud. I dropped to my knees and hurriedly scooped its contents back before anyone noticed. It had been six months since I'd left Alex. I should have known he'd be here. Victoria had sixty homicide detectives, but only a few were rostered on each night. Most cops hated working the graveyard shift. Alex would volunteer.

Behind him, under the streetlights on the other side of the road, all of Williamstown was watching from dressing gowns and overcoats.

Alex looked up and saw me. I had no choice but to wave.

As he approached, the strength of the floodlights had flattened his round features and transformed his face into a single plane. When he got closer, I saw that new lines had appeared around the large brown eyes and full mouth. Beneath the lower lashes were black half moons. In the six months since I last worked with him, his face had aged five years. Even his hair looked tired—lank instead of the coarse waves I remembered.

'She's ready to be printed,' I said, 'but it has to be done now.'

His brown eyes moved over me. I knew what he saw. Six months away had left me a little heavier and lengthened my blonde hair to just below my shoulders. But I still felt too short, too thin and too pale.

He was about to speak.

I took control. 'Her ridges will fade within half an hour. They're too pulpy.' I held out the girl's hand for him to see.

He stared at his feet, avoiding the girl. 'I'll get Catherine to do it,' he finally said.

'No. I'll take care of her. But I need your help.'

'That's not a good idea.'

'Are you okay?' His skin had faded from pale to grey.

'Yes, well no.' Then: 'I guess I just don't have the stomach I used to have.'

Alex had been picking through human remains for over ten years. He was trained to look for the story of a body and a scene. What had six months done to him?

'Alex? What-'

'Forget it, I'm fine.' He wiped his hands down his thighs and squatted in front of the girl. He was one head taller than me.

From my silver equipment case, I removed a Durester Printake ink strip and a small wooden chopping board. I ripped the top plastic layer from the strip and spread the remaining sheet onto the board. I rested the board on Alex's knee and took the girl's right wrist. As my fingers closed around it, the flesh beneath her skin shifted like the pulp of an aged tomato. She had begun to bloat. I held her arm so that the hand was outstretched, palm down. Her wrist was light and the bones inside as thin as paperbark.

Alex held the ink strip in place. I rolled her right hand thumb across the surface, then moved the finger over the space marked right thumb on a cardboard print card. I repeated the procedure with each of her left hand's digits.

'How's your wife?' I asked.

'Gone. You've been away a long time.' His eyes searched my face.

'Six months without this type of work is not long enough.'

'Sometimes I think it's worse when you take a break. You have to desensitise all over again.'

I wanted to tell him that for the girl's sake, I wouldn't let myself grow cold.

'What did the coroner say?' I asked.

'Small calibre shot to the heart. No damage to the skin on the palms or knuckles so it doesn't look like she put up a fight.'

I looked up. 'He removes her fingertips while she's alive, and she doesn't put up a fight? And where's all the blood from the shot to the heart?'

'Dr Greenberg thinks she was close to death when she was shot. But there's no sign of any other injury. Except the hands.'

I started printing the right hand. 'Why bother shooting her if she was close to death?'

'I don't know. Greenberg's going to put a priority order on the toxicology. He's betting she was drugged, probably more strongly than the killer realised.'

'So the killer didn't know she was close to death.'

'Exactly.'

I nodded at the evidence marker. 'What was at her feet?'

'A hollow piece of wood carved with aboriginal markings. We don't know what its significance is yet.'

I went back to rolling the right fingers.

Alex watched me in silence, then shook his head. 'I don't get why the fingertip skin's missing. If he didn't want her identified, he should have tossed her into the bay or buried her in a secluded spot. Maybe he wanted the skin and nails on her fingers as a token.'

'Fingerprints as a souvenir is unheard of—once the skin dries it just shrinks and curls up. The fingerprints disappear,' I said.

'Greenberg said the outer layer of skin on each finger was removed in one piece.'

The smooth flaps of skin closing over the epidermal pulp had not left my mind. 'Yes, I saw that. Must have been a blade with an unserrated edge.'

'A scalpel?'

'That's what I'm thinking. Not the type of thing your average Joe carries around. I gather she didn't have any I.D. on her?'

Alex glanced over my shoulder. 'Oh, no.'

'Arden!' The voice that called my surname was deep and disapproving. I knew whom it belonged to before I turned around.

Quickly I pulled a tissue from my pocket and smoothed it over the print card, then slipped the tissue into my overalls again.

I rose and turned to face Senior Sergeant Ron Peterson

'Why are you here?' he asked.

'I was paged in like everybody else,' I said.

'By who?' Peterson's voice was calmer than I expected, but his face was still too narrow and too pale even beneath the wash of the spotlight. Instead of the regulation crime scene overalls, he wore his usual dark blue suit with a dark shirt. Between the lapels of his black, calf length overcoat hung an aubergine-coloured tie. As he strode toward me, the wind billowed the coat open and his trousers flapped against his legs. He was still spider thin and catalogue neat.

The evidence collectors turned to stare at us.

Peterson stared back.

They dropped their eyes and returned to work.

I opened my mouth to say that it was just the standard department call out but Alex raised a hand.

'I assigned her,' he said as he rose to his full 185 centimetre height.

'You?' I said.

Peterson stopped a metre from us. Any closer and he'd be forced to look up at Alex. A gust of wind blew off the ocean and whipped the end of Peterson's tie over his shoulder. He pulled it back against his chest and tucked it inside his jacket.

'You assigned her?' he asked Alex.

'That's right,' Alex said. 'What's the problem?'

'The problem is you're not in charge of crime scenes.'

'Sarah's the only one who can read prints when the fingers are mutilated this badly—you know that.'

'No one can get an accurate print from a hand like that. We don't have time to waste on this.'

I stepped between them. 'It's taken less than an hour.'

Peterson stepped around me. 'And it will probably take another five hours in the lab. And just to get an inaccurate result. We don't need her prints to I.D. her.'

He ripped the identification tag from the bottom of Alex's jumper before I had time to reply.

'You're not working this, Pace,' Peterson said.

'What? You can't do that!' Alex yelled.

'Go home.'

'What's really going on here?' I asked.

Peterson ignored me. 'I've got four other detectives working this—and they're better than you, Pace.'

Alex stepped toward Peterson. The wind swept off the sea again and blew my hair into my eyes.

I put a hand on Alex's chest. 'It's not worth it. Meet me back at the office.' My hand jumped with his breathing.

His gaze shifted from Peterson to my face.

'Please,' I whispered.

His shoulders relaxed and he took a step back.

'Big mistake,' he told Peterson.

I turned my back on Alex and addressed Peterson. 'Her killer doesn't want us to identify her by prints. That means we have to.'

'Just leave. Don't even bother getting the ink off her fingers,' Peterson said. He straightened his tie.

'At least let me run her prints through the database,' I said.

'I'm reporting you for contamination of evidence.'

Alex's footsteps made soft thuds on the sand as he walked back to his car. The wind carried Peterson's tie over his shoulder again. This time he let it stay there.

I stripped off my gloves and threw them into the open case at my feet. 'For God's sake, her hands weren't even bagged. I should be reporting you.'

Peterson beckoned over a uniformed police officer leaning against the wall a few metres from where we stood.

I grabbed Peterson's sleeve. 'The nails are not a token. Whatever's beneath them would give him away.'

Peterson jerked his arm away with such force that it knocked my wallet out of my pocket. My credit cards and driver's license flew up into the air. The wind scattered the cards towards the crowd. Peterson watched the uniformed cop gather the cards and stuff them back into the wallet.

'You're a fingerprint technician, not a detective,' Peterson said. He levelled his right index finger at me. 'The fact that you seem to forget that is exactly why I don't want you doing my homicides. You seem to think you're a solo act, not a team member.'

The uniformed policeman reached us and handed me my wallet.

I slipped it back into my jacket pocket.

'Escort Ms Arden to her car,' Peterson said.

The officer blushed and waited.

I squatted in front of the girl and applied warm soapy water to her fingers with a sponge.

'You don't give up, do you?' He lowered himself down on haunches until his face was a few millimetres from mine. 'Well guess what? I'm not going to let you embarrass me with your little theories.' His breath smelled of mint and mouthwash. 'I'm on the way up because I run the tightest scenes in the state. I don't tolerate breaking of procedure.'

9

I held out the girl's print card. 'Then include this in your procedures.'

He turned to the officer. 'Wait for her by the road.'

When the lad had gone, Peterson snatched the card from me and tore it up into two neat pieces. 'You should be thanking me for this. I've just saved you the embarrassment of being wrong.'

I watched the halves flutter to the ground.

He rose. 'Give your badge number to the Constable. You're never working one of my scenes again.'

I knew what this meant. In three months the position of State Coordinator of Forensic Investigations would be up for grabs. Rumour said Peterson would get the job after having been passed over twice in the last ten years. Every crime scene in Victoria would be in his control.

'The killer will be under our nose,' I said and picked up my case.

'Not your nose,' Peterson said.

Alex was by the roadside talking to the young officer.

I turned my back and walked away.

But I was not walking away from the girl.

She and I now shared a trait.

I have no fingerprints either.

3

It was just after a quarter past five when I arrived at the St Kilda Road Police Complex.

I stepped out of the car and drew my coat against the icy wind. The handle of my metal case turned my palm cold the moment I pulled it from the car.

St Kilda Road is more a grand, elm-lined boulevard than a street, but at night it loses its gentility. Trees become camouflage, the arcs of streetlights don't pool wide enough to penetrate dark spots, and the walkways are wind tunnels that blind you with your own hair and clothes.

While I waited for Alex to arrive, I sat in the shelter of an illuminated spot on the front steps of the building. There was a long night ahead of me and I needed to soak up as much fresh air as I could before I submerged myself into the ninhydrin-fumed seventeenth floor.

I pulled out the tissue I'd used to copy the girl's prints and examined it. The nationwide computer databank needed only the outline of a fingerprint to generate a match. The usual procedure is to sketch the fixed ridge points used for classification of a fingerprint from record card to tracing paper, and then to scan these ridges into the AFAIS databank. The inked lines on the tissue were a little blotchy, but I could clean these up on screen. Years of translating a full fingerprint into five or six bold lines had trained my eye to spot significant characteristics immediately. First, however, I'd have to scan them and reverse the image.

She had six ulnar loops, three whorls, and twinned loops

rising to an arch. Skin irregularities on her left pinkie, fourth, index and pointer fingerprints were obvious. They showed as long, white interruptions in the black ink. I had seen these many times before. The marks of a musician.

In the centre of her right index pad was a star-shaped blotch. Had the ink smudged or was it a scab that had formed over a fresh wound?

My vision blurred slightly, and I realised I was losing the battle against sleep. I let my head rest against the wall and closed my eyes. Suddenly, I was in a dream. My mother stood before me. The old women floated behind her, whispering to each other. She told me again that my fingertips were her fault. I forced a clinical tone to my voice as I said the phrases she hated to hear. *An imbalance in the amniotic fluids, the failure of the dermis to wrinkle.* Forget your science, she told me, it's the science that closes your mind. It was the man who gave me you. He untied my knots and I let him. After he'd left they said he was a man of the cloth. He gave you the finger curse. And I let him.

A car revved down St Kilda Road, and I woke with a start. The dream was still fresh. I shook my head to clear it away. My mother's superstitions about my condition and my job would drive me mad someday.

While my mother saw my disease as a curse, I saw it as a gift. I was born to be a fingerprinter. Science tells me that three months into my mother's belly the skin on my fingers should have arched, whorled or looped into thin lines. Instead, I entered the world with a dermis of broken ridges.

My bedmates in the Riverina nursery ward had fingertips like the gentle roll of desert sand, but mine were like the cracked bed of a dry river. When a doctor discovered this difference, the visits began. At first they were simply regular examinations by city specialists. Soon they progressed into acid peels, the filing away of skin and a biopsy of the epidermis on my index finger. During the procedures, the doctors would distract me by letting me look at the old black and white pictures in manuals. By the age of twelve I could recite statistics on every ridge configuration. After sixteen years of experimental treatment, I was glad when my mother fled the doctors and buried us in the anonymity of a small town outside Perth. Suddenly instead of being the freak that drew city scientists, I was just a kid who could name her friends' fingerpatterns.

It was in this new home that my passion for dactylology grew. I moved beyond classifying patterns into analysing the content that made up the residue of a print. I secretly saved for and bought an old microscope and a new chemistry kit. These revealed that latents the locals left on their whisky glasses held traces of weatherboard paint and cooking flours. I learned to read occupation from the imprints. A farmer's ridges were sanded down by the gripping of rusty ploughs. In the shearer's hands, I could see the grooved edges of sheep hooves. Shearing was in their blood and the scent of wool's lanoline on the webbing between their fingers. The wool spinners' ridges were flat with weak definition. The wool oil makes their hands too soft for identification. As my skills built, I began to read emotions in the impressions: an oedema of the ridges when circulation is suppressed by sorrow, the blurred lines left by the throb of an angry pulse, the bold lines made by a heart in love.

I graduated from my forensic science degree with honours and took my knowledge to the only place where I could use it: the police force. My mother had moved back to the Victorian Riverina. She wanted to make peace with the past, she said. I had stayed in Perth to work.

'Hey,' Alex called. He was crossing the road.

I stood up and walked over to meet him on the nature strip.

'Look,' I handed him the tissue and pointed to the marks. 'She played the violin. Musicians indentations. Definitely a four stringed instrument. The marks are too close to the nail to be from guitar strings, unless she had lousy technique. If her prints are on record, I'll be able to tell for sure from the right thumb. The coroner should find an impression on her neck where the violin was nestled as she played.'

13

He stood still and stared down at the tissue. 'But how do you know? You didn't even have her skin to print.'

'The indentations were deep, so deep, I'd say she's been playing even before she reached primary school.'

'What type of kid plays the violin at five?'

'One with pushy parents,' I said. 'Or parents that were musicians themselves.'

He gave me back the tissue and we started across the footpath. 'You should go home,' he said. 'Why don't you just let me run the prints?'

'Because these need cleaning up, and even if I do clean them up and let you run them, you won't get a direct match. If I see her prints on the computer, I'll know them.'

He smiled grimly and shook his head. 'You haven't changed.'

'What do you mean?'

'Peterson was right. You get too involved.'

His words hit a nerve I thought I'd severed half a year ago. 'Too involved? I can't believe I'm hearing this.' Getting too involved was not my problem. My issue was something else and I was surprised he hadn't worked it out yet. I grabbed my case from the step.

'Don't get shitty with me, Sarah. Everyone knows why you had to leave. No sleep, no food, no life. You couldn't deal with the job anymore.'

'The job?' I stared at him in shock. I had left because of him. How could he not see that? 'Don't you dare tell me how I feel, especially if you can't even get it right.'

'Then stop making me guess.'

'For Christ's sake—'

'You disappear for six months without explanation, and I can't ask questions?'

'This is not about us.' I hurried up the steps to the entrance of the building. My reflection trailed me in the mirrored glass of foyer windows. These cold office blocks, with their facades designed to reveal more of the outside than the inside world, made me uneasy.

Alex followed me up the steps. I paused at the door while he caught up with me.

'And since when is it wrong to get involved?' I said.

'I called you out to get the prints from the girl's fingers, not to solve the whole crime in one night. You've done what we needed you to. Run them through the machine and go home before Peterson suspends you.'

'I'm not afraid of Peterson. He's been an explosion waiting for a match ever since he got passed over for promotion. That's why his people work so well. They're scared of the bang.'

'If I were you, I'd be scared of his bang because it's gotten louder while you were away,' he said. 'One of his technicians accidentally contaminated some blood work. Peterson got his arse kicked and now he's hell bent on throwing the procedure book at everyone. In a very loud voice.'

'But you're obviously not afraid of him.'

The electric doors opened and we stepped inside.

'It's different for me,' Alex said. 'You work for him, I don't.'

'He's detective in charge of the crime scene. Am I going mad or didn't he just pull you from the case?'

'From the scene, not from the case. The only one who can throw me off an investigation or suspend me is the Commissioner.'

A guard sat in the security box by the electronic sensor gate, flipping through a magazine. He glanced up as we passed, stared at our identification badges, and then returned to his magazine.

We stepped into the elevator and moved up to the seventeenth floor.

'Since Peterson's never going to let me work his scenes again, what does it matter if I get suspended,' I said.

Alex thought for a moment. 'We could go over Peterson's head.'

'To the person who's about to hand over their job to Peterson? By the time our request gets processed Peterson will have got his promotion. He'll be the one who has to sign the form!'

We stepped out of the elevator. The moment I opened the thick glass doors of the fingerprint department, the steely odour of ninhydrin spilt over me and out into the corridor.

'How can Peterson make State Coordinator after the bad blood work and getting passed over once before?'

'You should see the other contenders.'

4

'Twenty hits. Only six females,' I told him as I set the men's prints aside and examined the women's.

We had the Fingerprint floor to ourselves. Alex wandered over to the window facing the ocean side of South Melbourne and stared out. We all shared the same view, just at different heights. I knew his eyes were tracing the curves of the Westgate Bridge. It's only from the half moon of shore from Port Melbourne to South Melbourne that the lie of the bridge's shape is exposed. When you're travelling across its asphalt, the road ahead appeared as straight as a railway sleeper. But from here it's a serpent, a line of two mirrored curves forming an 'S'.

'Each of the six women whose prints I've brought up have the same number of ridges and general configurations as the girl,' I told him.

'Can you narrow it down from six?'

'Doing it as we speak. It's all in the differences.' I didn't go into detail, didn't tell him that these differences were in the positions of the main characteristics—a loop too much to the right, leading into a delta way too high to be hers; a core too small; a tented arch so broad that the computer mistook it for a radial loop. Within two minutes I had disregarded three of the prints and printed a hard copy of the remaining three.

I laid the copies out on one of the seven conference tables that lined the centre of the room.

It took me only four minutes to identify her hands. Her distinctive arch was what I remembered. The ridges formed two loops, one beginning on the thumb's side of the hand, the other at the ulnar bone's. They rose until they met face to face but didn't touch.

The computer image of her right index pad had no star-shaped mark. Yet the prints I'd taken tonight did. She must have injured her index finger within the last few days.

Alex stood behind me, hands resting on the back of my chair. He leaned over my shoulder to watch the screen. He smelled of warm wood and cinnamon.

My eyelids dropped and re-opened in the space of a breath. This cologne was my first intimate gift to him—wrapped in brown paper illustrated with 16th century cartographers' drawings and offered on a Sunday in an old, vinegar-fumed lane in Chinatown. My tongue remembered the ginger in his kiss.

I cleared my throat.

'Emma Faber,' I read from the printout. 'Twenty-four years old. Address 2/150 Mariner Street, St Kilda.'

Alex slid into the seat next to me.

I went on, 'Arrested and charged with disrupting the peace and resisting arrest two months ago at a land rights protest. Probation.' A memory tugged at me. 'Hang on, that thing you found at Emma's feet. What was it?'

'We don't know. Some wooden thing.'

'With aboriginal markings on it?'

His eyes widened. 'Hey, that's right.'

'Maybe someone didn't like her messing with aboriginal issues. We need to check if she was some kind of known activist.'

He shook his head. 'There's nothing on the arrest record. And it's her first.' He pointed at the printout I was holding.

'I wonder who the arresting officer was?' I read the page again.

'I can answer that.'

I stared at him.

18

He said, 'It was almost me.'

'Almost you?' I remembered how he claimed to feel queasy around the body. 'You recognised her at the beach, didn't you?'

'I wasn't sure though. That's why I needed you.' He stretched back in his chair. 'I'd met her and her father before the protest. The body of a man was found in the alley behind her house. I was called out. It turned out to be a junkie so we dropped it, but I had to interview her to settle the paperwork. Her father had come to sit in on the interview. She gave me coffee, we all chatted.'

'What was your take on the father?'

'A caring guy. He didn't get in the way, just listened to make sure I wasn't hassling Emma. He's in construction, owns a company that throws up high rises and carparks. Anyway, a week later, I was rounding up protesters at the Aboriginal rally. She was supposed to be one of my arrests.'

I checked the signature at the bottom of the page. 'Hang on, it says Constable Mead of Footscray made the arrest.'

'I said I was supposed to. I knew she was a good kid and that a rap sheet might kill her chances of a decent job. So I let her go. But Mead picked her up a few minutes later.'

I examined the page more closely. 'Wait, there's another signature beneath it.'

'Two signatures?'

I handed him the printout.

He read the second signature. 'Peterson!'

'But you're both homicide. What were you doing at a land rights protest?'

'We'd just finished working a scene in Port Melbourne and went over to the river to take a look at the protest. There were rumours that the gathering might heat up like the World Economic Forum riots. Peterson's name on the rap sheet is probably nothing. Ring up Constable Mead and ask him about it.'

'Good idea.' I leaned back in the chair. 'Can we pull out Emma's file?'

'I'll need to make an official request. We should have it by ten o'clock today.'

'Okay.'

I closed my eyes against the feelings of despair and waste that lived inside me when I worked murders. 'So, who's going to tell her parents?' I asked.

'Peterson will have to organise that.'

I filed all our paperwork away.

'Hey,' he pointed directly across the dark blanket that was the bay. 'See those two highrises? That's Williamstown there, right opposite us. The beach where Emma's body was found is tucked in a cove around the corner, facing the open bay.'

I followed his finger. An orange beacon flashed on the surface of the water, followed by another a few kilometres down the coast. They marked the shipping path that starts at the ocean mouth of Port Phillip Bay and cuts across the bay to the entrance of the Yarra River. Yet another beacon lit the underbelly of the bridge and threw an orange glow over Williamstown's shoreline.

My eyes followed the river upstream. From the banks, thick beams of light skimmed the surface of the river.

'That's strange,' I said.

'What's strange?'

'Those searchlights.'

'That's the geologists.'

'Geologists?'

'There's been some weird changes in the currents during the last month.'

'Yeah?'

'The ocean's seeping into the mouth of the river.'

I shifted my gaze from the lights to his face. 'A river flowing backwards? No way!'

'Not really. They think the river's broken into an underground stream that empties into another part of the bay.'

The beams roamed the surface of the water. Even from this height I could make out small triangles of surging waves. No strength of light could make the water look anything but black.

'Why are they working at night?'

'It's the only time the shipping doesn't disrupt the current.'

'Williamstown is at the mouth of the river,' I said, thinking aloud.

Alex glanced at his watch. 'It's nearly sunrise. Come on, lets get out of there.'

Alex walked me the few short steps to my car. Even though the bay was nearly ten kilometres away, its scent was heavy in the air—a tickle of salt and sand that inflamed my sinuses; the stench of discarded bait, and the chemical headiness of jet-ski fuel. My head ached from tiredness.

I said, 'You should have told me that it was you who assigned me.'

'Would you have worked the case?'

'Maybe not.'

'Then I did the right thing. You're the only person who can find prints where there's none.' He leaned back against my car. 'Can we go somewhere to talk?'

We had never really talked about our break-up, but I could feel he'd wanted to back at the crime scene. Could I trek through an anatomy of it tonight? How could I talk about anything with clarity when I'd spent the evening holding what was left of Emma Faber's bloodied hand?

I said, 'Call me tomorrow, okay? I just can't tonight.'

'Sarah?' he reached out and touched my arm.

I remembered his wife answering my knock on his door. She wore bedroom hair and his khaki jumper.

'I just need to get tonight out of my head first,' I said.

He stepped back from the curb.

'Call me,' I mimed through the window.

He nodded.

I pulled into the early morning traffic and drove off.

5

I'd fallen in love with Alex's fingerprints two months before I met him.

After my transfer from Perth to Melbourne, I was kept off the streets for a week and introduced to the geography of my floor—job roster on the whiteboard in the operations room, prints recorded on index cards arranged in drawers marked by the year the impression was taken, the login details of the computer networks, and the layout of the laboratory. My desk was a three-legged table with faux silky-oak grain laminate. Three plastic crates took the place of the fourth leg and camouflaged a sticky black stain on the brown carpet that smelt like sour milk. From my chair I had a view of the men's toilet. If the door was left open, I could smell the urinal.

I found Alex's prints in the lab. Catherine was pulling a black Smith and Wesson .38 out of the large Perspex cube used to contain superglue fumes that polymerised the water and sebaceous deposits in fingerprints. It had been a month since I'd last been in a lab, but I felt immediately at home. The landscape of fingerprint science is the same no matter where you work—ninhydrin air, superglue residue flaking like old skin from the white Formica benchtops, the rattling beat of fume cupboard fans. I slipped on an off-white lab coat that was too long at the sleeves and covered in the purple and brown stains of sloppy chemistry.

Catherine placed the gun on a white sheet of butcher paper and rolled off her white plastic gloves.

I was standing behind her.

She said, 'A dick from homicide goes to see what the local chickenhawk knows about a dead underage hooker. Chickenhawk gets nervous and pulls a gun. The cop wrestles control of the gun, but the guy screams it was the cop who drew the weapon. Check it out.' She nodded down at the gun.

I moved in beside her and peered down at the lines and curves the superglue had formed on the muzzle.

She went on, 'The dicks prints are on the card by your elbow.'

I picked up the card and examined Alex Pace's fingerprints.

She said, 'I tested the gun's butt and the muzzle. Cop's prints are on the muzzle, not the butt's grip. He's in the clear.'

But I was still staring at Alex's print card. 'These can't be right,' I said.

She shrugged. 'I took them myself when he started.'

Only five percent of people have an arch as one of their ten patterns. Yet he had an arch on every finger on his right hand.

Catherine leaned back against the bench and looked over my shoulder at the card. 'Strange, aren't they?'

In the centre of his right thumb was an ulnar arch as sharp as the point of a blade. Ridges circled the pattern like waves in a pond rushing from the drop of a stone. His pointer was a plain arch with ridges that rose and met in the shape of a bullet. The index finger was a mixture of a loop and tented arch that merged to look like the letter 'S' laid horizontally. His ring finger was another plain arch as rounded as a handcuff's loop.

Catherine tapped a finger on the left side of the card. 'It gets weirder. The left hand classifications are your standard, dull old loops, but his papillary lines are the longest I've ever seen.'

Before fingerprinting was a science, elongated papillary ridges were seen as signs of passion. If hands lived a life of lust, it could be read in the shape of their lines.

A man with one handful of pyramids and another of curves. The extraordinary and the ordinary in a single person.

She rolled her eyes. 'That's Alex for you.'

I stepped around her and peered down at the fine white ridges on the barrel of the gun. They were barely visible compared to the thick lines on the handle.

'His prints are light,' I said.

'Tell me about it. It's taken me two days just to get them to show. A guy points a gun at me, I'd be sweating so much that my prints would glow in the dark.'

It was all those arches, I thought. Five examples of perfect balance and symmetry. All lines connecting. How could a man with five arches be anything but focussed? He had obviously subdued the influence of the curves.

I waved the card in the air. 'If you're finished with this, I'll refile it.'

'Thanks.'

Using the edge of the butcher paper as a makeshift glove, Catherine pushed the gun into an open space on the bench and set up the equipment needed to photograph the prints on its barrel and butt.

On my way to the filing cabinets I stopped by the photocopy room. It was empty. I slipped Alex's record card into the machine and made a copy. I returned the original and discreetly tucked the duplicate into the inside pocket of my bag.

Within a week I knew his every crease and curve. Each night I'd sit at my small pine desk with a jeweller's magnifier clamped to my left eye. Beneath the tungsten of a lamp, I had searched his patterns for clues about his life. The pucker of a scar on the right side of the highest ridge of his left index. The commonest spot for a cut from a cooking knife. He had to be right handed.

He had old man's hands. Ridges like grain in a timber plank, curves like the knots that sink in aging wood. Cutting across the ink on each fingerpad were the narrow, oval, white spaces made by creases in the epidermis. A lifetime of dry hands. Constant exposure to wind could sap a finger's moisture and leave the surface this cracked. So could frequent immersion in water. I wondered if he were an outdoor type. At the base of his thumbs was a roll of skin, an extra millimetre of flesh eased down the length of the finger by decades of gravity. It reminded me of the way medieval stained glass windows swell at the sill. He had to be at least thirty when the prints were taken.

I wished I could check for signs of love, but with a single set of prints, it was impossible. I needed an object he had touched. Love could only be detected through comparison and flawless testing. It was my theory that the swelling of the heart produces a mixture of minerals and acids in the pores that is different from those found in a normal fingerprint. There is more creatine and more uric acid, but fewer amino acids. Passion's sweat is so strong you never need to dust it with black powder or expose it by lumalight. Its mark is always visible, never latent. Love defines a fingerprint like a tattoo stains the skin.

I was wrong about Alex subduing the curves.

I finally met him two months later when I was called out on a cool spring morning to fingerprint the body of an eight-year-old boy found in the muddy Burnley backwash of the Yarra. October storms had swollen the river, its force a cannonball that had rolled the body into the duckweed shallows.

Peterson was supervising the removal of the body from the water. The mother was up on the bank, locked in the dimpled arms of a pudgy cop with skin as sallow as boiling butter. Peterson's blunt instructions carried across the marshy plain and up to where the mother stood. I cringed as I heard him order the body be brought in with hooks. A bullet had turned the boy's chest into a rotting black hole.

A dark haired cop flew down the bank at us. When he reached our plateau I saw he was taller than Peterson, but also rounder. While Peterson's face and limbs were long planes, this man's were swelling lines. The controlled curves, I decided, of a man whose body wanted to be bigger than its master allowed.

25

'Hey, keep it down,' the man said. His eyes never left Peterson's face but Peterson's were everywhere. 'The last thing the mother needs is to hear you talking about her child like he's a side of beef.'

Peterson seemed like a coiled spring about to leap. He grabbed the flapping tie with his left hand and pinned it to his narrow chest. 'Get back up there, Pace. And why is the mother still hanging around?'

Pace. Alex Pace? I wanted to grab this tall man's hand and turn it over to examine the finger pads.

His right hand clenched into a fist at his side and his left rose to rest on the slight curve of his hip. One arm a loop, the other an arch.

Alex said, 'She needs to see this for herself, or she'll always wonder what really happened to him.' His voice was low and smooth but the triceps of his right arm strained against his white overalls as his fist clenched even tighter. His calmness was obviously an effort.

Peterson threw his arms in the air. The tie flew back over his right shoulder again. 'Needs to see this? Since when do we let family see us picking over the bodies? You want her to watch the autopsy too?' He turned to me. 'After the other technicians are finished, you can print him here on the bank.'

I swung to face Peterson, my arms folded across my chest. 'I am not printing this kid in front of his mother. I don't care if I have to do it at the morgue at 3 a.m., just as long as she's not there to see it.' I turned to Alex. 'And I don't know what weird theory you're following, but to get this kid's prints, I have to slice off the skin on his hand and wear it like a glove. You understand me? Somehow I don't think that's going to help her grieve.'

I picked up my case and fled—from the boy with the hole of hate in his chest, from this detective whose fingers bore too many curves.

The next time I saw Alex I was browsing in a second hand bookstore on Barkly Street, St Kilda, a seven-minute tram ride from my office. I always came to St Kilda when I wanted to avoid running into the people I worked with. Through a fingerprinter's eyes, St Kilda was a place where thieves were either too smacked out to wear gloves or so stoned that they dropped them before escaping. We spent too many hours collecting easy prints in this suburb of decaying window sills, maze-like alleys and uncontrollable drugs to want to spend our leisure time here too. I assumed it was the same for homicide detectives.

Alex was standing in the textbook section, flipping through a yellowing Oxford atlas. The woody dust from old, cheap paper pulp breezed across the room at me each time he turned a page.

I had entered the shop simply to escape the geometry of the morning's work. I had been manually comparing each delta and bifurcation of a latent print found at a robbery the week before with the loops and whirls of the twenty matches the computer had selected. Unless I took my break in a place of uneven shapes, I would go line mad.

I tapped him on the shoulder.

He turned to face me. 'Sarah!'

He must have read my surprise at his knowing my name, because he suddenly turned back to the book case and slipped the atlas between two similar sized volumes. When he faced me again, his cheeks were flushed.

'I'm Alex,' he said and offered his right hand.

'I remember.'

His fingers were warm. I pictured the imprint of the curves on my skin, and then coolness as they faded. Fingerprints on skin last only a few moments.

'How's the boy's mother?' I asked.

'Better.' It had been two months since his body had been found. 'I dropped in to see her yesterday.'

'The case is still open?'

He nodded and ran a hand through his hair. The curls were clipped now, ordered and controlled. 'I want to apologise about the other day.'

I held up a hand. 'You do your job well—that's all that matters.'

'So do you.' He cleared his throat. 'What time are you due back?'

'Fifty minutes.'

'Coffee?'

I smiled. 'Okay.'

Homicide's night shift met in the coffee room at 11.00 p.m. to assign cases and swap stories. At 11.15 that night I sneaked upstairs to their working area with a pair of tweezers and a paper bag in my pocket.

There were sixteen desks, all cluttered but unmanned. I looked for signs of Alex in each. My eye lingered on one carrel located two desks from the window that overlooked the sea. On it sat a wooden world globe used as a paperweight for a stack of blank report forms. I saw his thoroughness in the yellow highlighted sentences of interview transcripts, his kindness in a floral, thank-you card from a victim's sister. And on the top right corner of his desk, adhered with sticky tape, his sorrow in a school photograph of the blond, freckled boy we'd fished from the river.

I turned from these things and looked for something he would not miss. The piece of paper he'd hastily scribbled my phone number on was now a coaster for his dark blue, lacquered coffee mug. A thick ring of moisture had blurred the ink. The digits were unreadable. A teledex sat by his phone. When I opened it to the entries beginning with 'S' I saw my name and number in black pen. I lifted the mug and used the tweezers to transfer the piece of paper into my paperbag.

My heart's first theft.

6

I arrived outside my single-fronted weatherboard house in South Melbourne with a promise that I would forget Alex and Emma Faber for a few hours.

The wind tore through the acacias lining my side fence and beat against the car so hard it rocked. I bent my head low and pushed through the wind until I made it inside.

Bess started frantically scratching at the back door. I let her in. She gave me a welcoming sniff and then plodded along the wooden floorboards to my bedroom, her caramel Cocker Spaniel hair trailing along the ground. She was heavy with pups and would give birth any day now.

After locking the back door, I gave it an extra tug to check it was secure. Burglars seemed to like the house as much as I did. It had been built in the 1920's, decades before the need for a term like 'break-and-enter'. I'd fallen in love with its side-hinged windows and stained-glass door panels the moment the agent ushered me through the front door. Within a week the house was mine. By the end of the year, it'd been broken into twice. I bought an alarm system, but thieves stole that too. Mum offered me garlic and thyme sachets to hang in the doorways for protection. I'd refused on the grounds that I'd never come across a burglar with fangs in South Melbourne.

I slipped into my dark brown pyjamas, then removed nine cabbage leaves from the fridge and pounded them with a meat tenderiser. When they had turned a deep, bruised green and crosshatched lines of cellulose began to appear, I scraped the leaves into a saucepan and slowly let them warm up. As soon as heat made them transparent, I spooned them out onto nine strips of white bandage. I spread the vegetable across the surface as if I were buttering bread, and then coiled a strip of bandage around each fingertip. My skin tickled as the cabbage began to draw sweat.

Mum had sent me this remedy in her latest letter. She said she'd concocted it for a neighbour with eczema and thought its extracting properties might also be good for coaxing my skin's pebbled surface into folds and ripples. I knew, however, that she'd created the recipe just for me. After all, the disease on my fingertips had begun in the womb. Her womb.

Tomorrow I would unwrap the bandages and grip a glass, touch the edges of the laminated kitchen table, and press my finger flat on wax. She'd be calling me at 8.00 am to check if it worked. Of course it wouldn't. Skin specialists had been experimenting with my fingertips ever since the hospital recorded my prints as a newborn. If science had failed to alter my pebbled patterns, what chance did my mother have? And what did it matter? I still had enough friction ridges on my fingertips to grip a wet beer glass. Sure, my prints fell outside the standard classifications on loops, whorls and arches but they were still unique enough to identify me.

Yet I still applied Mum's ointments and checked for signs of a normal print. At night I've dreamed of growing up without thimbles over my thumbs. I've caught myself envying women who can pass through winter without hiding their hands in gloves. When the cold made my surgical scars tighten and sting, I've found myself swearing with the words Mum uses to undo curses. Sometimes, late at night when my reasoning was shaky, I even dusted all my home's surfaces in the hope of finding changes in my fingerpads.

When I first began to powder my house, I found what seemed to be my pebbled thumb print in places I had never touched. It appeared at knee level on the fridge door, on the leg of a bedside table, along the porcelain underbelly of the toilet bowl. Once I'd found this print, I became obsessed and dusted any low surface that I suspected would preserve a latent.

It was only when I photographed these marks that I noticed their differences from my print. They were too large to be my finger, as wide as both my index and pointer together. Instead of the uneven oval typical of a latent, they were the shape of an hourglass.

I took the Polaroids to work and searched through the department's archives of reference books on imprints. Fingerprinters, I'm afraid, don't reserve inking just for fingers. I'd flicked through hundreds of pages on the residue marks left by shoe tips, rodents, and children's tongues before I finally found a print that matched my photographs. It was on a yellowing page between an example of a bear's paw print and a reproduction of a man's heel mark on pig's skin. The image was labelled 'Dog's Nose'. The patterns on a dog's nose, the excerpt read, were thought to be as individual as the ridges on a human finger.

When I returned home, I added four drops of water to the surface of a standard ink strip, then smoothed it lightly over Bess's nose as I tickled the underside of her chin. I rolled coarse butcher paper from one nostril to another, then wiped her nose clean with diluted dog shampoo. The wet, suede-like texture of her nose gave as clear an impression as a nervous burglar's finger. Her pattern was like my own—as cracked as baked earth, thousands of tiny specks black on the page with white valleys between.

It had been three years since I'd printed Bess's nose. The residues we left behind were still so similar that only height and magnification let me tell them apart.

I climbed into bed.

Bess settled across the doorway like a barricade.

A dream came swiftly. I saw myself standing on the footpath under Princess Bridge. The brown flow of the Yarra River passed by my feet. Thick waves of stinking faeces and rotting seagull carcasses floated upstream towards the city instead of out to the bay. The thumping of tyres on the road above my head echoed off the iron pylons so loudly that I had to clamp my hands over my ears. I stepped down to the river's edge and looked across to the high-rises lining the opposite bank. Black garbage bags were piled against the mirrored windows of the lower floors. One by one they slowly rolled down the bank and slipped into the river with barely a splash. They floated upstream in a river that let nothing of the city's waste wash away. The earth beneath me crumbled. I tried to scramble up to the footpath, but my feet couldn't grip the ground. I fell backwards into the river with a scream.

Bess's sharp bark startled me from the dream. I sat upright and watched her claw at the bamboo blinds. Cats howled and hissed, and I heard the frantic scratching of claws on the wooden fence and then a thud as something hit the grass. Bess's barking faded to a whine, and she sat with her head cocked.

I rolled the bedsheets back and stepped down to the floorboards. As soon as I drew the blind away from the wall, Bess pushed her nose against the window and growled. It was still dark but the misty arc of light from the street lamps spilled over the pavement outside and lit the edge of the garden. The yard was empty. I let the blind fall gently back over the window.

Suddenly there was a crash from the backyard, loud as a gunshot. Bess stumbled through the house as if it were on fire.

I followed her to the rear door and tried to quiet her frantic barking. Just a garbage can, my mind screamed. Cats. Cats. I slammed the porch light on and peered out the small window beside the sink.

A man in the yard. Pressed back against the shed, frozen by the sudden flood of light. He seemed to stare straight at me, and I instinctively stepped back from the window.

In a flash, I saw myself as Emma Faber, slumped lifeless against a beach wall, fingertips flayed, blood dripping on my black Mary Janes.

The hand of common sense gripped my shoulders. *He can't see you, the light's too bright, he's out there and you're safe in here, get a good look at him, pull yourself together.*

He ran straight for the rear fence and scrambled over it into

32

the alley.

I slumped against the wall.

Long shaggy brown hair, dreadlocks maybe, head just reaching the top of the fence so he'd be about one seventy tall, clothes ragged like a homeless guy—just a homeless guy.

I knew I should be writing this down. I would, just as soon as I caught my breath. A few seconds were all I needed.

The image of me as Emma Faber flashed before me again. I was wearing the clothes she was found in, slumped against the wall of the beach, fingertips a bloody pulp.

I leaned over the sink and emptied my stomach.

7

I woke up exhausted. Each time I'd closed my eyes, I'd became Emma Faber.

Alex also used to get restless whenever he was working on a case that touched him—night sweats, whimpered apologies, fists slamming against the bedhead in his sleep. He said the homicide squad had a name for it. Proxy guilt. Mum called it sleeping with the dead.

This morning I worked away that guilt by assembling and reassembling my fingerprinting kit. Wrapped in a white robe and shut in my narrow, windowless workroom, I buried myself in the impersonal smells and textures of my tools. I passed an hour unclogging and conditioning the bristles of my squirrel, camel and pony-haired brushes, and numbed my mind with the rhythm of scrubbing off superglue residue from my fume cupboard. Refilling the kit's 2oz tubs with tart, metallic smelling powder reminded me that I was a technician, not a detective. It reassured me that I couldn't be blamed if my tools failed to find the latents Emma Faber needed in order to rest peacefully—that she had no right to hound me in my dreams.

A car pulled into the driveway.

I hugged my bathrobe tightly for warmth and hurried to the lounge room window. Fog hung low over the street, turning the cars and houses into shapes behind a rice paper screen. I could make out the front-end of Alex's Falcon.

I groaned as I looked down at the white bathrobe stained with clots of black fingerprint powder and the black bedsocks speckled with Bess's brown fur. I ripped the bandages from my fingers and tried to forget the stench of boiled cabbage.

Hadn't I made it clear last night that I wasn't ready to discuss our past? Memories still tumbled out of rooms as I passed, still floated like smoke in the places he'd liked to sit. It had taken me six months to learn to ignore these memories. If I let him inside, he would leave new ones behind.

I opened the door.

He said, 'Ugh, this place still smells the same.'

Bess plodded up to him, her tail wagging. He bent low and patted her on the head.

'It's just the aluminium in the powders. I was restocking my kit.' I leaned against the doorframe, arms folded. 'What's the matter?'

He brushed the morning drizzle off the shoulders of his dark blue suit. The lapel of his jacket shifted, and I caught a glimpse of a yellow suspender strap against the white of his shirt. I wondered when he'd had time to change.

'The coroner rushed through the toxicology report on Emma Faber,' he said. 'A sedative called Zaparin was found in her system. It may have been used to subdue her before the gunshot.'

Alex had already hooked me with his new findings, but I purposely distanced myself. 'I'm late for work. I start in an hour and I'm not even showered yet. Call me later to explain.'

'No time, I've got to see her parents. They've pointed a finger at the girl's boyfriend. Peterson wants to know if they've got anything to add. Plus I need to ask them if Emma used Zaparin.'

'So Peterson's eased up on you?'

'No. Campbell assigned me to follow up duties. And yes, Peterson's livid about it. After lunch we're taking a look around Emma's flat.'

'Who's taking the prints?'

'Don't ask.'

'Who?'

He shook his head. 'Forget it, you're late.' He started back towards his car. 'I wanted you to come down to Emma's parents with me. Never mind that now.'

'You had breakfast?'

He hesitated half a second, then traced his steps back to the front door. 'What's cooking?'

'Your favourite.'

Some things were more interesting than resolve. The chance to ask Emma Faber's parents a few questions was one of them.

'How come this place is lit up like St Pat's?' he asked as he headed for the kitchen.

I looked around and noticed that the lights in the hallway, lounge and kitchen were on. Daylight pushed through the closed slats of the bamboo blinds. I switched all the lights off except the one in the kitchen and yanked up the loungeroom blinds. I opened my mouth to tell him about the man in the garden but changed my mind. Where I saw a man seeking shelter and searching for food, Alex would see a predator looking for an easy mark. Before I knew it, he'd have a bodyguard and a swot squad camouflaged in the trees.

I joined him in the kitchen and made scrambled eggs on toast with two strips of bacon. I slopped a dollop of hollandaise sauce on top of the eggs.

He stared at the black fingerprint dust on my robe. 'Restocking the kit at seven in the morning? Gotta be insomnia, right?'

I shook my head. In the eight months or so that we'd spent together, we'd learned to read mood from each other's habits. Now that it was over, it was easy to mistake familiarity for something more emotional.

I said, 'I might have to stop at a scene before I get to the office.'

He opened the fridge and removed a carton of orange juice.

'How common is the sedative?' I asked.

'Very. I don't think we'll get a lead there.'

'What about checking if the immediate family and acquaintances have got a prescription?'

'We will, but half of them will probably have a supply in their cupboard.'

36

I placed his eggs and bacon on the kitchen table and took a seat. I nodded at the chair opposite me and said, 'You can sit down, you know.'

He did.

I watched him pour a glass of juice. On the bottle I could see the smeared trails left by his fingers. At the end of the smudge was a clear impression of his pinkie. It was an ulnar loop, twenty ridges from the delta to the core. I hadn't seen his prints in six months but I remembered them so well, I could close my eyes, raise a finger and sketch them in the air— a hand of loops and a hand of arches. My mind tried to slip back again to the day I first saw them, the day I first wondered how he fought the influence of all those curves. Instead, I jumped to my feet and put the bottle back in the fridge.

'So who did you say was checking her place for prints?' I asked.

'Ben.'

'Ben? Baby Ben? He's only printed break-and-enters. How can a kid who's never even testified in court handle a murder case?'

Alex tugged at my robe. 'Sit down for this one. Peterson's supervising their collection.'

'Supervising? He's not even a fingerprinter! First his signature's on Emma's rap sheet, now this.'

'As head of crime scene, he's allowed to step on or over anyone he wants. After the blotch up with the blood work a few months back, he's on everyone's back like a fly.'

I sat down. 'I don't like the sound of this. Peterson's never shown interest in fingerprinting before. His job is to coordinate the teams of technicians, not stand over our shoulders and point at where to dust.' I chewed on a fingernail. 'If the prints at Emma's are so important that he wants to supervise, why send in someone as inexperienced as Ben?'

I had a sickening thought. Maybe a fuck-up was exactly what Peterson wanted.

Alex stopped eating his breakfast and waved a hand in front

of my face. 'Hello? Talk to me.'

I hesitated. How much should I share with Alex? My fear was that I'd cost Alex his job.

I decided to tread carefully: 'Peterson seems pretty paranoid about people undermining his authority. Maybe he's training Ben to be his ear inside the squad, someone to report back on who's blotching up, not following orders—someone he can trust to do what needs to be done.'

'Or Ben could be cover. While he's running around dusting door handles, Peterson cleans off a few prints with a damp rag. Peterson's the type of guy who owes a lot of favours. He could be using Ben to even one of them out. Or it could all be coincidence, and Peterson thinks the boy's got a gift for lifting prints.'

'Did you find out why Peterson was arresting officer on Emma's breach of peace rap?'

He toyed with the bacon. 'Yeah right, I'm gonna just walk up and ask him.'

'Maybe we're reading too much into Peterson's motives. He's worked too hard to throw it all away over a fingerprint or two.'

He looked doubtful.

I said, 'We'll just have to wait and see. There's nothing else we can do.'

'Yes, there is.'

'What?'

'You can go in to Emma's flat first.'

'In to Emma's flat? Before Peterson's squad? You mean like —'

'Go in without Peterson knowing. Collect a few things.'

I couldn't believe what I was hearing. 'An illegal entry? Are you crazy? I'd be contaminating the scene. Even if I found something, it could never be used.'

'It wouldn't be illegal. I'd assign you. It'd be like a presweep for prints. We'd record everything you found in the normal way to make sure it's all legal. We just won't file it unless you get caught.'

'If Peterson finds out, he'll report you.'

'I'll deal with that when it happens.'

I stared at him.

He gulped a mouthful of orange juice. 'I knew her, Sarah. And I don't trust her to Peterson. This will be one of his last cases before he gets promoted. He needs a clean and quick resolution. As long as the ends tie up, he won't care about what Emma actually went through. I owe it to the girl and her father to find out.'

'But you shouldn't be asking me to do this.'

'I know, but you're the only one I trust. Think of Baby Ben working on those prints. He could lose something that could close the case.'

It was true that the thought of Ben loose with a brush in Emma's flat was terrifying. 'I don't know.'

'Just think about it for a while.' He dabbed the corners of his mouth with a napkin and looked at his watch. 'Hey, you'd better get ready. We've got to get to the parents.'

'Okay. Can you grab my keys from the entry table and let Bess out back for a bit?'

On my way to the bathroom, I stopped at the phone and called Catherine at the office. She agreed to cover my shift until I got in. I'd work late to cover hers.

As I stood under the shower, waiting for the water to turn warm, I thought about Alex's suggestion. He was right; there would be nothing illegal about doing a presweep of Emma's flat as long as it was documented. It was Alex deliberately crossing Peterson that worried me. All that was questionable about Peterson so far was his judgement. Alex was the one who was acting unprofessionally. If Peterson protested hard enough, it could cost Alex his job.

Yet I could understand Alex's request. Alex's emotions were like a landmine— hidden just beneath the surface and easily tripped. This was why he always over-identified with his cases and why his solve rate was one of the highest in the squad. The fact that he'd known Emma Faber would make it even more difficult for him. It was no surprise he couldn't follow the straight lines that Peterson laid out. With a handful of curves, how could Alex be any other way?

If I didn't help him, he would try to circumvent Peterson on his own.

And end his career.

When I stepped back into the kitchen—showered and dressed—Alex was sitting at the kitchen table, reading the newspaper. The breakfast dishes were on the drying rack. Beside the paper was my driver's license.

I picked it up.

'What are you doing with this?' I asked.

'You must have dropped it on the back steps.'

'The back steps?'

'Right next to Bess's fish.' He closed the newspaper. 'You should just give her the flesh, not the whole fish. No wonder she didn't eat it.'

'Fish? What fish?'

'There's a thin silver fish on the doorstep.'

'You found my driver's license and a fish on my back steps?'

'Isn't that what I just said?'

'I couldn't have dropped my driver's license out there. I haven't been in the backyard for two days.' Suddenly I remembered Peterson knocking my wallet out of my pocket. 'Last night at the beach my cards flew out of my wallet. My license would have been amongst them.'

'So how did it get back here?'

'A young cop picked up the cards.'

'That's it then. He must have missed one, and someone else found it and dropped it back to you.'

'Why on the back steps? Why not come to the front door? And what about the fish? I didn't leave it there.' For a second I considered checking the license for prints, but realised there was no point. Both Alex and I had handled the small, plastic card since it had appeared. What about the man I had seen in my backyard? Could he have been at the beach that day?

Alex looked pointedly at his watch. 'Of course it was the cop. Anyway, you got your license back. Let's move, we need to get to the Fabers.'

I nodded absently.

8

I recognised Michael and Elizabeth Faber's street the moment Alex's car entered the quiet boulevard. I had attended two break-and-enters in this suburb the previous year. To a fingerprinter, Brighton is a suburb of gloves. The difference between the break-ins here and to the west are the fingerprints left behind. Brighton's crime scenes rarely had any. Only the most learned and talented of thieves could overcome the sophisticated anti-intruder devices that protected these mansions. This type of thief never leaves prints because he always wears gloves. The gloveless few rarely leave prints either, nor do the occupants, thanks to obsessive cleaning by domestic staff. The other fingerprint technicians claimed dusting a house without prints is like moving amongst ghosts. I felt at home.

The Faber's house was hidden behind a high hedge and an iron gate.

Alex buzzed an intercom mounted on a fence post.

A male voiced responded from the box. 'Yes?'

'It's Detective Alex Pace.'

'One moment.'

The iron gate slowly rolled open.

We walked up an agapanthus-lined driveway. The house was a typical Georgian style mansion—three storey without balconies and small rectangular windows with more height than width. The only modification for the Australian sun was a porch that ran across the front of the house and wrapped around the sides.

'According to Peterson's men,' Alex said, 'the parents last

saw Emma about two weeks ago. The night Emma died, her mother was at a friend's and her father working late. Plenty of witnesses.'

A few metres in front of us, a woman in black slacks and a tailored, red shirt was sweeping the wooden floorboards beneath the porch with a fan-shaped straw broom.

Alex slowed his pace and said, 'I think you should let me do the talking.'

I nodded. I was the fingerprinter; Alex was the brain picker. I had no desire to swap roles.

We drew closer. I recognised Emma's hands on her mother —bones long, the span of the hand narrow but the wrists surprisingly broad. Hands are inherited from one parent, never both.

The woman looked up. I first saw shoulder length, honey-coloured hair and well-cared-for skin, then grieving eyes with their puffy lids and angry red capillaries spidering out from the irises. Creases folded the thin skin at the outer edges of the lashes. I focused on the movements of her hands. She stopped sweeping and leaned the broom against the white rendering of the side of the house. The left hand rose to her hair and patted down imaginary stray strands. As her fingers touched the midpoint of the strand's length, the edges that cupped her shoulder moved en mass. Despite the trauma of her daughter's death, she still cared enough about her appearance to use hairspray. I took this as the desire for normality in the face of grief. Men shine their shoes before leaving for the morgue to identify a body; women take a half hour to apply full makeup knowing that their tears will carry it away. Elizabeth Faber had probably been sweeping that porch for hours. No matter how deep our tragedy, we do not want to appear unprepared. This is where the guilty give themselves away.

The hand darted back to her side nervously.

I glanced at her fingernails. The thumbs had been manicured to a rounded tip, the other fingers equally long, but raggedly torn—the fingernails of grief.

Alex offered his hand. 'Mrs Faber.'

Elizabeth Faber sat on the edge of a stern, brown leather armchair, rolling the edge of her red shirt into tiny bundles between her thumb and first finger. We sat opposite her on the Chesterfield, our backs to a bay window with a view of their rear yard. Elizabeth looked past Alex's shoulder and over the expanse of manicured back lawn.

'I'll make this as quick as possible,' Alex said.

Elizabeth nodded. Her face and neck were still. Only the fingers bothering the red shirt moved.

The door opened behind her, and a tall, slim man in his early fifties entered the room. Dressed in tan chinos, a white polo shirt, and a red baseball cap, he looked like he'd been negotiating a deal on the 18th par, not suffering through a day of mourning. The only oddity was the one-day growth shadowing his jaw. The eyelids were swollen and the rims of the eyes purple. His skin was the colour of bleach and creased like linen. On his lower lip were small rectangular indentations surrounded by the discolourations of bruising. I'd seen this before with grieving men—the biting of the lip to suppress tears.

I rose to greet him but he gestured for me to remain seated. He crossed the floor with long, relaxed strides and gripped Alex's hand. Then mine as Alex introduced me. I noticed Faber had shut the lounge room door behind him.

'I won't say it's good to see you again, Detective,' he said.

'Call me Alex.'

'Your people just left an hour or so ago.'

He sat swiftly down on the far left side of the three-seater lounge, an elbow crooked along the arm rest, the other stretched along the top of the couch. He removed the cap and laid it on the coffee table. He crossed his legs.

'Have you found that boyfriend of hers?' Elizabeth asked.

Michael's hand flew out, palm up towards his wife. 'Now, hang on a second.'

I removed a notepad and pen from my jacket pocket. 'His name?'

Michael gave me a disgusted look. 'That boy has enough grief to deal with without you people poking at him every few hours. We gave the other detectives his address. Surely that's enough.'

Elizabeth turned to him. 'All she wants is his name. If he's done nothing wrong, then he'll be all right.' She turned back to me. 'Charlie Hunt. She met him at university.'

'What's his address?' Alex said.

Michael jumped to his feet and paced to the window.

I watched as he angrily stuffed his hands in his pockets.

Elizabeth ignored him. 'Beaconsfield Parade. A big old dump called Mansfield. Top floor, looking towards the beach. Number three-hundred-and-something.'

'You've been there?' Alex asked.

'Certainly not. That place should be condemned. If it weren't an aboriginal co-op house, it'd have been pulled down years ago. A waterfront site that size is worth well over a million.'

'Charlie's an aboriginal?' I asked.

'Yes.'

I continued: 'I take it you don't approve of Emma seeing him?' Out of the corner of my eye I watched Michael's back. His shoulders were squared, loose pockets bulging where each hand had formed a fist.

'Charlie is just a kid who still has ideals,' Michael said to the window.

'Charlie's trouble,' Elizabeth said. 'I'm a solicitor. I've done enough legal aid work to know a deviant when I see one. What mother wants her daughter going out with a man who's always getting arrested?'

'He's been in trouble with the police?' Alex asked.

Elizabeth let out a huff. 'Just about every branch.'

Michael turned to face his wife. 'Oh, come on, Liz, don't exaggerate. So Charlie has a social conscience and gets arrested for exercising it.'

'It's not social conscience he has, it's pure hate.'

'You make him sound like a terrorist,' Michael said. 'That

45

legal aid work of yours has turned you against the world.' He met Alex's eyes. 'Her firm makes all their lawyers do at least one pro-bono per year. And she hates every second of it.'

There was an awkward silence.

'Do you know of anyone who would want to harm Emma?' Alex finally asked.

Michael looked at Elizabeth.

'No,' she said, 'not that I know of. Everyone seemed to like her. She and Charlie had their arguments and he was a little rough—'

'She means rough as in abrupt,' Michael interrupted. 'But he wouldn't hurt her.'

Elizabeth's jaw set in a hard line. 'I mean exactly what I said.'

'Do you have any other children?' Alex asked.

They were silent for a few seconds.

'We have a son. Grant,' Michael said.

'Have you contacted him about Emma's death yet?'

'I haven't.' Michael looked at his wife. 'Have you?'

She shook her head. 'I thought I'd wait until mid-morning. Let him get a decent sleep first.'

'Were they close?' Alex asked.

'Not really. He's ten or so years older than Emma,' Michael said.

'We'll need to talk to him,' Alex said.

Elizabeth wrung her hands. 'That other detective said he'd do it.'

'What detective?'

'The tall one.'

Alex and I exchanged glances.

'Peterson?' Alex said.

'That's it—Peterson.'

Michael shifted uncomfortably in his seat. 'Have you discovered anything more about her hands. Why she had no, you know...' His voice trailed off.

'Fingerprints?' I prompted.

He nodded.

46

'Not yet,' Alex said. 'The coroner found traces of a drug in Emma's system. Do you know if she used Zaparin?'

'What type of drug is that?' Elizabeth asked.

'A sedative.'

'Emma refused to take medication,' Elizabeth said. 'Not normal medication, anyway. She only took homeopathic stuff.'

'Not even an aspirin?' Alex asked.

'Never. I know because she was always trying to switch me over to natural remedies.'

'Have you ever used Zaparin?' I asked her.

Alex shot me a look of warning.

'No, I've never heard of it,' she said.

Michael put a hand on his wife's knee. 'Wait a minute. Why do you want to know if my wife uses it? No, don't tell me. Let me guess. And your next question is going to be *where were we last night?*

Elizabeth removed her husband's hand. 'It's all right, Michael. I don't mind answering their questions.'

'Well, I do. It was bad enough to be asked once. Am I going to be suspected of my own daughter's death until one of you lot gets off his butt and actually finds who did it? Here, write this down. I worked late that night. A dozen people saw me there. My wife was at her friend's house. June...June...'

'June McNaughton,' Elizabeth said.

'That's it. Now I think it's time you people left us alone.'

Alex rose. 'I'm sorry. You're right. I think you've been through enough.'

Elizabeth Faber walked us to the door. 'I'm sorry about my husband.'

Alex held up a hand. 'No, don't be. This is an impossible time for both of you.'

She offered him a weak smile, and then her hand.

He took it.

'I thought you were going to stay in the background,' Alex complained.

We were walking back to the car.

47

'Sorry.'

'Of all the things to ask—'

His mobile phone rang.

I left him to the call and leaned against the door of the car. The smell of wood smoke curled out of the house across the street. It drifted through my lungs and teased my memory. This was the smell of my mother's town at twilight in winter. I looked up to the sky. Graphite-coloured clouds hung low. Rain would be here soon.

'We've got a lead,' Alex announced when he returned. 'The wooden thing we found at Emma's feet had a fingerprint on it.'

'A fingerprint? Who tested it?'

'Catherine did this morning.'

I felt a surge of relief. Catherine was one of our best printers and the closest thing I had to a good friend. Even if Peterson booted me off the eleventh floor forever, Catherine would still be my ear to the ground.

'Did she get a hit?'

'Yes. Guess who.'

I studied his face. 'Charlie Hunt?'

'Yep, and Emma's too.'

'That was easy.'

Alex grinned. 'Just the way I like it.' He face turned serious. 'Any more thoughts on going into Emma's flat?'

'Like I have a choice.'

'Of course you do.'

'Yeah, right.'

'No one will know you've been there—in and out in ten minutes.'

I had the feeling it wouldn't be that simple.

9

Alex dropped me home. I changed into my standard fingerprinter's outfit—black trousers, black jacket and dark blue shirt. It had cost me three beige suits before I'd learned that black dusting powder slipped through every join and zip of my overalls. The powder clung to dark clothes too, but at least no one noticed. I slipped a rainproof spicer over my jacket.

The phone rang. The caller I.D. displayed the number of my mother, Beryl. I considered letting the answering machine take the call, but I knew she wouldn't be content simply leaving a message—she'd ring my mobile, my office extension, and then every member of my department. The 'B' in Beryl stood for badger, beleaguer and berate. I snatched the handset from the kitchen phone.

'Did you wear the cabbage?' she asked.

'Morning Mum. Yes, I did wear the cabbage.'

'Did it work?'

'It made my fingers itch.'

'That's good. Were there any changes?'

'Of course there were no changes! Why don't you try these concoctions on yourself first, and only if they work—'

'But I'm—'

'Yeah, yeah, I know, you're not the one who's cursed.'

Silence followed, but I could almost see her smiling down the line. She loved to hear me admit I'm cursed.

Finally she said: 'Make sure you check your skin again tonight. The poppet was unearthed this morning.'

'Huh?'

'The doll I stuffed with nettles and buried under the elm—the curse breaker. The Coopers' dog dug it up.'

'Tell me this isn't the reason you're ringing?'

'It's a sign.'

'Yeah, a sign that the Coopers don't feed their dog.'

'Don't joke about this. A poppet only unearths when a curse is undone.'

'Then that's good news, right? So what's with the doom-and-gloom voice?'

'There's more.' She paused and then drew a shaky breath. 'An old man drowned in the Murray last night. They found his clothes and a bible under a tree.'

Her words slipped out of focus as I struggled to breathe. I'd inked enough floaters to know what they'd found—a body bloated to twice its size, skin a mottle of grey and purple, dermis so loose over the fingers that to take a print we'd have to cut it off and wear it like a glove. I knew she was implying the body might be Dad, but my father could not look like that. His body would be thin like mine, skin tight and pale. He'd be wearing my face, not the mask of decomposition.

With the phone clamped between my shoulder and ear, I opened the fridge door and leaned in. The cold air was like an electric shock. Within a few seconds my heart found its rhythm again.

'Sarah?'

I wiped my palms on my trousers. 'A bible? His bible?'

'Just a bible, they said. The police think the man was in his late sixties. It's him, I can feel it. All the signs are right. I felt the pain again last night, same as I did the day before he left.'

'Oh, come on!'

'You think I'm exaggerating? Listen to this. I dreamed of a change in the tides last night. Then they found him. Can that be coincidence?'

'You don't know it's him for sure.'

'And the night before I dreamed of a river that broke its banks and drowned a town.'

She'd dreamed of a river too? I took a deep breath and

forced myself to think rationally. Mum lived in a superstitious town so victimised by harsh weather that folks lit fires to bring rain. She probably had ten 'visions' a night, all omens and symbols. Of course we'd hit on the same subject eventually. But there was no way I was going to mention my river dream. She was anxious enough.

I tried to keep my voice even. 'So you predicted someone would drown—that doesn't mean it was him.'

'You still have the letter he gave me, don't you? You could get the hospital up here to send you a copy of the body's prints. You could compare them with the ones on the letter.'

I willed my fear into anger. 'What does it matter if he's dead? If I don't care, why should you?'

'It's different for you—you never knew him. And you do care, blast it.'

'How can I care about a man who deserted us? And don't tell me you loved him cause that's crap. You barely knew him either. For twenty-five years you wouldn't even tell me his name, now you ring me up every two days because you've seen some whacko sign of where he is.' We'd had this argument too many times.

'Maybe if he's dead, the curse will end.'

'You and your curses! It's not a curse to have no fingerprints. You're the only one who makes me feel cursed.'

More silence.

I wanted to bang my head against the fridge door. 'Sorry Mum, I didn't mean that. I just—why do you always have to look for him? You spent one month together. One month!'

'I only do it for you.'

'And if you found him? What would you say? Here's our daughter's address, send her a birthday card on July 4th, and while you're at it can you whisper some mumbo jumbo to give her back her fingerprints?'

She said nothing. I pictured her skinny fingers working at the coconut beads around her neck as if they were a rosary, sliding them along their loose string one at a time. If I examined the prints on the necklace, their edges would be blurred. Anger makes the pulse surge and vibrates a fingertip's ridges. I knew I should have apologised or at least changed the subject before the argument ended in the same old place. But I wouldn't.

'And Mum,'

'What?'

'I love you, okay? But priests don't cast curses.'

10

I drove through hail the size of ten-cent coins and thought about my father. The few things that Mum had told me about him were vague; he only wore wing-tipped shoes imported from Chicago and hid a thin silver flask in the breast pocket of his jacket. His voice was so deep that the wooden floorboards of the stage vibrated when he spoke. A devil so charming he'd swept aside all my mother's knots and spells, then abandoned her with me in her belly. These snippets were all I had of the father I never knew, the father I would never know.

I stuck by the decision I had made twenty years ago. I would not look for him. I would not call the Riverina Regional Hospital. I would not have the drowned man's fingerprints sent to my office. To me, my father died before I was born. What did it matter if they found his body this week? It had to be lack of sleep, not grief, that had disabled me in the kitchen. Tiredness had made me as sensitive as exposed bone.

I cruised past Emma's place and parked four houses away. I'd lived in an apartment block like hers when I was a student back in Perth. Realtors pitched it as 'New York-Style Living'— one hundred and twenty bucks a week for a few rooms in a graffiti covered tenement with unlit stairwells, psychotic neighbours and all night police sirens. I'd lasted two years. Emma had been here four.

The hail had melted to rain by the time I hurried past the lone police cruiser parked on the street. A middle-aged uniformed cop with a boxer's nose sat in the driver's seat. He was writing on a black clipboard, probably filling in an attendance report. His duty was to nab intruders who tried to sneak into the flat before the forensic technicians arrived. No media, no nosy neighbours and no off-duty fingerprinters. I was travelling light—gloves, a brush, 2 oz tub of multipurpose powder and a J-strip adhesive in my pockets. Hopefully he'd think I was just a resident entering my building or he'd have to sign me in and make me wait for the rest of the crew. So far I'd gotten lucky. He should have been standing outside Emma's door.

I pulled on the hood of my slicker and thanked God for the rain.

He looked up as I approached the mansion's gate, then down again when I passed it. I waited a few seconds, then glanced over my shoulder in his direction. His head was still down, pen moving over the clipboard.

I crept back to the gate, slipped through the entrance and hurried to the foyer of the apartments. Only for Alex and the fingerprintless girl would I do this.

The foyer was so dark that for a few seconds it felt as if someone had thrown a blanket over my head. I paused to let my eyes adjust and within a few seconds my vision returned to normal.

A stench like wet dog's fur coming from the carpet made me gag. The muted strains of a television drifted down from the floor above. Gradually I made out three numbered doors and a concrete staircase.

The first door was Emma's. No security grill— just a wooden door with a round lock. I slipped on the gloves and jiggled the handle. It wouldn't turn. I pushed hard and peered into the crack. There was no sign of a deadbolt.

The latch was visible so I knew I could open the door. My tool was a U-shaped strip of aluminium I'd cut from a Coke can and folded over and over for strength. I hooked the latch with the edge of my tool and wiggled the aluminium into a position that let me pull the latch from its hole.

54

Suddenly I heard a sound like the crackle of leather.

I spun around. The patrol cop was standing just inside the foyer, squinting into the dark. Splinters of rain slid down between the spikes of his hair. He was older than I'd first thought, with a sagging bulldog's face and tired eyes. As he waited for his eyes to adjust, his hand drifted to his utility belt and hovered just above the butt of his gun.

'Hey!' His voice bounced off the walls and leapt back at him. The hand was still lingering by the gun as the other waved me away from the door. 'What are you doing?'

I turned my back on him and yanked the metal from the lock. The latch slipped back into place. I hid the metal up my sleeve. When I turned to face him again, I had a small brush and a tiny tub of powder in my hand.

'The rest of the techies here yet?' I asked.

He stared at the brush for a few seconds, then folded his arms across his chest. 'You're the first. You were supposed to give me your I.D. number when you got here.'

'I'm not in. I wasn't going in.' I turned back to the door and dabbed the brush in the powder.

'Yeah, but you're supposed to give me your I.D number.'

'Fine, I'll give it to you now.' I set the brush and tub of powder on the floor and took out my wallet.

'But I've got to take it down.'

I stared at him as if he were a wayward child. 'So, take it down.'

'You'll have to come back to the car.'

I returned the wallet to my pocket. 'Look, I've got another two jobs after this one, you know how it is. I'll stop by your car on the way out.'

'Forget it. I thought you weren't supposed to touch anything until the photographer arrives?'

'I'm the fingerprinter! I know what I can touch and not touch.'

'Yeah, well, I have to secure the scene.'

'Secure the scene? God, tell me *you* haven't touched anything.'

'Of course I haven't touched anything!'

I picked up my brush and pot of powder. 'You lot have no idea how much of our time you waste. Didn't go near the place, you always say. But what do we find on the windows? Your prints. On the car? Your prints.'

He took a step towards me. 'I told you I didn't touch anything.'

I noticed for the first time how much taller than me he was. And how his hand had crept back down to the butt of his gun. I lifted my chin and pretended not to be intimidated. 'Then secure your scene instead of growling at me. Without touching anything.'

'You have to wait out front.'

'Oh, for God's sake!' I pushed past him and stormed out of the foyer. He was absolutely right, of course, and I felt rotten for giving him a hard time.

'Hey!' His voice followed me across the yard.

'All right, all right. I'll wait in my car,' I called over my shoulder. Instead of heading back to my car, I circled the block on foot. There had to be a back way into the apartment block.

11

Sure enough, I found a cobblestoned lane that ran along the rear of Emma's apartment block. From behind, the building looked even more run down—sheets of black plastic slapped against broken windows and gaping holes ripped in the flywire back doors. A splintered wooden staircase led to the second and third floors. A television blared from somewhere on the top floor. Above the lane's sickly stench of jasmine and cat's urine, the smell of sewerage banked up in the flooded drains.

I heaved my torso over the fence and tumbled to the ground on one knee.

'Shit,' I yelped.

I opened my eyes to find an old woman cowering behind an open rubbish bin. She was standing less than a metre from where I was.

'The police are out front,' she croaked. Her hands gripped the fraying edge of her off-white cardigan in fear. 'One holler and they'll be all over you.'

'I don't think so.' I stumbled to my feet and pulled out my I.D.

She stepped out from behind the bin, scooted around what looked like a rusting car axel and took the card. She examined it while I checked out the yard. It was all concrete, only about ten metres long and a few more wide but dotted with little piles of rubbish and broken furniture. If Emma's apartment was the same I'd need a tetanus shot.

The old woman looked up. She was prune faced with white hair floating above her head like fairy floss. I guessed she was about seventy. Her brown polyester slacks flapped around her legs and pooled over her shoes.

'You're police?' she said as she grabbed her slacks by the waist and hiked them up. The space between us suddenly smelled of camphor.

'Yes,' I said.

'Then why are you coming over the back fence? And don't cops have a badge with some star thingy on it.'

'Can I have my I.D. back. Please.'

She moved the card closer to her chest.

I leaned forward and snatched the I.D. off her. I'd already had my dose of little old lady today and wasn't going to take a spoonful more.

I said, 'Look, I'm in a hurry. Which is Emma Faber's back door?'

She squared her shoulders and folded her arms across her chest. 'Number one, 'round the right side of the building.'

I started across the yard, carefully stepping around a three-seater couch that had been stripped to its springs.

'And you tell that girl to keep her garbage to herself,' she yelled after me.

The television on the top floor suddenly cut out.

I paused and turned back to her. 'What did you say?'

'She's always throwing her garbage in my bin, and I'm tired of tossing it back. Look!'

She leaned into the bin and pulled out a box of sanitary napkins and a pair of white latex gloves. They waved above her head like a flag.

Finding latex gloves always makes me suspicious. Whenever I find gloves, I tend to be in close proximity to broken windows and jemmied locks. Thieves find it hard to grab jewellery in gardening leathers, and woollen mitts don't provide the traction you need to wield a crow bar. Latex, however, is perfect. It gives a burglar a natural sense of touch and lets him separate sheets of paper—and money—with minimal effort.

Perfect is also how I'd describe the prints that we always

find on the inside of the gloves. Burgling a house is a stressful affair, and naturally the thief is feeling more nervous than normal. So he sweats. The lack of air circulation in the glove combines with the increase in body heat to create even more perspiration. The talcum in the interior of the glove then soaks up amino acids and oils to produce a finger pattern. Add a little ninhydrin and a purple-toned print appears.

I grabbed her arm. 'Hold them still for a minute, I want to read the label.'

She lowered her hands.

Stamped into the base of the gloves was the trademark 'Labaid.'

'Whoa,' I breathed. Labaid was not the type of brand found on a supermarket shelf. We used them in the lab at work because they were one of the strongest on the market. They were so hard to get in Australia that we had to import them from the United States.

Being an anthropology student, Emma had no reason to spend time in a lab. I was willing to bet that she—like most people—had never worn latex lab gloves. If the glove weren't Emma's, then the print wouldn't be either.

Then I saw it.

A red stain on one of the gloves.

I snatched them from the old lady. 'Police property.'

Her eyes narrowed so tightly they nearly disappeared in the folds of her face. 'So what's that girl done now?'

'How well do you know her?' I asked as I pulled the paper bag from my pocket Carefully, I slipped the gloves in the bag.

'She's just a neighbour. Whatever she did, I don't know anything about it.'

'What's your name?'

'Jane.'

'Jane, what I'm going to tell you may be a shock.'

'A shock? Takes a lot to shock me.'

'She was murdered,' I said gently.

'Well, she was a strange one.'

I stared at her. 'That's all you can say?'

She shrugged. 'Told you I didn't shock easily. I'll tell you something else, too. She's been acting mighty strange lately. Worse than normal, I mean. If you let me come in with you, I'll show you where she keeps her spare key.'

The smell of clove hit me the moment Jane swung open the door.

Jane laughed when she saw me wrinkle my nose. 'Stinks, doesn't it.' She nodded at a row of jars on a counter just beside the door. 'She had a thing for herbs.'

'Stay outside,' I said.

I stepped past her and checked the place out quickly. It was a standard low rent unit: peeling backdoor set into the scuff-marked wall of a small kitchenette that made up the corner of the lounge, corridor leading past a bathroom with a toilet seat squashed between a shower and a basin. The bedroom at the end of the passage looked out into the yard we'd just left.

I tried to absorb as much of Emma's lifestyle as I could. Broadsheet newspapers were scattered along a shabby, wooden coffee table in the lounge, most open at the first few pages. This I interpreted as an interest in national news rather than international affairs or finance. A pile of books sat on the edge of the table. Spread over the books was an open copy of the Green Left Weekly, a newspaper that reported on socialist and ecological issues. It was popular with students and professional protest groups. I picked it up by the corner to check the date. It was last week's issue.

Beneath the newspaper I found two glasses. One was upright, the other knocked on its side. I peered into the bottom of the standing glass. It was clear, with none of the sticky residue left behind by soft drinks. I concluded it had held only water.

I returned to the kitchen and searched through the cupboards until I found two plastic bags. Using a section of the plastic as a glove, I slipped the glasses into a bag each and set them down by the back door.

Two glasses side by side were a good bet that Emma was

entertaining someone. Had one been tipped over in a struggle? The loungeroom didn't look ruffled. There were no other glasses left around so it seemed that Emma cleaned up after herself pretty quickly. There was no proof, but I'd be willing to bet that the two glasses were used the night she died. If they held two different prints, the print that was not hers could belong to the person who'd shared Emma's last evening.

I turned my attention back to the room. Textbooks on anthropology and aboriginal culture and a few paperbacks by Patrick White and Catherine Susanna Prichard sat on an unpolished pine bookshelf. A single couch covered with a blue batik throw rug faced a seventies style TV. An answering machine sat on a table by the front door. I pressed play. There was a message from a man who sounded in his twenties. 'Hi, it's me. I thought you were coming over tonight. Call me back at home.'

Jane came up behind me. 'That's probably her young man.'

'I told you to stay outside.'

'It's cold out there,' She pulled her cardigan shut. 'I'm not as young as I look. And don't you think I'd look a bit suspicious hanging around the back door.'

'All right, all right, but stay in the kitchen.'

Emma's bedroom was untidy. A few days worth of soiled clothes had been thrown on the floor beside the bed. Her small wooden desk was covered with a few of the window-faced envelopes that usually hold bills, more anthropology books, crumpled notepads and dirty drinking glasses. I slid open the drawers, but found only stationery and study notes. A small windup alarm clock and a textbook on environmental biology sat on her bedside table. I fossicked through its drawer, looking for anything that could be Zaparin. There was only little bottle of tea tree oil, a jar of chemical-free makeup remover and some facial wipes. A few batik dresses, casual shirts and trousers, two above the knee black skirts, and a navy blue business jacket and matching skirt filled her wardrobe.

My nose drew me back to the kitchen. I scanned the jars and recognised lemon grass, cumin and bergamot. The last jar held a light pink, cream-like substance. 'What's that one?' I asked Jane.

She reached out a hand towards it.

'No!' I yelled, but it was too late. The jar was in her hands, lid off.

'Smells like calamine lotion.'

'You can't touch anything,' I said.

'Why not? I've been in here a dozen times. My fingerprints will be over everything anyway. She used to pay me to clean things up a bit.'

'How often?' I asked.

'Just occasionally.'

'When was the last time you were in here?'

'Last week. Thursday.'

Eight days before Emma died. 'Does anything look different?'

'Yeah, it was clean when I left.'

I grabbed a tea towel from the bench and wrapped it over my hand so I could open the cupboard doors without leaving prints. I didn't have classifiable prints like the rest of the world, but my colleagues would immediately recognise the pebbled pattern my fingerpads left behind. My prints were so unique, they needed no classification.

I hurriedly checked for what looked like a medicine cabinet. I found some adhesive strips and a few tubes of herbal ointment on a high shelf above the stove. There was nothing that could have been Zaparin and no latex gloves. Emma's mother had been right—no pharmaceuticals.

I opened the fridge.

Dishes clattered to my left. I turned to see Jane removing a large frying pan from the cupboard beneath the sink.

'It's mine,' she protested. 'Emma borrowed it a few weeks ago.'

'The police have to go through all this. You can't take anything.'

'Well excuse me, but haven't you already broken the law by walking through that door?'

I tried to keep the surprise from my face.

'I wasn't born yesterday, you know. If you were allowed in here, you wouldn't be creeping around.'

'My job is none of your business, but I'm warning you that if you take that pan, you're breaking the law.'

'It's coming home.' She tucked it under her arm.

'Then so are you.' I pointed to the door. 'Now!'

Jane's attention was caught by something in the fridge behind me. 'Where's her test tubes?'

I turned back to the fridge and stared inside. 'Her what?'

'She used to have one of those wooden racks with test tubes in it. Each tube was labelled.'

'Labelled with what?'

'Dates—like June 8, June 15, June 22. She was real particular about me not touching them. Told me off for slamming the door and making them rattle.'

Why would an anthropology student keep test tubes in her fridge?

I grabbed Jane by the arm. 'Change of plan. You're staying.'

'Damn right I am. Who knows what else of mine this girl's still got.'

'I want you to take a look around and tell me if you see anything else that's different.'

She glanced around the room. 'Looks normal to me.'

'Where does she keep her violin?'

'In the bedroom. But I haven't seen it for a while.'

'It wasn't here when you were last over?'

She shook her head. 'No. Maybe it's getting repaired. I remember it looked really old.'

'Can you check the rest of the place?' I asked.

While she went through the unit room by room, I peeked out the front window to check if the technical teams had arrived yet. I could just make out the bonnet of a second cruiser parked across the road.

'Hurry up,' I called.

Jane returned a few minutes later. 'That wooden thing's missing from the top of her telly.'

'What wood thing?' I asked.

She made a shape with her hand. 'Small and long. Like a little log with no insides.'

'Did it have anything on it?'

'Yeah, Aboriginal paintings.'

I assumed this was the object that was found at Emma's feet.

'What did she use it for?' I asked.

'A telly antenna, I guess.'

I kept my frustration in check. 'So you don't know.'

'It was probably just an ornament.'

So Emma's killer had been in the apartment or Emma had given it to him. 'Okay. Just let me go through the bathroom cupboard, then we can go,' I said.

'I already have. She's out of toothpaste.'

'Any medication?'

'Not a single one. Judging by all the crap in the kitchen, she creates her own.'

Voices boomed out from the porch. Words were indistinguishable but the tones were rhythms I'd heard a hundred times before. The crime scene technicians were being allocated rooms and tasks. The photographer would be first in at any second.

I grabbed Jane's elbow and pushed her back into the kitchen and out the back door.

The scrape of a key inserted into a lock carried through the lounge.

I grabbed the plastic bags holding the gloves and wine glasses, then pulled the door shut and jammed the key into the lock. 'You keep going.'

Jane paused by the gate. 'What are you doing?'

'If the door's left unlocked, it'll look suspicious.' I turned the key and hurried to join her at the gate.

She pulled the gate closed behind me. 'So tell me again why you're hiding from the police?'

'For god's sake, I'm not hiding! I'm an unsworn officer. It's my job to find fingerprints, that's all.'

'I suppose I haven't seen you then, if the real police come looking.'

'Not unless they ask about me specifically.'

'What a shame! I like you better than the usual stiffs who beat on my door everytime Emma's done anything wrong.'

I stopped dead. 'The police have been here before?'

'Now and then.'

'Why?'

'I bailed her out once when she was thrown in the clink for demonstrating. She called me because she wanted some clean clothes and some money. I was the only one who knew where the key to her flat was. A cop came around asking why my name was on the form.'

'Do you remember his name?'

'Nope.'

'What else did he ask you?'

'Nothing. He just wanted to know how I knew Emma. I told him she was my neighbour, and he was happy with that.'

'Why were the police here the other times?'

'Silly things. She was always going to protests about aboriginals so the police knew where she lived. One time they came 'cause her boyfriend got into a fight with a guy on the street outside. Then about a year ago her place and a unit upstairs were robbed. The cops asked me if I saw anything.'

I looked back at the block of units and saw a light go on in Emma's apartment.

'That policeman that came around. What did he look like?'

'Tall and thin.'

'Would you recognise the name if I said it?'

'I might.'

'Anderson?'

She shook her head slowly. 'No, I don't think that was it. It was sort of like that though.'

'Peterson?'

Her face lit up. 'That's it! Peterson.'

12

I took the gloves and the glasses straight back to the office on St Kilda Road. As I'd expected, the floor was nearly empty. The squad room log registered two of the five on-duty fingerprinters as being at Emma's apartment. The third, Paul, was in the print lab processing the clothes that Emma had been found in. I searched for Catherine's name on the log. Disappointed, I saw she was listed as attending a B & E at a city corporate block on Collins Street. The log listed me as running background checks on the prints of employees new to the casino—punishment for being last into the office that day. I stared down at the bag in my hand. With someone in the lab, there was no escape. I'd have to save the gloves and glasses for later and get stuck into the casino job.

But first, I cut out the bloodstain and bagged it. Alex would have to arrange for it to be tested. I called the internal courier and filled in a chain of evidence sticker. I hoped Alex had already filled in the paperwork authorising my access to Emma's apartment.

I locked the gloves and glasses in my filing cabinet.

Before I dedicated myself to screening potential croupiers, I phoned Footscray Central and asked for Constable Mead.

I introduced myself and asked if he remembered working the protest two months ago.

His voice had the gruff suspicion of an aged cop. 'Down past the docklands, right?'

'That's it.'

'Yeah, we overcommitted our numbers to it. We were afraid professional protesters would hijack the whole event. Once they get involved, things turn ugly. But it was quiet. A few arrests, but mainly to get them to move on.'

'You made one. A young woman.'

'Yeah. And?'

'She was murdered the night before last. You'd signed an arrest form but so had another cop called Peterson. I wondered why that was?'

'That's why you're asking? You just wondered?'

'I'm looking for the whole picture here, that's all.'

'Then why not ask Peterson?'

'I will ask him, but I thought I'd ask you first. He's a detective. I don't want to waste his time on small details.'

'So you've decided to waste mine instead.'

'Look, all I want to know is why he co-signed. If you were pulled off the arrest because of something you did, that's between you and Peterson. I'm not interested in what you did —just give me a sense of why you were pulled off.'

'It's nothing I did. Anyone will tell you that. He just rolled up and went through the arrest paperwork until he found something he was looking for.' He sighed. 'Look, you want my opinion?'

'That's why I'm calling.'

'He didn't know her. I remember he had to call out to see who she was. He must have wanted her for something else. I assumed maybe she had priors or that he knew she was the ringleader or something.'

'Did you think she was the ringleader?'

'No. Peterson he wanted to speak to her for something, that's all I know. It seemed perfectly legitimate, and I think it's wrong for you to paint it otherwise. In fact, I think she even thanked him afterwards.'

'Why?'

'Well, a few of them got thrown in the clink for a few hours. Maybe he decided she could go free.'

Silence fell between us as I thought about his words.

'Look,' he said, 'if you're finished, I've got work to do. I'm not happy talking about other cops. And you shouldn't be either.'

'You're right. Okay, thanks.' I hung up.

No doubt Peterson was going to get a phone call from Footscray Central in a few minutes.

I sat down at one of the six computers and began the slog of scanning casino worker's prints into the computer. My left foot tapped against the leg of the chair. I was still pumped with adrenalin from sneaking into Emma's place and finding the gloves and glasses. It was going to be a long afternoon.

I was half an hour into the job when Alex called my mobile. 'The squad's at Emma's house.'

'I know,' I said. 'I saw them go in.'

'Did they see you?'

'No. I found a glove with what looks like blood on it.'

'A glove?'

'Latex. You're not going to believe this. In the girl's garbage.'

'How do you know they've related to the crime?'

'Who else is going to be using latex gloves?'

'A lot of people, judging by the amount of boxes on supermarket shelves.'

'They not a consumer brand. They're industrial export quality.'

'Why would the killer cut off Emma's fingerprints if he's going to leave a glove with his prints on it lying around.'

His words turned my stomach. He was right—something didn't make sense.

I said, 'I've couriered the stain up to you.'

'Good. I'll get the lab to see if it's a match with Emma's.'

'Did you ask Peterson why his name was on Emma's arrest record?'

'Yes. He claims he doesn't remember, and that he might have taken the protest call because he was in the area.'

'He doesn't remember her face?'

'No. That's not surprising given it was a few months ago.'

Once I'd fingerprinted someone, I rarely forgot their face. Detectives usually had even better memories. I bit my tongue and moved on. 'I spoke to Emma's neighbour, Jane Frommer. Does that name ring a bell?'

'Yeah, it does.'

'She bailed Emma out once. She says a cop came around asking questions about her relationship with Emma. Guess what that cops name was?'

'Not Peterson?'

'Peterson.'

'Why would he care whose name was on the release form?' Alex asked.

'You tell me.'

'Obviously he wanted more information about Emma. Maybe he thought she was involved in something more than a simple protest.'

'And we can't ask Peterson if he doesn't remember arresting her.'

'Maybe now that I've asked him about her, he'll give it more thought. It may jog his memory.'

Paul emerged from the lab, still wearing his white lab coat. He waved a hello then mimed eating.

I figured I had the lab to myself for at least half an hour.

'Gotta go,' I whispered and hung up.

13

The lab was tomb silent. I wriggled my hands into a pair of latex gloves and laid the ones I'd found at Emma's on the workbench. I held my hand above the fingers of the used glove and noticed that it was a larger size than my own. A search of the storage cupboards in the lab yielded a box of large sized gloves. I measured them against the glove from Emma's bin. They were the same size.

I'd held Emma's thin hand in my own—bulbous, bruised and skinless. The feel of her hands would never leave me.

But her hands were too small.

These were not her gloves.

To check for a print, I had to work out whether the gloves were inside out or right side out. When a wearer peels the gloves off, the inside is usually turned outward, but I couldn't risk making a mistake. If I handled the wrong side, I could accidentally destroy the print. I gently felt the surface of the gloves, feeling for the slip of alkali against my fingers. This would be the talcum powder that lined the inside.

Sure enough, the latex felt smooth and slick against my own gloved hand. This was the side that had moulded around the wearer's hand.

Using a lumalight, I shone beams of light from visible luminescence to ultraviolet over the gloves. The glove's surface glowed a greenish blue. What in visible light was a seamless film of plastic became like a rainforest floor dense with overlapping leaves and pine twigs. Plastic, like skin, was simply a chain of fibres.

I looked for the moist residues of finger pattern, but found none. I snapped off the lumalight and restored the lab to bulb light. Hopefully, superglue would detect a print.

Picking up the glove with a pair of metal tweezers, I placed it inside the fanning fume cabinet and spread superglue over its surface with a spatula, taking special care to cover every speck of surface area on the fingers and lower palm. This is where the wearer would most likely have sweated out a print. A palm impression is as individual as a fingerprint. The final step was to place the gloves in a large Perspex cube that would contain the fumes.

It would take a few hours for the glue to polymerise onto the mix of water and sebaceous deposits left by the wearer. I locked the box away in my filing cabinet drawer and pulled out the two glasses.

From my own kit I removed a squirrel haired brush. I dipped the brush into black powder and dusted the first glass. I began at the rim of the glass and rolled the brush handle clockwise and anti-clockwise between my thumb and pointer finger. Moving across and down at the same time while twirling the brush was the only movement that would not cut through the latent print's ridge structure.

I recognised Emma's index print even before I'd cleaned off the excess powder. Her twinned loops flowed up and stopped just below the centre point of the pattern. Twinned loops raised to an arch occurred in only a tiny percentage of the population. The star-shaped blotch marked the centre of the pattern. Separately, these characteristics were rare. Together, they could only be Emma Faber's. She had definitely touched this glass

I kept checking for prints.

A thumb impression can usually be found on the side opposite to the section that was cupped against the palm. Holding the base, I rotated the glass but could find no more prints. I would only have one to work from.

I concentrated on the loops. The print was not complete.

Only the pad's centre detail showed. No fingertip, nothing below the delta. I photographed the print with a colour Polaroid and cleaned the excess powder from the glass with a small, thin brush. I danced the bristles lightly along the ridges of the print. Too heavy a pressure can compress the lines and curves of a print; too forceful a stroke can alter their flow. Under a weighty hand, an ulnar loop can become radial; an arch can become a whirl. A single twist of a bristle can add a bifurcation where there were only straight ridges. A wayward strand of squirrel hair can transform an eight-ridged pattern into a nine. I had seen an unsteady hand create a new identity from someone else's fingerprints.

Still wearing the eyeglass, I traced the ridges until the excess powder disappeared. Under magnification the lined characteristics were bolder. Lines swelled upwards and plunged down to accommodate the broadening curve of the loops. Creases in the deltas at the origin of each loop could be traced and counted. Nine ridges in exactly the same formation as those I had reconstructed from Emma's print. There was no doubt these were Emma's.

I turned my attention to the second glass. I dusted it in the same manner as the first, always twisting clockwise and then anticlockwise and then clockwise again, always moving across and down. The powder began to cling and lines emerged. As the print grew, it seemed that this was Emma's as well—a loop moving in the same direction as Emma's, radiating from the same position in the fingerpad. Blurred lines moved away in the opposite direction. This had to be the second loop. I shifted the glass to catch the lines from as different angle. This amount of blurring would normally render a print unreadable but because I knew every crease and curve of Emma's finger, I might let my imagination, not my eye, read her print.

In Australia, there must be eight points of similarity between two prints to call them a match. Here I had only two —the two origin points of the loop.

Legally, I could not attribute this second print to Emma.

I was glad about this. I did not want this print to belong to

Emma. I wanted it to be the residue of the person who had shared Emma's last hours.

And possibly her last moments.

Of course, I was forbidden to think like this. It's unscientific to hope something into actuality.

I photographed the print and added it to Emma's file. By the time I'd cleaned up the lab the clock showed I'd been at it for half an hour. Paul was due back any minute. I scooted back into the partitioned area and sat down at my desk. I fed the rest of the casino workers' prints into the computer and printed out a progress list. In the hour since I'd entered the first scan, the database had only found two hits out of the seventy sets of prints I'd entered. At this rate it would take two days.

I was eating a six-inch roll with salad and vinaigrette at the Subway a few doors down from the office when Alex called me on my mobile.

'I've left an envelope in your pigeon-hole,' he said. Inside is the background check on Michael Faber.'

I filled him in on what I had found on the items I'd taken from Emma's house and mentioned that the neighbour claimed an aboriginal item was missing from the top of the television. 'And we need to ask the parents what they know about the test tubes,' I added.

'I think we'll have trouble getting them to talk to us again. Anyone one else she knew who could shed light on the test tubes?'

'There's a message on her answering machine from a man she was supposed to meet. The neighbour thinks it's Charlie's voice. He may know,' I cradled the phone between my shoulder and my ear and continued eating.

'Peterson sent a team over to the boy's place. No sign of him. Looks like he's done a runner,' Alex said.

I swallowed a clump of bread roll. 'Really? That looks bad. Has anyone printed his flat?'

'No, why should we? Peterson's already got a match on

your database between Charlie's print and the print on the Aboriginal token found at Emma's feet. We know we'll find Emma's prints at his flat because he was his girlfriend. There's nothing to be learned.'

'There's always something to be learned from prints. What if I find the prints of Emma's brother there, or one of her parents. Changes the picture a little, doesn't it?'

'You don't have authorisation from Peterson to go into Charlie's place.'

'But I don't need it. If Peterson sent someone over that meant he had a warrant. And if he has a warrant, that would cover fingerprints.'

'Sarah-'

'I'm not saying I'm going in.' With one hand, I tossed the remains of the roll in the bin and stood up to return back to the office. 'It was just a thought.'

No one works on the fingerprint floor at night. On-call staff stay at home to answer their beeper but few fingerprints require identification so urgently that they are traded for sleep.

The ninhydrin was stale in the air and below it I could smell the acrid fume of cigarettes. The building was now strictly no smoking but somehow the blinds and carpet seemed to have the stain of cinder and nicotine. If I left papers on my desk overnight, by morning I'd have to brush off flecks of grey dust. Obviously some colleagues could not kick the habit.

Paul had gone home hours ago. The panel on my desk phone was flashing to indicate that someone had left a message on my voice mail. It was my mother. Ring me when you get a chance, she said. She must have called when I was eating dinner. I checked my pigeonhole. Inside was a light yellow manila envelope. In the corner of the envelope was my name scribbled in Alex's loopy hand.

I pulled a set of gloves from the box on my desk and wriggled my fingers into them. I grabbed a pair of tweezers and a brown evidence bag from the supply trolley. With the tweezers, I lifted the envelope from the drawer and carefully removed the contents. Holding it delicately by the corners, I folded it in two and slipped it into the brown bag.

Alex's prints had always been strong but towards the end of our relationship they had grown bolder. I wondered what I would find tonight.

Love defines a fingerprint like a tattoo stains the skin.

I switched off the lights in the main room and took the brown bag and the papers he'd given me into the lab. I sprayed the envelope. After I'd removed my gloves and rubbed Vaseline into the tiny scars on my fingertips to stop the skin from drying out, I sat down by the fume cupboard and read about Emma Faber's father.

Michael Faber was the president of Vic Environs, one of the state's largest construction organisations. Unlike the executives of other high-profile, Melbourne-based building companies, he was not tied to the firm by family or marriage. He had bought the company out when it was undervalued and strengthened its fiscal position by winning a number of key contracts to construct Victoria's new maze of ring roads. His wife had contributed most of the buy-out funds.

Alex's notes then descended into a standard background check. No criminal record or breaches of contract serious enough to result in the need for a criminal file. Although it was doubtful that Michael would gain monetarily through Emma's death, Alex had run a financial check as a precaution. Vic Environs had filed a tax return of $3.5 million last July, with just under $1 million in losses. A credit check had been performed on both the company and Faber himself. The man's record was triple A, the company's equally good, although it had a considerable list of debtors. There was no indication that payment had ever been reneged.

I folded the papers and slipped them into my briefcase.

From the offices outside the lab, I heard the long squeal of a filing cabinet drawer closing.

I jumped to my feet and swung open the lab door.

The lights were still off in the main room.

Something in the darkness shifted.

I gasped and snapped off the lab's light.

Any staff working on my floor would have just flicked on the master light and yelled out to let me know they were there.

Whoever was here didn't want to be seen.

With my back against the wall, I slid away from the main room.

My head suddenly throbbed from the force of my pulse.

I laid a hand on my chest and made myself breath deeply.

Not now, I willed my lungs, no time for a fit of breathlessness.

Think logically.

Should I slip into the lab and lock myself inside?

The intruder knew I was in the lab—the light shining under the door would have cast illumination over a quarter of the main room and let him see what he was doing. He must have expected easy access to whatever he was looking for. So easy that it didn't worry him that I was working in the lab.

I peered into the darkness again, trying to detect movement.

Everything was still.

I ran across the floor and flicked the main lights on.

A man dressed in dark clothes slipped out the swinging entrance doors.

'Hey!' I rushed to the doorway and stepped into the foyer.

It was empty.

The elevators were still at ground floor.

I pushed open the stairwell door and heard footsteps echoing up the vertical concrete tunnel.

'Hey!' I yelled again.

A door slammed and the footsteps stopped.

He had fled to another floor.

I leaned against the wall and tried to breathe.

14

Once my lungs had steadied, I checked all the filing cabinets to see which one was open.

Only mine was unlocked.

I pulled out the Perspex cube that held the glove. Superglue fumes had clouded the inside of the plastic, making it impossible to see the glove within.

There was a mark on the brown bag that held the drinking glasses I'd recovered from Emma's coffee table.

It was a small black smudge, half the size of a five-cent piece in circumference.

I recognised it immediately. I'd spent ten years searching knife handles and gun butts for this collection of half lines and gentle curves.

A partial thumb print—faint and incomplete.

To the naked eye, there were only a few ridges. I knew my own rippled print by sight. This was not mine.

I left the door open and wriggled my hands into a pair of latex gloves. With metal tweezers, I lifted the bag up by the edges as if it were infected. Which, ironically, it now was.

I placed the bag on my desk and checked the yellow suspension files that hung at the back of the drawer. Emma Faber's was still first. I had left it unlabelled on purpose, although that now seemed a futile gesture. One look inside and it would be obvious who the subject was. I removed the file and spread it open on the desk.

The Polaroids of the fingerprint on the glass were still there. Gently, I picked them up with the tweezers, carried them into the lab, and turned on the lumalight. Frequency by frequency, I ran the light over the photos until I found what I had suspected was there.

Another print.

Faint like the thumbprint on the brown bag but with a few ridge characteristics that I could name. Someone had managed to open my filing cabinet and had quickly looked though the contents. The print impression was light and barely visible even under luminescence. The photo and the bag had obviously not been handled for long, and by someone who was not nervous about discovery.

I sat down at my desk and flipped through Emma's file. There was little here of any value. The fingerprint on the glasses were her own, and the notes I had taken so far had yielded nothing significant. I doubted the details of Emma's wear patterns would mean anything to anyone except myself.

The only unknown was the glove.

I closed the file, pulled the Perspex cube over, and tried to see through the fog of glue. The resins had so densely coated the walls that visibility was impossible.

Panic closed my lungs again.

How did I know the glove was still inside?

With my left hand, I turned the cube and examined the hinges. They were sealed, the latch still locked.

That meant nothing. The cube was designed for containment, not security.

Yet if I opened it, the air let in would halt the glue's adherence to the amino acids of the print. It had been processing for three hours, not quite long enough. It needed a minimum of four hours, otherwise I'd be left with half a print, or at best, a complete but ill-defined one. The final hour was the most crucial.

I set the cube back down on the desk. There was little I could do. I would just have to wait and hope that the glove had not been removed or exposed to air.

One thing was certain. There was no way I was leaving the cube or my files here in the cabinet. While they revealed little, they did announce that I was working on the case. Somebody now knew. The question was who and how he found out.

I pulled open the filing cabinet drawer again and quickly checked the content of the other files. This was my first case since I'd returned from leave, so the rest of the files were cold cases—either closed or surrendered to other members of the department.

I quickly identified each file.

It struck me then that I was only assuming that it was the Faber case that had attracted someone to my drawer. Just because the other files were closed or reallocated, it didn't mean they were worthless. But if someone wanted access to these files, why not just ask me?

Still wearing my gloves, I snatched up all the files and carried them into the lab. One by one I tested each file under the lumalamp for fingerprints. On the thicker files, I found a few sets of fingerprints. I could identify all of them. I'd learnt the imprints of my colleagues as quickly as I'd learnt their names.

There was no single print that emerged on all the files, and certainly no repeat of the partial I had found on the Faber file and the brown bag.

So the intruder had come to look for the Faber files.

I scanned the partial into the computer. Normally it would be impossible to get a result on such a small segment of print. However, by choosing digital enhancement parameters I could control the focus of the search.

I asked the computer to search only amongst active members of the Victoria Police and hit the enter key.

While I waited for a result, I felt my hands starting to shake from the adrenalin of the break-in. To distract myself, I forced myself to think about the person I had been trying to avoid.

Alex.

15

For a year, I thought Alex and I were slowly falling in love. I had done all the things that people in love do: revealed the things I usually hid and neglected to hide the things that were too revealing.

And I stole his fingerprints.

Initially it was to test the strength of his emotions for me. He was strange sometimes, with his long stares out windows and sudden silences. I assumed his mind was haunted with the crime scene photographs of his latest case, or the unsure words of a witness. Or perhaps heavy with his feelings for me. He would not talk about these moods, so I used the only tool of clairvoyance that I knew—his fingerprints. I tried to read what his touch left behind, but I was looking with my heart and not my eyes. He was like a partial latent that I had let my imagination fill in. Where there was a straight line I saw a bifurcation. When an impression was strong, I saw passion instead of turmoil. Sometimes I would find another set of prints on his pen or on his telephone. I began to collect the marks that filled his life. I knew the residues of his best friend, his occasional cleaning lady, and his mother. There was another group of patterns that I would find everywhere but could not name. They seemed to settle over his things like a layer of perfume. One day I tested the handle of his bedroom door and found them there too. They were all thick lines, swollen with power.

It was Catherine who finally told me. He had been married for four years. He was separated, she said, but the wife was still around.

I asked him and he said they were over. Yes, she came to his house sometimes, but only as a friend.

How, I wondered, could he have hidden a wife for a year?

I realised then that she had not been hidden.

Again, I had simply been looking with my heart instead of my eyes.

I went to his house to tell him I needed time alone, that I had applied for leave and would be going away. I needed time to slow my emotions down, to assess whether he was in love with me too. His wife answered the door wearing his jumper and bedroom hair.

I fled but he followed. It's not as it seems, he argued, don't run.

But I did. I ran just as Mum and I had ran from the Riverina to small towns near Perth, and like I had ran from Perth to Melbourne when Mum moved back to look for Dad. This time I ran to a small border town between South and Western Australia. I stayed with a former colleague from Perth and promised myself I would never again let imagination fill in the lines of a fingerprint. I had the feeling it was a promise I would not keep.

While the database was checking the intruder's prints, I examined Alex's envelope.

His lines were deep and dark, every ridge countable. Countable, I reminded myself, not readable.

I was doing this out of clinical curiosity, not love.

Still, my heart began to beat a little faster and I felt my face grow warm.

I tore up the envelope and threw the pieces in the bin.

By the time I packed the files and the drinking glasses into my briefcase, an hour had passed since I'd discovered the print on the files.

I carried the Perspex cube into the lab and switched on the fume cupboard. While it was warming up, I loaded a Polaroid with film and set the camera on the bench.

I unlatched the cube and exhaled in relief. The glove was still in there.

With metal tweezers, I pulled the glove out and sat it on a wooden chopping board. The glue had crusted over the print, but its angles and turns were clearly visible. In the middle of the print was the same star-shaped blotch that I had detected in Emma's print.

For a second I thought I was looking at her print again. Had she worn the glove herself after all? I felt a flash of foolishness. Why had I jumped so quickly to the conclusion that the gloves would belong to an intruder just because they were too large for Emma? I had worn gloves that were too large many times when we were out of small ones. Simply because Emma's neighbour had found a few household items displaced didn't mean that someone had slipped on gloves and removed evidence.

I fitted an eyepiece and examined the print at a magnification. But instead of Emma's distinctive twinned loop, the lines swelled in divergence from the side of the finger into a broad circle that ringed the white pulp of the finger. Such roundness could only mean a whorl. Yet the star-shaped botch had obscured the spiralling central point of the pattern.

Whipping off the eyepiece, I held the glove up against my own hand. The print was on the inside of the thumb. The print from the drinking glass had been from Emma's index finger.

What if she had worn the gloves on the wrong fingers?

No, the mark I was seeing was definitely someone's thumb. My years of experience examining fingers had taught me that thumb prints are the most easily distinguished from the other digits. Only on the thumbs do the ridges at the extreme tip, or what we call the distal limit, slope towards the ulnar bone. I knew a thumb print when I saw one. This was one.

And not Emma's.

With such an incomplete image, there was little point running it through the database. Far too many possible matches would be chosen by the computer.

I fitted an eyeglass and examined the print again.

A smudge of glue had adhered to the blotch. My first instinct was to peel it off, but as I ran my finger over the line, I could feel smaller glue residues around it. The polypropylene had stuck to some smaller, barely distinct, secretions.

I increased the magnification of the eye lens to full and tried to detect a pattern in the glue stains. I traced my tweezer point along each of the lines, searching for an intersection where they converged or even crossed.

Two thin lines running across the centre of the pulp seemed to run parallel and then joined into a rounded tip, like a loop. Yet every loop has at least one rod running through it. If these lines were actually papillary ridges, they couldn't be a loop without a rod. I ran the tweezers inside the loop and searched for the slightest change in texture that would indicate a raised line. The tweezers edge jumped slightly as I drew it across the surface of the glove. There was something raised there, but too low a wall to be detected.

I grabbed a pot of gentian violet from the supply cupboard and lightly brushed the liquid over the ridges.

In a few seconds, the shallow ridge grew visible. After switching off the lights, I switched the lumalight to ultraviolet to better see the gentian violet's staining.

A rod appeared through the centre of the loop in the middle of the fingerpad. It was short, severing after a few millimetres. It could easily have been a dash—a short abrupt line that led nowhere.

I examined the rest of the print, but no further glue adherences were visible with the lumalight still shining. I photographed the impressions on the glove and then took more shots in visible light.

Despite finding these new lines, I knew they were still too few to run through the database. As I cleaned up the lab, my mind drifted over the statistics of fingerprint nominations I had learned. This new pattern was a whorl on the thumb. While whorls were most frequent on the right ring finger, and second most common on the left, they were not rare on thumbs.

A lifetime in the profession teaches dactylologists that finger lines have associations as organised yet cryptic as a Masonic codebook. Each finger has a personality and each ridge a social position. The thumb is the most gregarious of the phalanges. It's deviance is its brand. A single fingerprint on a plane of glass can be immediately nominated as a thumb by the wayward lines at its tip. The thumb's edge will rebel against all patterns in its effort to create a run of ulnar leaning lines. It is greedy too, spreading its creases across a larger surface than the other fingers and competing to create the highest number of ridge counts from delta to core.

But the thumb pays dearly for its dominance. While it may be the most eager to leave its impression, it has the weakest of detectable prints. We brace our lives with our thumbs, it steadies our newspapers as we turn the page and applies the most pressure when we hold a pen. It is the anchor to our teacups and beer glasses. It steadies us when we hold onto a bar on the bus and provides the traction we need to turn our car's steering wheel. A life of friction erases its character and wears down its ridges.

But no amount of ridge wear could create a blotch in the centre of the print. To create a blotch when inked, the mark must be raised.

How could two individuals both have the same mark on a finger of their hands?

Why on her index and the unknown person's thumb?

I switched off the lights in the lab and packed all the files and photographs into my briefcase. I had expected the fingerprint on the glove to be the clue that gave me a name to start investigating but instead it offered me only more mystery.

I recorded what I had found in my small notepad and checked whether the computer had returned a result on the print I had found on my folder.

It had.

I stared at the name on the screen, unbelieving.

Peterson!

But why? As head of crime scenes, he could ask to see my files at any time. Why would he need to sneak through my files. And why run away when I caught him?

What was he looking for that was so secret?

I printed a full copy of his prints and then packed up. Time to head home.

But first, I decided, I would drive past Charlie Hunt's place.

Elizabeth Faber had ignited my curiosity about Charlie and the world he resided in. By going on the run, Charlie had transformed that curiosity into an urge to see what he had to hide. Peterson's invasion of my files implied I was close to something that made him, or someone close to him, nervous. This combination of compulsions chipping away at me meant that I wouldn't be able to just log off, head home to bed, and tune out for the next six hours.

I would cruise past. If the place looked empty, I might even take a peek through the windows and collect a few prints from the exterior.

16

By moonlight, 'Mansfield' was a four-storey shadow with a tiny yard of low weeds. It was run down in a gentle way—metal balconies chewed by the ocean air, bricks bombed streaky white by seagulls, garden shaggy but not overrun. It looked a little downmarket compared to the twenty-floor condo to the left and the three-storey art deco apartments on the right, but it was hardly the state-funded squat Elizabeth Faber made it out to be.

A police cruiser was parked a few properties down. I parked my own car a block away. My mobile phone rang.

'Mum, be quick. I'm on a job,' I lied.

'It's past nine o'clock!'

I tried to be patient. 'I'm on shift. What's wrong?'

'I need you to come up to the Riverina.'

'What? Why?'

'I can't be alone now.'

'Why?'

'I'm having dreams about the river. The body they found in the river has started people talking again. The townspeople are starting to avoid me. Someone painted a word on my letterbox.'

I knew what that word was. Kids had been painting it on our box ever since I was a kid. 'Look mum, I can't come down right now. Go and stay with Doris Reddy for a couple of days.'

'But I want you—'

'No, I told you, I can't.' I pulled out my last resort. 'Use one of your charms if you're worried. That one with the rosemary is always a winner.'

'Don't make fun of me!'

'Mum, I've got to go. I'll call you tomorrow.'

She sniffed out a goodbye.

I hung up and considered the police car. There was no way I could just stroll up to Charlie's floor and start knocking on doors, peeking through windows, or start spreading powder around with the cops watching.

On impulse, I dialled 000.

'Hello? I want to report someone breaking into a house in Armstrong Street, St Kilda.' Armstrong Street was about five blocks away from where the cruiser stood.

'Your name?'

'Alison Chambers. I live at 24 Armstrong Street. I just saw a guy in a black tracksuit climb over the fence of number 30.' I gave a few more bogus details and watched as the cruiser pulled away from the curve a few minutes later.

I jumped out of my car and hurried up to the top floor.

Ten or so windows looked out over the gaping jaws of Luna Park and the bay beyond.

All of them had curtains. No blanket-across-the-window evidence of transient lifestyle here. Footsteps had cut a swathe through the weeds and I followed them to a rusting fire escape on the city side of the building. Ascending was like climbing the iron walkways of a navy cruiser. Each footfall rang out with a clang.

Charlie Hunt's flat had a rotting wooden door and a one-by-one metre window shaded by Venetian blinds. The door seemed out of place against the neatness of the blinds. As I knocked, the wood felt damp and porous beneath my knuckles. With each rap the hinges rattled and the nails that anchored them wriggled in their holes. It was still locked, yet Peterson's men had already been through the place. It should have been open or affixed with a temporary lock. Someone must have already erected a makeshift door.

I paused and put an ear to the wood.

Silence.

As I stepped away from the door, my foot slipped in the iron decking.

I fell forward.

Instinctively, my hands flew against the door to brace myself. My body weight followed.

The door shuddered and then splintered at the lock.

It flew open.

I froze.

The light in the next apartment snapped on.

Curtains ruffled and a hand curled around their edge.

Quickly, I stepped into Charlie Hunt's apartment and closed the door behind me.

I heard a window fly open on the floor above. 'Bloody pigs, he's not here. Piss off.. You break another door and you'll be paying for it.' The window slammed shut again.

I leaned against the door and looked through the darkness at the apartment before me. There were no signs of a police search. Peterson's men probably only had permission to bring Hunt in for questioning.

A small kitchenette stood to my left in front of the window. I could make out a grimy oven and cook top, a small section of empty benchtop with two cupboards beneath, and an oval-shaped 1960's style fridge wedged into a corner.

To my right stood a double seater lounge with batik-style throw rugs and an armchair with its back facing me. In front of that, a small wood panelled TV with a set of rabbit ear antenna resting on the top. On a small, low wooden table between the lounges were framed photographs and an orange lamp. I switched on the lamp and knelt down to examine the pictures under its gentle glow. Face to face with the table, I could smell dust. Dust is a fingerprinter's favourite environment. The light was too soft to detect any impressions but I couldn't risk turning the large overhead bulb on. I grabbed the lamp and tilted it over the surface of the table.

A history of touch was suddenly revealed.

Emma's fingerprints were the first I saw. They were on the far side of the table, in front of the two seater lounge. I tried to detect which fingers the marks belonged to. All four of the left hand, except the thumb, were as clear as if she'd rubbed her hand over carbon. The outline of the thumb's phalange was visible, but tilted to the side. It was a typical left hand print: pinkie, fourth, index and pointer with pads flat, but with lines light and fine. A low pressure, low emulsion impression.

I held the light closer to the marks. The centre of the index was missing, the strange star- shaped blotch in its place. Emma's prints.

The other side of the table carried two whole hand prints and ten or so singles. I pulled the instant camera from my handbag and snapped a shot.

All loops.

Definitely Charlie Hunt's.

These were not the prints on the glove or on the glass I'd recovered from Emma's apartment.

I returned the lamp to its position on the table and examined the photos. In the first, I recognised Emma Faber immediately. The thin young man with a dark ponytail and his arm around Emma's shoulder had to be Charlie Hunt. They were standing next to a campsite set against thick woods. Both were dressed in shorts, t-shirts and hiking boots.

They appeared in another two photographs. In the larger photo, Emma was standing in a picket line in the centre of a suburban street, holding a sign that read 'Land Rights Now.' She wore army cargo pants and a black bonds t-shirt. The black haired boy I assumed to be Charlie Hunt was nowhere in sight. In the next they were standing next to a sign I could barely read. I slipped the photo from its frame and dropped it in my handbag.

I picked up the next one. Taken in this room, it showed Charlie and an older woman sitting together in the couch. Her smile and thick dark curly hair were Charlie's and I assumed they were mother and son. I replaced it and looked around again.

A thin sheet with Aboriginal water motifs hung across the doorway behind the two seater lounge. I walked through it to an unmade bed covered haphazardly with clothes. An old mahogany coloured wardrobe stood against the wall with its doors hanging open. Most of the hangers were empty. The single bedside table hung open, its contents spilled out onto the carpet. I peered down at what was on the floor: a tube of tinea cream, an unopened box of condoms, a grey sleeper's eye mask, a silver watch whose hands were still, and a book about Melbourne's historic aboriginal sites.

I sensed the contrast between the two rooms immediately. The kitchen and lounge so neat and organised; the bedroom a hurricane's path. A hurricane called Peterson's men? But even if Peterson's men broke the rules, they would have searched the lounge, not just the bedroom. A police search was methodical and ordered. Dumping a wardrobe's contents on the bed was not good procedure.

My attention drifted back to the bed. My eye looked for patterns in the way the clothes were arranged. T-shirts and long sleeved sloppy joes were strewn towards the foot of the bed, underwear and socks in the centre. The final third of the bed was clear.

Enough room for a suitcase or bag.

Someone packing clothes and personal things in a hurry.

Charlie Hunt fleeing before the police came calling.

I checked the tiny bathroom adjoining the bedroom. Mirrored vanity, cupboards hanging open, a tube of toothpaste but no toothbrush, an empty towel rack. No razor or shaving cream.

Charlie Hunt was on the run with his toothbrush, towel and shaving kit.

No need for towels or personal hygiene items in a hotel. If he was as active in the aboriginal rights movement as Elizabeth Faber had implied, he'd have a good network of fellow travellers to lie low with.

I moved back into the lounge and found the telephone on a low shelf of the corner table beside the sofa. Intending to check the phone for a redial function, I stepped up to the sidetable. My foot struck something. I squatted down to find a small leather bound address book. I picked it up and quickly flipped through it. The A's alone were so full that a leaf of paper had been stapled onto the back of the page. On the table was a bank statement for a home loan in Charlie's name. He owned this place? So much for Elizabeth Faber's theory on aboriginal housing co-ops.

I froze as I heard the fire escape rattle. I slipped the address book into my back pocket and rushed to the door to listen. Footsteps echoed against the steel steps and then dulled as they moved across the walkway that led to the apartments on this floor. I held my breath as they approached Charlie Hunt's door.

They stopped outside.

'Fuck,' muttered a male voice.

The door crept forward but stopped a few centimetres from my cheek.

I leapt away.

I scanned the room for somewhere to hide.

The bedroom.

I scrambled under the Aboriginal motif sheet that hung between the lounge and the bedroom.

17

The man quickly stepped into the flat.

I scrambled into the wardrobe. A thin beam of light crept through the doors and I could still see a strip of bed. Dust closed in around me.

A few beats of silence passed.

Finally I heard the soft thud of furniture being moved around in the lounge.

Suddenly the sheet in the doorway rustled. I shrank back against the rear wall of the wardrobe as the man entered my field of vision. I watched him bend over the bed and begin tossing the clothes to the floor.

I felt relieved when I caught a glimpse of black ponytail. This had to be Charlie Hunt. The sleeves of his red shirt were unevenly rolled up to his elbows and his dark cargo pants were so creased it looked like he'd slept in them. The wavy lines of a tattoo stained his forearm.

He dropped to his knees and peered under the bed. 'Bugger,' he spat out.

I pushed my way out of the wardrobe.

'Looking for this?' I pulled the phone book from my back pocket and held it in the air.

He jumped in fright.

'It's okay, Charlie. I'm not here to arrest you.'

His eyes darted to my hip.

'No gun,' I reassured him. 'You can have your book back.' I held it out to him.

He snatched it off me, then sidestepped into the doorway. 'You broke my door. That's illegal entry.' His voice was surprisingly deep for someone so thin.

'You're right. So anything you tell me is inadmissible.' I quickly moved beside him. 'Running is the worst thing you can do.'

'Emma's dead. I don't give a shit about what happens to me.'

'Then stay and help the police.'

'Yeah right. And what are you, a cop?'

'Would I be hiding in a wardrobe if I were a cop?' I explained who I was.

'You have no power of arrest?' he asked when I finished.

I shook my head.

He whipped the curtain aside with the back of his hand and stepped into the living room. 'Then I don't care who you are. I'm out of here.'

'Wait,' I hurried past him and stood with my back against the front door. 'I want to know what happened to Emma.'

'So do I. But I won't find out by sticking around here.' He reached past me to place a hand on the door knob. 'Get out of my way.'

I stood firm.

'I asked you to get out of my way.'

I ignored him. 'I think someone's been through her apartment. Things seem to be missing. I found a pair of latex gloves in a bin next to her house. The fingerprint in them isn't hers. I think it belongs to the person who killed her.'

His eyes widened and his hand fell from the door handle. 'What's this got to do with me?'

'I think you can help answer my questions.'

'How? If I knew who went through her place, don't you think I'd tell the police. I loved Emma, for Christ's sake.'

'Maybe you don't realise how much you know. It'll cost you nothing to talk to me.'

'It will if I stay here.'

'Come with me, we'll go somewhere else.'

'No, I need to disappear.'

'Meet me tomorrow morning then.'

'I don't know where I'll be tomorrow morning.'

'Then take my phone number.' I pulled out my wallet and used the pen on my Swiss army knife to scribble my phone number on the back of an old business card.

I handed the card to him, then asked, 'Emma had test tubes in her fridge. Why?'

He slipped the card into his back pocket. 'Water samples she took for me.'

'From where?'

'The Yarra River, upriver from the docklands site. A big real estate firm have bought up sites by the river, backing onto sacred land.' He stepped up to the window frame and lifted the edge of the curtain away from the glass. He peered nervously at the street below. 'See that car there? Out on the street?'

I looked out at the street.

'Just outside the circle of the streetlight.'

I could make out the smooth rise of a car bonnet. 'Yes.'

'Someone's been watching the flat all yesterday, and today too'

'Someone's been sitting in there for two days?'

'A big guy. The car's a blue Mitsubishi sedan.'

'Mitsubishi?' Too new for a PI but new enough for a cop car. Had they seen me enter? 'Did you get the plate number?'

'Of course. How could I miss it? It's got everyone in the place creeped out. FBQ 397. '

I pulled the curtain shut. 'Forget him,' I said as I committed the number to memory. 'Tell me about the real estate firm.'

'Rumour is they're digging beneath our land, running pipes beyond the perimeter of their own land and into ours.'

'What does river water have to do with this?'

'They claim they're using river water to blast rocks, then returning the water to the river. But we think they could be pumping the water tables of our land out and into the Yarra to make their excavation easier. By testing the water at the mouth of their outlet, Emma said she'd know if it's river water or a subterranean flow.'

'How does Emma's degree in anthropology qualify her to test water?'

'She worked for the Environmental Protection Agency part time during her uni years and did a minor in environmental science. She wanted to combine that and anthropology to help aboriginal culture maintain sustainable development out on the settlements.'

'The test tubes were gone when I checked her apartment today.'

His eyes left the street below and fixed on my face. 'Gone?'

'I take it you don't have them?'

'Maybe she gave them to her friend at the E.P.A.?' He stepped away from the window and sat down on the couch. 'But she called me yesterday afternoon and told me that she had something big to tell me. I assumed she meant she'd got the results from the water analysis back.'

'You didn't ask her?'

'She just said it was about the river's edge. That's what the site's called.'

I'd heard about the River's Edge development. It was an apartment complex planned for the land a few kilometres upriver from the dockland's development. The land had been little-used parkland for ten years. Commercial port trading and aerospace industries had built their own communities around it.

I pulled out my notebook. 'What's the name of her friend at the E.P.A.?'

'Janine Wood. She's a scientist at the marine biology branch. She also teaches out at Monash Uni.'

I scribbled the name down. 'Apparently there was something else missing from Emma's apartment.' I watched him carefully. 'The small wooden trinket she had on her T.V.'

He frowned as he thought for a moment. 'The mortuary post?'

'It had Aboriginal pictures painted on it.'

'And it was hollow?'

'Yeah, that's it.'

He flopped backwards onto the couch, looking stunned. His reaction seemed genuine.

'What is it?' I asked. 'What's it called?'

He took a deep breath. 'A mortuary post is where a tribesman's bones are kept after he dies. Some of them have pieces cut out so that the deceased can watch what goes on around them.'

'That's creepy.'

He nodded slowly. 'So you think the murderer's been in her apartment?'

'Like I said, some things seem to be missing. Does this mortuary post have any significance to murder?'

'No. I brought it back for her from Arnham land a few months ago. It was just a model. A tourist thing, you know. The real ones are a metre or so tall.'

'So not only aboriginals would know what it was for?'

'Anyone visiting a museum would see one. Are you sure it's missing? It might have just fallen behind the TV.'

'Maybe.'

There was no way I was going to tell him that we'd found it next to the body. After all, he was Peterson's nominated perp. Not that he seemed to be acting like one. Nothing about him spoke the language of lies—he met my eyes when we talked, his grief was in proportion to his fear of being arrested, there were no nervous ticks. He'd seemed surprised when I told him the mortuary post was missing. I was not getting guilty vibes.

I decided to dig a little deeper. 'What time did Emma call you?'

'About two p.m. She was going out with her brother that afternoon and then we were going to meet here at sixish. She didn't show. I called her apartment but I only got the machine. I thought she'd gotten caught up with her brother so I just waited for her. She hadn't seen him in ages because of some falling out he'd had with the family. I must have fallen asleep. The next thing I knew Sammie from downstairs was pounding on my door, yelling at me to wake up. I let him in and he told me he heard on the radio that Emma was dead.'

'You don't know if she did meet with her brother?'

'No idea.'

'Have you met her brother?'

'About twice. I met up with her after they'd had coffee once. She introduced us quickly.'

'What did you think of him?'

'Something about him was off. I felt uncomfortable around him.'

'Why?'

'I don't know. I didn't really give it much thought.'

'So what did you do when you heard Emma was dead.'

He shrugged a shoulder and was silent for a few seconds. 'I couldn't believe it, I guess,' he said finally. 'I called her phone, but the answering machine kicked in so I hung up. I tried to call Emma's parents to see if it was true but Doris, the housekeeper, said no-one was home. I didn't want to ask her in case it wasn't true. Sammie kept saying they were going to think I did it. I knew he was right, I guess. I stared to panic. Then I just took off.'

And came back for your phone book?'

'If the cops get that, I've got nowhere to go. Friends are all I have now.' His eyes reddened and he lowered his head. 'I can't believe someone would want to kill her.'

'You've got to contact the police, Charlie.'

He wiped a hand over his eyes. 'God, I know, I know. But what makes me angry is that while the cops are busy pinning this on me, Em's killer is out there.' He grabbed my arm. 'I don't know what it is, but you remind me of her.'

I pulled my arm back. I remembered the feeling of familiarity I'd had when I first saw her. And then there was the vision I'd had of me in her clothes after I'd seen the intruder in my yard.

'The cops are not gonna fight for her. No one will ever know what happened. You can't let them do that to her. She was something special.'

'The police will find—'

'No, they won't. You've got to be the one who finds the truth. I have this feeling about you, that you're the only one who can do it.'

'That's silly. I'm just a fingerprinter.'

'But you're here, aren't you? And you know I didn't kill her. I can see it in the way you're talking to me. So you're already ahead of the cops.' He rose. 'My lawyer's expecting me. I have to get moving.' He stepped past me and carefully opened the door.

'Wait,' I paced to the door and rested a hand on his elbow. 'Let me check it's quiet out there.' I poked my head across the frame and then quickly stepped out onto the platform. Cars raced past on Beaconsfield Parade. The moon had cast a glittering coat of white tinsel over the ocean. The yard below my feet was quiet except for the scratch of rose thorns against the wooden fence. There was no sign of the police cruiser.

'Hurry,' I whispered into the doorway.

'Remember,' he said as he darted past me, 'It's up to you to look after Emma now.' He took the stairs two at a time.

I watched as he paused at the bottom of the steps to pull a black beanie over his hair and ears. He hurried across the yard and disappeared onto the Parade.

I stepped back into his apartment and pulled a dishcloth from the hanging bar on the oven door. Cloth draped over my palm, I went into his bathroom and plucked the toothpaste tube from the jar it rested in. With a flip of my hand, I wrapped the cloth around the tube and fled the apartment.

18

Alex was waiting at the kerb in his dark blue Jeep Cherokee when I returned home. It was 11 pm. His front wheel was level with the wattle on my nature strip. Tiny yellow balls of pollen had floated down to cover the roof of his car.

'I found Charlie Hunt,' I said as he got out and stretched.

'Don't tell me he came back to his flat?'

'He walked in on me.'

He stopped dead. 'Are you okay?'

'Of course.'

'I thought he'd be too smart to come back.' He grabbed my arm. 'Sarah, I'm so sorry. I should never have let you go in there.'

A gust of wind blew the wattles from the top of the car. They drifted down on us.

I moved away from him. 'It was my idea.'

'Hey, I got a result back on the stain from the glove. It's definitely Emma's blood.'

I shivered. 'Let's go inside.'

A breeze of cold air bit our cheeks as we stepped into the lounge.

'You've got a draught slipping in from somewhere,' he said.

'I know.'

I left him in the kitchen to make coffee. In the bathroom lab I unpacked the tube and photograph I'd seized from Charlie's flat and secured the tube in an evidence bag inside a lockable cabinet. From the narrow bathroom I could hear Bess scratching at the wire security door.

'Why didn't you call me when you found Charlie?' Alex called from the kitchen.

I let Bess into the house, locked the grill behind me and joined him in the kitchen. I could see the light on my answering machine flashing.

'He'll turn himself in,' I said as I hit the play button on the machine. I turned the volume down when I heard my mother's voice asking me to call her.

Alex watched as I erased the message. He said, 'Sure he'll turn himself in, when he's had enough time to invent a story.'

'Even if I did call you, by the time you arrived, he'd be long gone. It's not like I have the authority to hold him.'

'Why do you think he came back?'

'He forgot his telephone directory.'

'We've got a team tracking down his known acquaintances. We could have done with that address book.'

'I don't have the authority to seize property either.'

'Since when has that stopped you?'

I ignored the jibe. 'I told you, he'll turn himself in. He was talking about contacting his lawyer.'

'He won't be turning himself in if he killed her.'

'There's nothing to suggest he did. Her prints are on his coffee table but that's hardly a surprise given they were close friends. There were another set there, but I'd say they were his. Has someone interviewed the neighbours?'

'They said they saw him come in at 3.00 pm, then music until about 12.00 pm when the lights turned out.'

'There you go then.'

'Those neighbours don't have a high opinion of the police. For Charlie's sake the whole apartment block had better have seen him.'

I snapped my fingers as I remembered something. 'Hey, something that Elizabeth Faber said doesn't seem right.'

'Huh?'

'She implied the apartments were some type of housing estate.' I shook my head. 'They were too well maintained. And

I found a home loan statement in Charlie's name.'

'He owned his flat?'

'Just about. Did you do a record check on him?'

'He worked as an aboriginal aide worker. Been in the chink a few times for disorderly conduct and resisting arrest.'

'Protesting for aboriginal issues?'

'That type of thing.'

'No violent offences?'

'Not that he's been booked for. Except resisting arrest.'

'Who was the arresting officer?'

'Not Peterson, if that's what you're hoping. I did compare Hunt's record with Emma's though. Arrested the same night.'

'At the same rally?'

'Exactly. Same officer. Constable Mead from Footscray.'

I poured two cups of coffee, both decaf, and carried them to the lounge. Alex joined me on the sofa. The smell he brought into my house was never his own. It was the scent of other people's homes. Today it was jasmine rice and a spice like Morocco, the citrus sharpness of a family's toilet deodoriser and beneath it, the ammonia of the mortuary. I decided that when he left I'd search through my pantry until I found that spice.

'Where else did he get arrested?' I asked.

'Down by the river in Port Melbourne.'

'Near the new development?'

'Closer to the mouth of the river than that.'

I told him everything Charlie had said about the disputes at the site.

'Emma was arranging for the water to be tested for underground flow,' I said.

'Hence the test tubes?'

'The missing test tubes. I'm visiting the E.P.A. friend tomorrow. Charlie gave me his version of Emma's whereabouts on the night she died.' I filled him in.

'The estranged brother? That's interesting. Peterson got the brother's contact number off the parents. I assume he'll be interviewing the brother tomorrow.'

'I have to tell you something about Peterson.'

He sipped at his coffee. 'What?'

'Peterson's been fishing around in my filing cabinet. My locked filing cabinet. I found his prints on some paperwork.'

'That doesn't mean he's accessed the cabinet.'

'That print wasn't there before. And how else would he have touched the files?'

'You're telling me you never leave it open?'

'Very rarely.'

'Very rarely still means sometimes.'

'Very rarely means nearly never.'

He sighed as if he were dealing with a wayward child. 'Which files do you think he was looking at?'

'The ones on Emma Faber. Those and a few old case files were the only paperwork in there. The glasses and a Perspex cube with the glove in it were in there as well.'

'How do you know it was Emma's file he looked at?'

'It was her file that had the new print plus the other files are only active because they're due for court.'

'Maybe he wanted to check some details.'

'I was in the lab when he got into it. I just caught site of someone moving across the floor and down the fire stairs. Why not just ask me? And there was no fingerprint except on Emma's file.'

'Did you actually see Peterson?' I could hear the doubt in his voice. I didn't blame him. I'd think I was paranoid too.

'No. But the print means he was there.'

A worried expression crossed his face. 'Exactly what was in the file?

'Every note I'd made on the case.'

'Including when you got inside Emma's apartment?'

'That and the details of what happened when I visited her parents.'

He shrugged. 'What do you want me to say? Just be careful of him then.' He finished the last of his coffee and held it out to me. 'More of that would be great.'

As I took the cup from his hand I noticed an angry red welt

on his right pointer finger. I grabbed his hand and extended the finger. 'What's this?'

His forehead creased. 'What?'

I moved the skin around the perimeter of the mark with my fingers. The mark had flattened the ridges to a glassy oblong plane, narrow and slightly indented.

'Oh that. Target practice today. I'm up for retesting.'

'Do any more tomorrow and you'll rub it raw.'

He shrugged. 'Can't be helped.'

'I'll give you something for it.' I rose and fetched a jar of teatree oil from the pantry. 'This will help the skin callous. It'll make the skin tougher.'

'Sounds like an old wives tale.'

'You'll see.'

As he applied the oil I got up and brought him a box of tissues from the kitchen.

The draught made the edges of the tissue waver above the box like a flame. Alex watched me rub my hands together, then rub the woollen arms of my jumper.

He pulled out the tissue and wiped the excess oil from his fingertips.

I stared down at his hand. The length of his fingers had always captivated me. Broad knuckles, fingers ending in narrow, neatly rounded nail. Flesh bamboo brown, pores like a thousand splinters interlaced to create a mesh of skin. I wanted to count each one. Fine black hair as directional as rainfall seemed to grow not from the skin but over it. Somewhere in my memory was the tickle as it passed across my cheek..

'Who's Charlie Hunt's lawyer?' I asked.

'Kenneth Goodman. He's tied up with Ab Aid.'

'Charlie said he was supposed to meet him tonight.'

Alex nodded. 'We've got someone watching Goodman. We figured Charlie might try to make contact. Goodman doesn't encourage his clients to skip, but if we can grab Charlie tonight there'll be no risk of losing him.'

Bess shuffled from one end of the rug to the other.

'Have you eaten?' Alex asked.

'A bit.'

He rose. 'I'll fix you something.'

I held up a hand. 'No, it's too late.'

He sat down beside me again and pinched my waist.

'Hey!' I yelped.

'Just what I though. You're half the size you were when you left.'

'I'm okay.' I lifted my jumper slightly above the band of my jeans. His thumbprint had left a blob of red on my skin. I shifted to show him the mark.

He touched my lowest rib. 'You need to take better care of yourself.' He was so close I could smell the sea-scented shampoo he used. His hand slipped from my rib to the small of my back.

I pressed one hand against his chest and savoured the feel of him beneath my fingers. My hand moved with his lungs as his chest rose and fell.

I knew then that I still loved him. Going away had been futile. But now there was an extra emotion: distrust. I had walked out of our relationship because I feared he was still involved with his wife. They were divorced now, so what was stopping me? Surely I could trust him now. But he'd made no mention of his wife until I stumbled across her. What else would he not tell me?

He dropped his head and looked into my eyes.

I closed them. Then I turned my head away from him. I slipped my hand into the open neck of his shirt and trailed my palm across his chest to his shoulder. From there my hand moved down his arm until my fingertips found the man-made hollows of the raven's wings. I'd loved that tattoo with an intensity that could smudge its ink.

My touch knew the overlap of each feather and the sharp tip of each talon. It's wing span was the width of my knuckles, its height the length of my middle finger. Tracing its perimeter was to sketch a '+'.

Or a star.

I sat upright. 'A tattoo! Emma Faber had a tattoo on her finger.'

Alex stared at me.

'And so does the person who wore the glove I found.'

'A tattoo on the finger? Both of them?' He sat up straight.

'People get letters etched on each knuckle—there's no reason why a fingerpad couldn't be tattooed.'

'Why didn't it come up when you restored her prints the night we found her?' he asked.

If he was disappointed about me breaking the intimate moment, it didn't show.

'I guess it didn't penetrate the lower layers.'

He touched the raven on his arm. 'Tattoos go through to the third layer of skin. Even cursory decomposition doesn't erase them.'

'There was no marking on her dermal layer.'

'And you said the print from the glass had obscured ridges.' He slipped off his shirt and angled his shoulder at me. 'Sure, the needles make indentations, but they heal up pretty quick. The skin's texture stays the same.'

'Shoulder skin doesn't have papillary ridges.' I got up and walked into my study. From a bookshelf I plucked O'Donough's 'Anatomy of Ridges'.

Alex followed me into the study. He buttoned up his shirt as he stepped through the doorway.

I placed the unopened book on the desk. 'You said a tattoo needle makes indentations that heal quickly.'

'Yes.'

'It heals with a scab?'

'Kind of. More of a dry layer of skin.'

'That's got to be it.'

'It would have been recent if the dry skin hadn't fallen off yet.'

'How long does the scab last?'

'About a week. It flakes off bit by bit.'

'She died on a Friday night so she could have gotten it around Friday the week before.' I flipped open the

O'Donough and turned to the section on tattoos. Photos of finger length and whole hand tattoos were set in five pages of colour plates, including close ups at high magnification. There were no pictures of tattoo scars. The tattoos themselves varied from colourful designs that covered every visible space of skin from fingertip to wrist, to black Maori inspired motifs. 'It could have been something like this,' I tapped the Maori images. 'Small and ornate.'

'Something from a foreign culture?'

I thought of the eclectic collection of wall hangings and charms I'd seen at her house. 'Something a serious anthropology student would wear.'

Had her interest in Aboriginal culture included body markings?

I continued, 'The person who wore the latex glove had the same mark on their finger. The same tattoo with the same development of scarring.'

Alex cleared his throat. 'I don't mean to question your skill, but you're sure the print in the glove wasn't Emma's?'

'Absolutely. Completely different ridge detail. There's wasn't much detail left on the glove, but enough to compare with Emma's. The mark was on Emma's index, but on the other person's thumb. The wearer must have got a tattoo done at the same time.'

Alex's pager buzzed from the lounge. He hurried out of the study. I returned the book to the shelf and listened as he rang headquarters.

From his conversation I could tell what had happened.

When he hung up I entered the lounge behind him. 'They've found Charlie Hunt,' I said.

'He and his lawyer turned themselves in.'

'I told you.'

'All right, all right.' He gathered up his clothes, then squeezed my hand. 'I'll keep you updated.'

I squeezed back. 'Okay.'

'If you're right about Peterson accessing your files, then he knows you've been sneaking around behind his back. I think

I'd better be the one to visit Emma's friend at the E.P.A.'

'You won't get a chance—not with Charlie being brought in, interviewing Elizabeth Faber's friend and going back to Emma's.'

'Well, the E.P.A. can wait another day. It's got nothing to do with you anyway. Listen, I've got to go.'

'It's nearly midnight. When do you sleep?'

'At my desk when everyone's at lunch.'

I laughed but my mind was already on Janine Wood. He was right that I had no license to question Janine Wood. The fact that Alex wouldn't have known they existed if I hadn't broken into Emma's house with Jane Frommer was irrelevant. I remembered Charlie Hunt's plea that I was the only one who could help Emma. Why did I feel this too?

Yet there was little I could do. The test tubes were part of Peterson's investigation now.

Or were they?

I grabbed Alex's arm when he was about to step out the door. 'Did you report the test tubes were missing?'

'Not yet.'

'Whoever accessed my filing cabinet will know about them.'

'I'll file the paperwork to approve your entry first thing tomorrow.'

I laughed. 'You're good at being sneaky.'

'I'd say it rubbed off from you. Anyway, I have to be sneaky to get you out of trouble.'

'Hey! You pulled me into this case.'

His face grew serious. 'For print analysis. Remember that, Sarah.' He took my hand and pulled me close. 'Take care.' His lips touched my cheek and lingered there for a moment.

I watched him pass through the doorway and disappear into the darkness of my driveway.

I stood in my makeshift lab and watched as white powder revealed a thumb and first finger on the black felt pen that had rolled under the coffee table—Alex's pen.

The barrel had absorbed a neat centre strip of his thumb

pattern. His ulnar loop's turning point was so strong I could feel the rise and valley of the ridge when I traced it with my nail. Ridges surrounded it like ripples spreading from a stone dropped in water.

The impression was good. Lines as black as kanji painted with a teardrop bristled brush, canyons cut as clean as ocean rockface.

I checked the variables that make a print most defined. Room temperature was comfortable, but not warm enough to induce sweat. I could thank the draught for that. He had washed his hands in the kitchen so his fingerpads were clean of the particles a day of touch gathered. Of course, rinsing the fingers of their natural oils will cause the glands to briefly overproduce. The skin's physiology demands it always be moist, but this excess merely returns the ridges to their normal definition. Without the gland's burst of lubrication, there would be no fingerprint at all.

So why had his ridges left such strong lines?

He had rubbed teatree oil on the graze caused by the gun. That could cause more prominent ridges, but not lines this strong. It could only be one thing.

My heart beat faster.

I pressed my hand against the table top and then dusted the places my fingers had touched. The mark of my dry, pebbled print had not altered. There were no white lines, no valleys and peaks. Not even love had left its mark.

A quick powder of Charlie Hunt's toothpaste tube revealed a mix of thumb prints and index portions at the end of the tube. This told me he was a palm squeezer, using the centre of the underside of his hand to grip the tube while his thumb and index applied squeezing pressure. The sides of the tube revealed a weave of lines as distinct as the fibres in linen cloth. This is the kiss of the palm as it closes its embrace and brands an image of its warm epidermis on the plastic tube.

Charlie Hunt's thumb was an oval loop more circular than

Alex's and without the bleed of lines that usually seeps from the centre of the pad to the side of the first joint. The loop was ringed by a perfect circle and that circle surrounded by another, and that by another until the loop was trapped like prey.

His index was also a loop, but with a standard ulnar sweep. Two centre rods stood parallel within the loop like the slash of a bear's claw in a tree trunk.

Neither of the prints showed any abnormalities. Charlie had not worn the glove I had found in Emma's rubbish bin. The markings around the thumb print was typical of a fleshy thumb: lengthy rolls in the lower part of the middle third of the print. These would be creases in the surface of his skin. The core of a print is usually crease free simply because the centre point of a fingerpad does not fold out, and the outermost edges of the ridge pattern do not have enough loose flesh to ripple. The area in between, however, is a pulpy mass that crumbles easily under weight. Compress the tip of a thumb and thin horizontal welts will appear.

I photographed Charlie's prints and threw the tube of toothpaste away. It could never be used as evidence because I'd acquired it in an illegal entry. All these prints could offer was an arrow indicating which way investigation should head.

With a cloth dipped in soapy water, I wiped Alex's pen clean of black powder. To remove the iron-like smell of the powder, I rubbed weak lemongrass tea over the barrel. I would slip the pen back among his things tomorrow.

I soaked my fingertips in pureed strawberry for ten minutes and then wrapped them in bandages. Strawberry has drawing properties and will call up the oils that my skin hides away. While the puree dried against my skin I curled up in the arm chair with Emma's file in my lap. I separated each piece of paper into one of three piles which I nicknames Best Bet, Second Shot and Last Straw. In the Best Bet pile I placed everything to do with Charlie Hunt. Alex was treating him as their best suspect, so I did too. The circumstantial facts seemed to lead to him: A history of violence and one of the last people to see Emma alive. His fingerprints didn't match the ones on the glove, but we had yet to prove the glove was anything other than coincidence. Charlie Hunt's prints would be all over Emma's apartment. There was no need for him to wear gloves. On the paperwork about Charlie I attached a sticky note and scribbled 'needs alibi checked: ask Alex.'

Next of the Best Bet pile was a piece of paper with the few scraps of information that Charlie had told me about Emma's brother. Grant Faber had met with his sister sometime between two and five the day she died. If Charlie was telling the truth, then Grant Faber was the last person to see Emma alive.

I fetched the white pages phone directory and checked under Faber for a 'G' listing. A number with a Windsor prefix was attributed to a G.M. Faber. I jotted the number down on the page of notes.

I sailed through the rest of the file. The notes I'd made about the possible tattoo on both Emma's print and on the glove went into the Second Shot heap. From my wallet I pulled out the photo of Charlie and Emma standing by the old sign. Maybe I could visit parlours in her area and flash the photo.

I grabbed the yellow pages and flipped through the entries until I reach tattoo parlours. They covered four pages—at least two pages of them within thirty five minutes of her apartment.

I chewed on my thumbnail. Surely a tattoo on the fingertip wasn't common. I could start at the beginning of the listings and phone each one to see if they recalled doing any recently.

The only things remaining in the file were the notes I'd jotted down about the marks on Emma's hands, the summary of what Elizabeth and Charlie Faber had said, and an outline of what I'd found at Emma's apartment.

I looked over my observations on Emma's fingerprints again. A line about marks consistent with recent playing of a small stringed instrument caught my eye. There had been no indication of a violin or violin stand anywhere in her apartment. I placed these notes in the 'last straw' pile.

The interview with Emma's parents had led me to Charlie Hunt and little else. I filed my notes on them under 'last straw' as well.

I checked my watch. It was now 1am and my shift at St Kilda Road began at 8.30. Seven and a half hours of sleep beckoned.

I hit the pillow like a rock.

19

I checked the roster in the squad room. It listed me as on call for the morning. A request for attendance to a home invasion in Footscray had already been pinned under my name. I checked the rest of the staff. Paul and Amir were also listed as on call. Under Paul's name a message had been scribbled in blue marker. I recognised Amir's scratchy script: 'B & E Richmond - 1310 Bridge Road. 8:15.'

Amir stepped up to the board and stopped beside me. He sipped coffee from a brown mug with a crack in the handle. Catherine and I had bet on what would happen when that handle finally broke. She wagered he'd just glue it back on. I predicted he'd just borrow everyone else's mugs. Buying a new one would be too much effort for a man who'd worn the same lab coat since university.

He smoothed down an eyebrow so overgrown it curled towards his forehead like a suture. 'I'm taking the Fisher murder again today. Cranbourne boys think they've located the girl's car.'

Twenty four year old Louise Fisher had disappeared from her Cranbourne apartment three days ago. The apartment showed no sign of forced entry or struggle, but lumalight tests had found a large amount of blood in the floorboards.

'Who's working the Centre?' I asked. One fingerprinter had to remain within the complex to do latent recovery or print searches for the other departments.

'Catherine. I think Homicide have just called her.'

I left Amir to study the whiteboard and hurried over to

Catherine's carrel. She was carefully packing brushes into a metal kit. Each brush had a little plastic sheath over the bristles. Hers were the only brushes that never went missing. Who would want to borrow a brush with a leopard print handle?

'Hi,' I said as I leaned against her carrel wall.

Her long black hair swung over her shoulder as she looked up. 'Girl! I'd heard you were back but I didn't believe it until I saw big Al wearing his lovesick face again. Although I should have known something was up when he finally got a haircut.' She lowered her voice. 'He's left his wife you know. I mean, really left. Don up in Homicide says she hasn't called the office since you took leave. There's a rumour that he went a little nuts when you split.'

I didn't know what to say. 'Yeah?'

'Not that he wasn't a bit nutty to start with. You'd have to be to actually volunteer to work nights all the time.' She took me in for a few seconds. 'I saw you working the dead girl at Williamstown beach the other night. Good way to settle back in.'

'I heard you were there, but I didn't see you.'

She rolled her eyes. 'Oh, I was there alright. Peterson had me dusting every piece of beach trash from Willi to Werribee. You got the fun bit though.'

'Yeah, I got to go head-on with Peterson,' I changed topic. 'You're stuck here today?'

'Don't remind me.' She playfully curled a few strands of hair around her finger. 'Hey, I've been summoned by your loverboy.'

'Shhh,' I looked around to check no one was nearby. Amir was still standing in front of the noticeboard. 'Why?'

'To print their suspected perp.'

'But we've got his prints on record from previous offences.'

'Your Al wanted them redone. Something about a new distinguishing characteristic on Hunt's finger?'

'Yeah? Want to swap jobs?' I asked.

Her raised eyebrow implied she was interested. Most

printers prefer to go out on site than tediously slog through the mountain of prints that always needed processing here on the floor. 'Depends. With what?'

'A break-and-enter in Richmond.'

'I'm sick of B and E's. They take forever.'

'It's with assault.'

'Assault?'

I watched the enthusiasm build. An assault was always more interesting than a break-and-enter because it meant the person assaulted could direct the fingerprinter to the areas the assailant may have touched. The actual time spent searching for prints was minimal compared to a standard burglary and the victim was usually so emotionally distressed that frequent breaks had to be taken. The fingerprinter may spend more time there, but as long as you could cope with the victim's grief, it was easy time where you felt your skills were actually helping someone. And it meant not having to print a hostile detainee that homicide had been prodding all night.

'The vics conscious?'

'And already pointing.'

'Sold to the lady in love,' Catherine said, handing me the small kit we use when printing people in the building. 'This is ready to go. No fornicating in the holding cells.'

'Shut up,' I hissed. I nodded towards the squad room. 'B and E details are up on the board.'

She laughed. 'You were supposed to protest that you're not in love. Guess I hit the mark.'

I shot her a dirty look and grabbed the kit.

'Hey wait.' She beckoned me into the carrel.

I stepped in and leaned on her desk.

She chewed on the end of her pen. 'So seriously,' she said out of the corner of her mouth. 'What's with you and the Faber case? I thought Peterson pulled you off it.'

'Not really.'

'Not really? What the hell's "not really"?'

'There's something about that case,' I shook my head. 'Too many strange things at once. Burial monuments, the staged scene, the missing fingerprints.' I decided not to tell her about the identification I felt with Emma.

'Well, it's a weird one, that's for sure. The whole frayed finger thing is way creepy. Why leave her body out if she's not meant to be identified.'

'I don't know. I think we need to forget about the usual motives for fingerprint removal here.'

'Nah, I reckon it's a token. Something for him to take home and jerk off over.' Her phone rang. She snatched the receiver from the cradle. 'Yeah? Okay, okay, someone will be up in a second. Keep your pants on.'

She nodded to me. 'You're up. Here,' she handed me a manila folder. 'I pulled Hunt's first set of prints from our files.'

I took them from her. 'Thanks.'

'Hey,' she called as I walked off. 'Your mother called.'

20

Homicide was empty when I pushed through its swinging doors. I looked to the right and checked the squad room. The tables were clean, the yellow Venetian blinds closed. When I emerged I could hear voices from the rooms deeper right. The interview rooms.

Vreeland and two other detectives were standing inside a small conference den next to the first interview room, watching through the mirrored glass. Charlie Hunt was slumped in a chair in the interview room. One arm rested on the table in front of him, the other a fist against his thigh. Strings of long black curls had fallen loose from their ponytail and were plastered down the side of his face like errant sideburns. His plaid red shirt was hanging open, revealing a black singlet top stained with sweat around the neck and in a thick line down the centre of his chest. I guessed it had been a long night.

Peterson stood at the opposite end of the table, his suit jacket off and draped over the chair behind him. His arms were crossed and he appeared to be waiting for Charlie to speak. Even through the glass and behind the three men, I could see the fabric beneath Peterson's arms was damp.

A dark haired, olive skinned man I didn't recognise sat next to Charlie. By his dapper dark blue suit with perfect sleeve and leg lengths, I guessed he was Charlie's lawyer.

'Fingerprints,' I said.

Vreeland and the other detective swung around to face me.

I raised my kit and swung it slightly towards them. Vreeland nodded at the narrow conference table to my right. 'Unpack your stuff there. They're nearly finished.'

It seemed the entire squad was there except Alex.

I opened my kit.

Peterson's voice came through a speaker above the window. 'You can't seriously think you'll get bail with a record like that.'

'There's nothing on his record to indicate a potential for flight,' the lawyer said as he tucked a bold red tie between the lapels of his suit.

'Only a potential for violence.'

'Fuck you!' Charlie spat, 'everyone knows I'd never hurt her.'

Peterson grabbed a sheet of paper from his end of the table and slid it across the surface to Charlie.

'Everybody? Oops, look what I found. The duty nurse from the Emergency ward where you brought Emma after you broke two of her ribs.'

'She did that rollerblading-'

'Blunt force trauma,' he read. 'Consistent with being kicked in the upper stomach.'

'Yeah, it was my foot that did it. But only because I tripped over her.' He slammed a hand down on the table so loud I jumped. 'I've already told you this. That nurse was racist. She just assumed that because I was an Aboriginal that I beat Emma.'

'Perhaps she saw that same nasty streak that you used against the two police officers during your protest by the river.'

'For God's sake, you're not listening to me! I was defending myself. There were five witnesses that said the cops set on me first.'

'The same five witnesses that just happened to swear you were home all night the evening of Emma's murder.'

'They live in my apartment block and we go to the same rallies.'

'So it's safe to say they're your mates.'

'Yes, you could say that. But they're not liars.'

'And being good mates is about sticking up for your friends.'

Charlie threw his hands in the air. 'Here we go again. I can't believe you're wasting your time persecuting me instead of looking for Emma's killer.'

'Quite a few people don't seem to think we're wasting our time.'

'Oh yeah?'

The lawyer stood up. 'These are nothing but allegations. I won't let you use them to rile Charlie.'

'No, lets hear them,' Charlie spat out. 'I want to hear what bullshit he'll spin next.'

'The young girl's parents, for one. Elizabeth Faber said it was obvious you'd injured Emma.'

'Obvious?' Charlie yelled. 'How? Did Emma actually tell her mother that I'd hurt her?'

'I can't reveal—'

'Of course she didn't. It's all bullshit, that's why.'

'Are you suggesting Elizabeth Faber is lying?'

'Elizabeth Faber only hears what she wants to hear. Emma crashed her car. Her mother assumed I was driving it. Emma fails an exam. Her mother decides it's my fault. That woman hated me from the moment I held Emma's hand.'

'The mother puts you through that much hell and you still stay with Emma? She must have been something.'

'She was.'

'Too good to lose, huh? Too precious to risk losing to some guy in the Northern Territory.'

'What?'

'Hey, I don't blame you. I'd be the same. Sometimes you've gotta put your foot down. Sometimes you've gotta get rough.'

'You're sick. I never laid a hand on her.'

'Never? You never even grabbed her by the arm? She was never so pigheaded that you gave her a little shove on the shoulder? A girl as strong minded as Emma? C'mon, she must have deserved it sometimes.'

'You must think I'm stupid. Don't even bother pulling this shit on me.' He stood up and turned to the lawyer in disgust. 'That's it, this is over—get me outta here.'

Peterson circled the table and shoved Charlie back into the chair. 'This isn't over until I say so,' he said smoothly, his face only millimetres from Charlie's.

'Then charge me, you fucker. Arrest me and lock me up so that I can sue your arse 'til you've got nothing left but the skin that covers it.'

'I suggest you refrain from physically handling my client, Detective,' the lawyer said calmly.

Charlie drew breath and spat. The blob of saliva landed on Peterson's shirt.

Peterson stepped over to the mirrored wall and tapped on it. 'Get this sorry shit back to the holding cell.' He removed a tissue from his pocket and dabbed at the saliva on his shirt.

21

The lunchroom became my refuge until I heard Peterson and Vreeland's voices fade away down the corridor. Peterson had not seen me and I wanted to keep it that way.

Charlie was sitting, arms folded across his chest, knees tight together, on the bottom bunk of the wired off area that acted as homicide's holding cell. The room was standard conference size, altered only by the thick security fence and gate that divided it into two. Twin bunks in a steel frame stood in a corner. A battered bamboo screen tried to hide a metal toilet seat.

This was a room designed to reject the imprint of skin. Its plasticised grey tiles repelled body fluids and spilt coffee. Its concrete walls layered with thick stainproof paint. The shine of the bunk's steel frame was worn down to the dried matt skin of beaten metals, and the toilet's seat dull aluminium was blackened from tarnish.

The only surface that would hold the patterns of skin was the window. But that too had bars narrow enough to prevent touch.

I had been in this room hundreds of times before and it never seemed to lose its sharp odour of sweat. Fear seemed to carve notches in the air like long timers do in walls. My breath always quickened with guilt when I entered, even though my conscience was clear.

Charlie looked up when I stepped in.

I dragged the card table over to the bars and then fetched one of the wooden folding chairs. 'I watched the last part of your interview.'

'Interview? Is that what you people call it? I supposed I was just 'assisting police with their inquiries' while I was at it, right?'

I said nothing.

'I'm going to wear this, I know it. You lot just want someone to peg it on.' His words were an accusation but his eyes were calm, his tone dead. Hope had fled hours ago.

'You'll be fine as long as you didn't do it.' I placed my kit on the table and began to unpack.

'No one seems to care about that bit.'

'Step up to the bars, please.' I laid the Durester Ink Strip on the edge closest to him and placed a fresh print card beside it.

He stood up. 'You're going to fingerprint me?'

'It's procedure.'

'You've already got my prints, remember? That's why you lot came knocking on my door.'

'Come up to the bars.

He approached me. 'You know I didn't kill her.'

I sat at the card table and slipped my hand through the bars. I turned my palm up. 'Give me your hand.'

He placed his hand face down on my mine, then suddenly tightened his grip. With a yank he pulled my hand towards him.

I stumbled out of my chair and fell shoulder first against the bars.

His face was so close I felt I could count the pores of his skin. The brown of his iris had turned black.

I met his eyes.

'I didn't kill Emma but I know you can find out who did. You're different to the other cops.'

He loosened his grip on my hand but still held it. His arm moved forward through the bars, pushing my own back to my side. 'Fingerprint me if it'll help.'

'You'll have to kneel down.'

He did as I asked.

I examined his fingers. There was no star-shaped mark. I rolled his thumb from left to right and then repeated the roll onto the print card.

'Did Emma have a tattoo on any of her fingers?'

He stared at me for a second or two. 'A tattoo?'

'Her fingerprints had a strange mark on them. I think it was a tattoo.'

'A tattoo?' He shook his head. 'Forget it, she didn't have a tattoo.'

I rolled his point across the ink and then over the card.

'She'd have told me if she'd have gotten a tattoo,' he said.

'How can you be sure? Had she talked about getting one?'

'No, but if she wanted one she would have. And why on her fingertip? That's a stupid place for a tattoo.'

'Do you know anyone else with a tattoo on their finger?'

'Nope.'

I printed the rest of his fingers in silence then passed him a rag to clean his fingers with. 'Where'd you get the tattoo in your arm done?' I asked him.

'They're tribal markings, not tattoos.' He passed back the rag.

'They look like tattoos to me.'

'They're not—regular tattooists can't do them.'

'Can I see one?'

'Sure.' He lifted his shirt. Across his left breast were four ochre coloured wavy lines, each about five centimetres long.

'They're done in a similar way to traditional Japanese tattoos. The actual tattooing is a ceremony, instead of using a motorised needle an inked stake is beat in with a hammer. The tattooist sings a tribal song as they beat the stake.'

'Did Emma show any interest in them?'

'Well, she said she liked them.' He lowered his shirt and sat back down on the edge of bunk. 'So, maybe she had a tattoo. What's the point?'

'Maybe there is no point. It's an end that no one else will be bothered tying up.'

'So why waste your time on it?'

'A print with a similar marking to Emma's was found on something in her bin. Similar markings but not her markings. This alone would be odd, but put it together with the removal of her fingerprints and you've got something downright weird. People don't remove fingertips when they kill people.'

'I didn't realise these things have rules,' he said.

'Rules? No. But definitely patterns of behaviour.'

'So, if there are patterns of behaviour, why haven't the cops noticed that mine don't include killing my girlfriend and cutting her fingerprints off?'

'They're thinking about different patterns of behaviour. The types that show a person is most likely to be killed by someone they know.'

'I'm not the only person in the world she knew,' he said.

'But you knew her best.'

'So its logical that I killed her?'

'Your lawyer must have told you that our case is only circumstantial at this stage.'

'Yeah, he said that. But I'm still in here, aren't I?'

I snapped the lock on my case shut and left my card on the table. 'If you think of anything that she said about getting tattooed, you'll tell me?'

'Sure. I'll use my personal phone line.' He waved his hand around the cell.

'Tell your lawyer.'

He spread out along the length of the bed and closed his eyes. 'Sure. Forget to lock the door on your way out, will ya.'

22

When I passed the interview room, I heard voices. Peterson's smooth baritone spilled over Vreeland's softer drawl. I estimated they'd be in post-mortem mode for at least another fifteen minutes. I moved into the squad room.

Beneath Alex's name on the whiteboard was the name June McNaughton and Emma's name in brackets. June McNaughton was Elizabeth Faber's alibi. I checked my watch. 10 a.m. Alex would be calling in to see her in an half an hour. I checked the detective's time log and copied down McNaughton's St Kilda address.

It was an old fingerprinters joke that in St Kilda fingerprints are found inside, not outside, the body. Hot fingers pressed against organs of desire, and the peak of a loop forced beneath the skin by the tip of a needle. Other suburbs suffered these imprints, but St Kilda's sea air seemed to make the lines and curves more readable.

I returned to the eleventh floor and checked the prints I'd just taken off Hunt against the set Catherine had given me. They hadn't changed. I'd known they hadn't the moment I'd turned his hand over in the cell.

I settled into my desk with the Yellow Pages phone directory.

I decided to begin with the tattooist closest to Emma's apartment. St Kilda alone listed seven, and nearby Bentleigh listed four.

An hour later, I concluded I had been right in assuming that a tattoo on the fingerpad was rare. None of the local parlours I'd called had inked a design on that part of the body in the past few weeks. Nine of the eleven had never done one at all.

I realised I'd have no option other than ringing each tattooist in the directory.

The phone rang before I could call the first number. Line four lit up, meaning that the call was internal.

It was Emmanuel Wilson from Fraud. 'I've got some documents for you to test.'

I rolled my eyes and checked the time. 11.15. The moment anyone said fraud I smelled ninhydrin. Fraud squad was notorious for the volume of paperwork they demanded we check. We already had a separate department within our floor to do ninhydrin sprays on visa and credit card purchase receipts. Each member of our squad was rostered one day a fortnight to test and match the requests. After only one day of fraud work, unemployment seemed more satisfying. Any extra work that fraud gave us was usually suspected fake contracts or altered cheques. Thank god fraudsters were moving onto the internet. Wilson's people were yet to request we fingerprint a keyboard. Knowing the zealots who made up the fraud department, that wouldn't last.

I took the details from Wilson and promised to call him back when the internal courier arrived with the documents. After I'd hung up, I glanced down at my notepad and saw that I'd doodled a sketch of the tattooed lines that I'd seen on Charlie Hunt's chest.

Emma had planned to join an aboriginal community. Maybe she wanted to experience as much of their lifestyle and culture as she could before she joined—that could include tattooing.

I dialled the number given in the phone book for the tattooists' registry board.

A woman answered.

I introduced myself. 'Do you know if anyone in Melbourne does Aboriginal or Japanese tattooing?'

'Aboriginal or Japanese tattooing? I'm not sure. Hang on a moment.'

I heard tapping against a keyboard.

'There's none listed on the database, but I'll check with Pete.' She put me on hold but was back a few seconds later.

'Pete's heard of a guy in the city. A little shop beneath an arcade between Collins and Flinders lane. Roo's Tattoos.'

I thanked her and hung up.

From the corridor, the elevator bell sounded. I looked up to see one of our internal couriers, childlike in their shorts, long socks and short sleeve shirts, pulling a trolley into the corridor. I rose and waved him into the desk area. 'Something for Sarah Arden?'

He checked a list. 'Yep.'

'Just here will be fine,' I said.

'The message with it says they need the results by close of business today.'

'Oh. Right then.' I signed for it and tossed it on my desk.

As soon as the courier had disappeared back into the corridor, I called Roo's Tattoos.

A man with a sandpaper larynx answered with the name of the shop. I introduced myself and told him what I needed to know.

'Yeah, I inked a fingertip,' he said.

'When?'

'About...' He paused. I assumed he was counting backwards. 'About five days ago.'

'To who?'

'A girl. She came in with a guy.'

'What did she look like?'

'Tallish, maybe around 158. Blonde.'

'That's her. What did the guy look like?'

'Taller. Around 165ish. Muscular. Light brown hair cut real short, like a buzzcut.'

'You got both their names?'

'Just one. It's in my files.'

I blew a kiss to the heavens. 'What image did you tattoo?'

'A bunch of squiggly lines. The guy was thinking about getting one too so I let him take the image home with him.'

'So you only did one tattoo?'

'Yep.'

'I'm going to come down to see it in about an hour.'

'I'll be here.'

I treated the fraud squad's pile of papers and left them to develop in a fume cupboard in the lab.

As I stepped out of the lab I heard a voice from the squad room. Through the glass windows of the squad room I could see Paul and Amir marking off the job's they had attended. I walked up behind them. 'No new jobs have come in.'

Paul wagged a piece of white paper at me. 'Getaway vehicle in a bank robbery recovered in Carnegie. I picked it up off the radio on the way in.' Paul was our most senior printer. He wore the signs of an old dabsman—fingers ninhydrin red, a cloud of black powder in his cough. This stain and hack would be his retirement gift from the police force.

I snatched the paper from his hand. 'I'll cover it.'

Amir stared at me in surprise. 'Whoa. I thought you wanted to stay in today.'

'Don't sweat, I already did homicide's guest and sprayed fraud's latest volume.'

Amir groaned. 'Not fraud.'

'They called it in half an hour ago. I'll feed the prints in later tonight.'

Amir looked relieved. 'Oh, okay then.'

Paul slapped him on the shoulder. 'Don't worry. Something else will come in.'

I cleared my desk, grabbed a kit, and headed out.

I parked the car near the morgue and made my way through the cafes and restaurants that lined the river. Elizabeth Faber was sitting on the Doberville Hotel's boardwalk. Opposite her was a tall man with carefully-styled grey hair. She laughed and raised her glass to him. I assumed he was a business partner until I noticed he was wearing casual navy pants and a long sleeved polo shirt. Must be a client, I thought. I watched the river bubble past them for a few seconds, then manoeuvred myself past the lunchtime crowds that spilled from Southbank's restaurants. I crossed the bridge over the river.

The bridge became an underpass that snaked beneath the tons of steel and iron of Flinders Street Railway Station.

I passed the white tiled walls inset with the half-metre-by-half-metre galleries once used to water horses. Brown stains of trickling water running from roof to ceiling warned that the river remembered it had owned this space once. When the rains swelled the river's flow and reduced its banks, muddy water would spill down the entrance steps and reclaim the subway.

I hurried through the tunnel and emerged, blinking, into the late morning sun.

I felt a strange sense of relief to be above ground and out of the river's reach.

23

Royal Arcade was a funky indoor lane. Hovels furnished as shops sold retro curios to side-burned men in loose black shirts, baggy slacks and thick soled, lace-up shoes. Women in black hipster flairs and tight shirts sipped lattes over street magazines in tiny cafes with exotic names like *Maigret* and *Hacienda*.

I felt as out of place in my navy trousers and white shirt as a banker at a folk festival. Midway down the arcade I found a sign on the wall beside a descending staircase. Hidden beneath my footsteps, like an artist's garret, was Roo's Tattoos.

I climbed down the two flights of stairs and paused at the last step to view the room before me. Two mamasans hugged the corners of the room to my left and to the right four exhibition boards held samples of ink designs. Two metres in front of me Japanese ricepaper screens spread across the room, separating what I assumed was the operating theatre from the waiting parlour.

As I stepped off the last stair and into the room, a doorbell like chime rang out and a man emerged from a break in the screen carrying a large cardboard box marked 'gloves'. He was pencil thin in black straight legged jeans and a fitted black singlet and wore a face that had weathered too many Australian summers. His arms from shoulder to elbow were a swirl of black and white ink.

'Hey there,' he drawled as he set the box on the floor.

I recognised the three-pack-a-day voice from the phone. I

held out my hand. 'Sarah Arden.'

As he shook my hand, I sensed him assessing my conservative dress. 'Hang on a sec,' he said as he slipped back behind the divider.

He returned a few seconds later with a sheet of paper. 'This is what you're looking for.' He handed me a piece of white photocopy paper with a spiral drawn on it. Four thick lines radiated a centimetre into the outer swirl of the spiral as if an X had been sketched through it.

'Do you know what it means?' I asked.

'The girl said it was a motif representing the sharing of blood.'

'Sharing of blood?'

'Like blood brothers. Members of the same tribe.'

Blood brothers. Charlie said Emma had reunited with her brother. Or Charlie could be lying and it may have symbolised their friendship.

'What did her friend look like?' I asked.

'Tall, around 170 cm, hair cropped close to his head.'

'Do you think the guy could have been her brother?'

He stared up at the ceiling for a moment then shrugged. 'Maybe. They weren't holding hands or anything like that. I had them pegged as friends.'

'They didn't look alike?'

'No, not really. They did make unlikely friends though.'

'What do you mean?'

'She was really easy going. More with it. He was stuffy.'

'Like conservative?'

He squatted down and started unpacking the contents of the box onto a work bench. 'Yeah, guess you could say that,' he said as he stacked.'

I waited but he didn't elaborate.

I noticed the brand of gloves he was manoevering. Plasticoat. Not Labaid.

'She didn't use his name?' I asked.

'No.'

'Where else could he have got the tattoo done?'

'Maybe a normal parlour. I do mainly Japanese style, which uses a hammer instead of a machine. It's a slower process that makes a lot of noise and hurts like hell. I don't reckon he'd have got it done through. When he asked if I did paint ons, I realised he was going to chicken out.'

He straightened up. 'Okay, I'm guessing the girl's dead?'

'She was murdered.'

He nodded slowly. 'I thought I recognised her photo in this morning's paper. I only take first names when I book people. The name was the same. Emma.'

I slipped the drawing into my bag. 'Why didn't you call the police?'

'I wanted to think about it first.'

'What's to think about? Surely you realised we'd want to know about the man she was with.'

'In my business, you learn to keep your mouth shut. Especially when a guy like that comes in.'

I bristled. 'Guy like what?'

He rubbed at a smudge of ink on his singlet top, eyes down. 'Let's just say her friend made me a little nervous.'

'Why?'

'I'd never seen him before but I knew his type. I saw the way he walked, the way he looked around.'

'What are you trying to say here?'

His tindered skin grew even tighter.

I backed off. 'Look, whatever you say to me is confidential.'

'I don't think so.' He sighed and the skin loosened in resignation.

He looked me in the eye. 'He was a cop.'

24

'**A** cop?' I could hear Alex fumble with the phone as he nearly dropped it.

I said, 'He recognised the attitude, the walk, the gaze.'

'I wouldn't swear by that.'

'Come on, don't tell me you can't pick a plainclothed cop in a crowd.'

'Sometimes, sure. But not always.'

'Well, I guess this was a sometimes.'

I listened to Alex's breathing. 'Can't be,' he said finally. 'Peterson was handling the brother. If he was a cop, Peterson would have made a big deal out of it.' I could hear Alex tapping a pen against the desk. 'You know, Peterson hasn't said anything about the brother at all.'

'How can that be possible? Hunt claims the brother was the last one to see Emma alive.'

'If I wasn't on the way to Shepparton, I'd get the brother's address and talk to him myself.'

'Shepparton? That's three hours drive from here!'

'There's a body in a dam. Peterson's assigned me here for a few days.'

The days ahead suddenly seemed impossibly long. 'You can't approach the brother. How would it look if he had two visits in two days from two different detectives? You could alert him that he's a suspect,' I said.

'Peterson should have informed him of that already. Or the family may have. By the way, I talked to Elizabeth Faber's alibi, the friend she visited the night Emma died. She verifies that Elizabeth came over about eight and stayed until about 11.30.'

'If Emma died between 9 and 11.00 that leaves her in the clear.'

His voice was resigned. 'So we're back to either Charlie Hunt or the brother.'

'What's going on with Charlie?'

'Nothing. Peterson's still holding him.'

'What about if I go to see the brother? I've got a reason to. I usually get the prints of family members as part of the elimination process. It's part of my job.'

'No way!' His voice was so loud in my ear that I jumped.

He continued, 'Charlie Hunt could have done anything to you up in his apartment. I'm not sending you into a situation like that again.'

'I'll go to the brother's office. There'll be plenty of people around.'

'No.'

'Alex, you know this has to be done quietly and without causing suspicion. The minute you walk in there, Faber will be on guard. If Peterson's protecting him, he may call Faber before you even get there.'

'No. We have to do this by the book.'

'Just like Peterson's been doing? I thought you were on Emma Faber's side.'

'I am,' he said.

'Then do it for her.'

'It's not that easy.'

'It is for me,' I snapped.

I hung up before he had time to reply.

25

From my car I called Grant Faber's home number. It rang out a few times, then an answering machine kicked in.

A stiff but articulate recording announced that Grant could be contacted at two alternative numbers, one a mobile and the other his work line.

I dialled the work line. A woman answered with 'G.F. Investigations.'

Investigations. It made sense – a natural career path for an ex-cop.

'Grant Faber please.'

'Who's calling?'

'Sarah Arden from the fingerprint branch of the Victoria Police.'

She transferred the call and he picked it up on the fourth ring.

'Grant Faber.' The voice was confident and unconcerned.

'I'm calling about your sister, Emma.'

'Yes?'

A sickening thought struck me. Elizabeth Faber had said she would call her son to inform him about Emma's death. But what if she hadn't called him yet? Yesterday's paper had reported it, but he may not have read it. Peterson was supposed to have interviewed Grant, yet we had heard nothing. What if he hadn't done that yet. Police are trained in grief management. I was not. I did not want to be the one to break the news of his sister's death.

'You're aware of what happened to Emma?'

'That she was killed? Of course.'

I offered condolences but he cut me off.

'Thank you for your kindness but it's a painful time right now. I hope you won't be offended if I ask you to get to the point of your call. To get through this I need to concentrate on other things.'

His reply was fair enough. Focusing on the everyday aspects of living, on the little things, are what keeps most people sane.

'I need to take your fingerprints, Mr Faber.'

A pause. 'What for?'

'There were some prints recovered at her flat. There's no point us running around thinking we have her killer's prints when they could belong to people who just visit often. When was the last time you saw Emma?'

A longer pause. 'Do you mind if I ask for your badge number? If you're going to start asking these types of questions then I have a right to know exactly who you are.'

'Of course.' I explained that I was a non-commissioned officer and recited my personnel number. I also gave him my phone number. 'So, the last time you saw Emma?'

'A few days before the night of her death.'

'So, Monday or maybe Tuesday?' I listened carefully. Charlie had said Emma was meeting her brother the night she died.

'Sorry, but I'm a little confused here. Aren't you from fingerprints?'

'I am.'

'But aren't the detectives supposed to question me before sending you out to do the dabs?'

'No one's contacted you?' I forced surprise into my voice.

'Isn't that what I just said?'

'Yes, sorry. I'm just doing as I was requested to do.' I changed my tactics. 'If the police haven't contacted you, then you probably don't know what progress they've made.'

'I'm in the dark.'

It was on the tip of my tongue to ask why he hadn't come forward and demanded to be put into the information loop. And if he'd been a cop, why hadn't he used his status as an ex-member to gain access to the details of the investigation. I forced myself to keep my mouth shut. No need to get his back up more than I already had.

'Well, I probably shouldn't be the one to tell you this, but since no one else has bothered,' I paused for effect, 'we've taken Emma's boyfriend into custody.'

'Charlie?' He was shocked.

'Yesterday.'

'You are kidding. On what grounds?'

'He was reported to have been violent towards her in the past. He'd been heard making threats.'

'Heard by who?'

'I can't reveal that.'

There were a few seconds of silence. Then, 'Has he been charged yet?'

'It's only a matter of time,' I said glibly.

'Then why do you need my prints?'

'Just as a precaution. We're eliminating prints from her apartment and Charlie Hunt said that you were supposed to meet Emma the night she died.'

'I was, but I cancelled.' His voice quivered. 'I'll never forgive myself for that. If you check her answering machine there'll be a message from me saying I couldn't make it. Unless she erased it. I was at home all night sorting through a pile of paperwork. I had a client pressing me to get some loose ends tied up so I had to lock myself away to get it done.'

'It's not my duty to check on alibis.'

'Well, you've got mine now. I guess I shouldn't be surprised that you're looking at Charlie.'

'Why?'

'He was a bit rough, always roping her into attending protests.'

'Hmmm.'

'What's wrong?'

'Nothing. I probably shouldn't discuss any more. It's up to the detectives to pass on information to you.'

There was silence. I assumed he was thinking.

'You want to fingerprint me, no problem. I've got a free spot now, until 1.30. You could come to my office.'

'That'd be great.' I took down the address. It was an office space in the Rialto Complex. 'Business must be good if you can afford the Rialto.'

'I do okay.'

Grant Faber's office was on the twenty-eighth floor of the fifty-five storey business centre and tourist attraction. Renowned as the tallest building in Melbourne, the Rialto Towers boasted a 360° viewing deck on the top floor, a five star hotel and a shopping mall.

His receptionist guided me past documents piled high against the wall into a room with a mahogany executive desk and a deep black leather recliner. Boxes in various stages of unpacking littered the floor. Behind the desk stretched a floor to ceiling window with views across the eastern side of the city and the Dandenong Ranges.

A thirty-something man with tightly-cropped brown hair and skin as pitted as rainforest wood stepped out from a side door. He was wiping his hands on a strip of paper towel.

'Sarah Arden,' the receptionist announced.

Grant Faber crumpled the towel into a ball and tossed it into a black wire bin at the left of the desk. He offered a hand.

I glanced down at the fingers on his right hand before I grasped it.

No tattoo.

The receptionist retreated and he gestured to a black leather chair similar to his own that stood opposite his desk.

'You'll have to excuse the mess. I've just moved in.' He moved a brown leather briefcase from the desktop to the floor.

I smiled and nodded at the scene behind him. 'Quite a view.'

He swivelled his chair to face the window. 'When you can see it. If there's a bit of low cloud it's like looking at a wall.' He turned back to me. 'Do you want a cup of coffee?'

'That would be great.'

He jumped out of the chair and switched on a percolator that sat on a bookshelf to my right. 'I'm really sorry,' he said, 'but I've just got off the phone with my lawyer.'

I looked up in surprise.

'He's advised me not to be printed yet, not until the investigating officer informs me it's required. I'm sorry. There was no time to call you back. I'm sorry to have wasted your time.'

I shrugged my shoulders. 'You'll have to be printed eventually. I'd have thought you'd rather do it here than at a police station.'

'Of course I would, but I think my lawyer knows best.'

'Suit yourself. I'll still have that coffee, if that's okay.'

He smiled. 'I owe you that.'

Pushing Grant Faber to give his prints today would be more trouble than it was worth. The last thing I needed was Faber's lawyer calling Peterson to complain. The complaint I could handle, but the more Peterson knew about my dallying in the investigation, the more likely he'd bar me from it.

'So how's Charlie holding up?' he asked as he poured Evian water into the machine.

'It's not looking good for him. You said you weren't happy with the way he treated Emma. What did you mean?'

'Well, she had a decent career in front of her as an anthropological researcher. There's always government grants going to that sort of thing. He should have kept her out of his protests. The last thing she needed was a record.'

I watched him closely. 'Who told you she had a record?'

'She did. She got in trouble once and called me up. I know a few people in the force and so called around.'

'You got her off the hook?'

'Not really. She's still got a record.'

'Who do you know?'

138

He blinked in surprise. 'You want me to name everyone I know in the police force?'

I laughed, trying to cover my unease. 'Of course not. I'm just curious who you'd call to keep someone out of jail.'

'Look, this was a long time ago. Emma hated talking about it.' He shook his head sadly. 'So Charlie's in the clink.'

I followed his change in conversation amicably. 'Did you know him well?'

'Ah, no. I only met him a few times when I ran into Emma at cafés or in the street. My family was never one for bringing your partners along to dinner. Anyway, I was estranged from the family. Emma and I hadn't spoken for a long time.'

'When did you reunite?'

'A month ago. But with Emma only. Our parents are a different story.'

He added milk to the coffee without asking if I took it white, then placed it on the edge of the desk closest to me. He took a sip of his own.

'I couldn't help but notice that Emma had a mark on her fingertip.'

He placed his cup on the desk with too much force. Coffee slopped onto a pile of printed papers.

I jumped up and pulled a tissue from my pocket. I tried to mop up the liquid.

He quickly raised the paper on his desk into the air. 'There's towels in the ensuite,' he nodded at the door he'd emerged from when I'd first entered the room.

I slipped into the tiny room. A shower, toilet and hand sink lined the walls. I pulled a fluffy blue towel from a rack, then quickly folded it into four. I noticed reddish smudges, too brown to be blood, close to the corner. I returned to his desk and mopped up the coffee.

'I was told Emma's finger skin was...' his voice trailed off.

'Removed,' I said briskly. 'Yes, but we could still detect an irregularity in the centre of one of her fingers. I traced the mark back to a tattoo she received on Tuesday, four days before she died.' I clicked my fingers. 'Hey, could that be the day you saw her last.'

His face was impassive, 'Ah, the tattoo,' he said slowly.

'You knew about that?'

'I was with her when she got it. It was some tribal thing. Charlie was always pushing the abo culture thing on her. Teaching her the stories and weird rites of passage.'

I looked at him sceptically. 'The tattoo design is a symbol for blood relations.'

'Then the two of them probably did some thumb pricking, blood exchanging thing.'

'He doesn't have the mark.'

'Oh.'

I charged ahead. 'Let me get this right. You went with her to get the tattoo but you don't know what it was all about?'

'Like I said, it was some Aboriginal thing. I didn't really care. I just went with her because it was the only time she was in the city. We met for lunch first.'

'I see. Did Charlie know she was getting the tattoo?'

'I have no idea.'

'Tell me, you're a private investigator, right? What do you think happened to your sister?'

'Hey,' he held up his hands. 'I do spouse trailing and background checks on potential employees. I don't touch cases under investigation by the police.'

'Not even your own sister?'

'I didn't say I don't have suspicions.'

'Oh?'

'Obviously I'd thought of Charlie, but he seemed harmless. I've been thinking about it more now that you said he was arrested. I guess it makes sense. It's usually the ones closest to you, right? But I'd been thinking about someone Emma mentioned. She said she was being hassled by this hermit that hangs around the river. He lived near where they were protesting.'

'He lives by the river?'

'In the parkland there, I think.'

'What did she say that made you think she was being

hassled?'

'She said he kept coming up to her and touching her. They used to camp out there at night sometimes. One night she woke up to find him stepping into her tent. She screamed and he ran away. She even saw him hanging around her apartment.'

'What's his name?'

'She didn't know. He was just some hobo, I think.'

'Did she say what he looked like?'

'No. Oh yeah, she mentioned he stank of fish.'

'Fish?' My mind leap back to the morning Alex found the fish at my back door. The night after I'd spotted the man in my back yard. 'All she said was that he stank of fish? That's it?'

'Yeah.'

'Did anyone else see the incident in her tent?'

He shrugged. 'Maybe Charlie.'

'You should tell the investigating officer this.'

'I will. If I ever hear from them. What's the officer's name?'

'Peterson.'

I thought I detected a flicker in his expression.

'Do you know Peterson?' I asked.

He stood up and moved back behind his desk. 'What makes you ask that?'

'The look on your face.'

He blinked rapidly.

'When did you leave the force?' I asked casually.

He stared at me.

I picked up my case and rose.

He stood as well and then walked slowly to the door.

'I left two years ago,' he said, 'I was stationed at Green Heights. Peterson was my senior sergeant.'

26

I arrived at Carnegie twenty minutes after I'd left Grant's office. The Constable in charge said nothing about my lateness. There were never enough fingerprinters to promptly cover all of Melbourne so we often take up to an hour to respond to a call.

The car was a Holden Commodore. A favourite among thieves.

Within forty minutes I'd dusted the car and retrieved two different thumb prints. One was all over the driver's door, the steering wheel and the boot. The other covered the passenger side door handle. One would be the owner's. The other would belong to his regular passenger.

There was no damage to the doors from levering tools.

'How did they get inside?' I asked the constable.

He pointed to the base of the window. 'The rubber's compressed here. We think they used a strip of flat cord.'

'That's slow.'

'Not if you're used to doing it.'

I laid down my brush. 'There's no point dusting any more. This is a crime with gloves.'

By the time I arrived back at St Kilda Road it was 3.00 pm. Catherine was at her desk sifting through printouts, and I could hear Amir's and Paul's voices through the thin walls of the lab.

'Peterson was here looking for you,' Catherine said.

'Did he say what he wanted?' I asked as I dumped my kit on my desk.

'You. Immediately.'

'Great.'

'What's going on?'

I sat down next to her. 'Have you ever worked a case where you sense there's more than what you see? A piece of evidence that will get buried under the details? And no matter what else you're working on, finding what you can't see is all you think about?'

She shrugged. 'Of course. We all have that feeling. It's like waking up from a dream that you know you had but can't remember. Underneath every second of work you do that day, your subconscious is trying to piece it together. It's our job to solve mysteries from the residue that people leave behind. But to be able to bring what we've found to court we have to follow procedures. Lose your procedures and you've lost the case.' She rose.

'Wait,' I said. 'I want to ask you something. Were you ever stationed at Green Heights?'.

Fingerprinters were only based at Seaford, here in the city at St Kilda Road, Shepparton or Geelong. Catherine, however, had been a sworn officer who had started at the academy and spent six years as a constable.

'Nah. Footscray was my beat, then Altona North. I could ring around to see who worked Green Heights.'

I feigned disinterest. 'Never mind.' I'd never sniff out the relationship between Grant and Peterson unless I kept my enquiries quiet.

'Hey,' Catherine snapped her fingers, 'wasn't Green Heights the station that got busted for glazier kickbacks?'

I thought for a few seconds. 'Yeah, I think it was.'

Details of the story came back to me. Police recommending specific glaziers to robbery victims with broken windows and taking a cut from the sale of new glass. Peterson had been cleared, but two junior officers hadn't been so fortunate.

I checked my voicemail. Alex had left a message saying that they had made no progress with Charlie Hunt. The frustration in his voice was obvious. Unless they could dig up something more on Charlie, he would be free in less than four hours. According to Alex, friends of Charlie, and even not so friendly acquaintances, had all reacted the same way to his arrest: surprise, and then confirmation that he would never hurt Emma, and eventually a reluctant admission that he had run-ins with the law.

I thought back to my encounter with Emma's brother. Grant Faber's reaction had been no different, except that he had warmed quickly to the idea that Hunt's temper may have flared further than he initially imagined. That, I decided, was the cop in Faber.

I requested Faber's prints from our employee database. It came up within fifteen minutes. They were a mix of arches and loops. His ridges were as jagged as the ridges of broken concrete, all sharp in bold angles. Like the teeth that guard the jaws of a cat.

There were no marks like those on the glove.

I headed up to Homicide to report to Peterson.

27

Peterson was sitting at his desk, office door open, signing a pile of reports. I stood in the doorway and knocked.

He looked surprised when he saw me. 'My god, you've followed an order. I was beginning to think that you worked solo—or are you just here to tell me that?'

I stepped into the office and sat down on the vinyl chair opposite him. 'What do you want to see me about?'

He pushed the paperwork to one side of his desk and nodded at the door behind me. 'Close that, will you,' he said briskly.

I leaned backwards and pushed the door shut with the edge of my fingers.

He sat upright and rubbed his back. 'I want you back on my team. Don't work against me.'

I stared at him in surprise. This was not what I had been expecting.

He spoke carefully and quietly. 'Don't think that I'm unaware of what you've been up to. You'd been removed from the Faber case, but your name keeps coming up. Sarah Arden visits Emma Faber's parents, Sarah Arden tries to get access to Emma Faber's apartment. Vreeland himself saw you driving out of Emma's street and the uniform confirmed he caught you hanging around. Then some paperwork turns up approving your entry, conveniently signed by Alex Pace. To top it off, I hear down the grapevine that you've contacted Grant Faber.'

'Who told you that?'

'The name doesn't matter.'

'Actually it does.' The only person who knew I'd been to see Grant was Alex. Unless Grant himself had told someone and word had spread from there.

'Grant called you, didn't he?' I asked.

'No, he didn't.'

'You worked with him at Green Heights. And the two of you were incriminated in the glaziers' kickback.'

His face froze for a few seconds.

'So were about five other people,' he said. 'We were cleared. Look,' he held out his hands in a sign of peace, 'we're on the same side here and to prove it, I'm going to confide in you. I'm taking a big risk doing this, but I think there's something you need to know before you keep charging into things that you don't understand.'

'So, enlighten me.'

'We're looking at Grant Faber over another matter.'

'What?'

'I can't tell you. I just need you to keep away from him for the time being.'

This was obviously just another attempt to get me off the case. He had seen that ordering me off hadn't worked. Now he had changed tact. I decided to change tact too. 'I might be able to do that. Under one condition though.'

Amusement flickered in his eyes. 'Oh?'

'Why is your name on Emma Faber's arrest warrant from six months ago?'

'This again! It was a protest. After the riots at the G7 meetings last year, we were worried it could turn nasty. Land rights is a flashpoint. I was returning from a scene in St Albans so I called in to help.'

'Help who?'

He stared at me, uncomprehending.

'There's a rumour that you were fixing a problem for someone.'

His eyes narrowed. 'Who said that?'

'I said it's a rumour. It doesn't matter who said it. Do you want my theory on it?'

'No.'

'You owe Grant Faber for something. You were stationed at Green Heights together. Maybe he was due a few beers, maybe he's got you for something that happened when you worked together, maybe its just an old buddy thing. Whatever it was, he called it in when his sister got arrested. So you took over her arrest and got her off. But Grant was worried about what she was really involved in. He thought the protest crowd might have sucked her up. He didn't want her blowing her scholarship so he asked you to check out how deeply involved she was with the protest scene. So you sniffed around her neighbours and known acquaintances, then reported back to Grant. Am I warm?'

'You've got an active imagination.'

'Then a few months later she turns up dead. This gets you thinking about who she was hanging around with, the names you turned up. You're a seasoned detective, you know the drill. Most people are killed by someone they know. So you start looking around her, searching for motive. You know that Grant is her brother and you're on favourable terms with him —you must be because you did him a favour six months ago —so you call him first thing.'

He shook his head. 'I'd stop there if I were you.'

'Yet he says no one's contacted him. Except me. So you didn't call him. That implies you're not on good terms with him. And if you're not on good terms with him, then he's one of the first people you should have suspected. Yet you didn't even mention to anyone that you knew Emma had a brother. You let us find out from the parents. And I find your fingerprints on my files in my locked filing cabinet.'

His jaw shifted slightly. The grinding of teeth. 'If that's what you think, then you're a fool.'

'From the outside it looks like you're trying to protect him.'

He leaned forward. 'Here's another scenario. If Grant had done anything wrong here, and note that I stress the 'if', then we can't run the investigation like we normally would. He was a cop, he knows the ins and outs. We need to tread carefully. I need to know everything that goes on, everything that's uncovered. You're the obstruction to this because you seem to be running your own investigation. I can't trust you because I never know what you're up to.'

'If you didn't keep me off the case and keep cutting me out of the loop then I wouldn't need to tip toe around behind your back,' I said.

'I've worked around you for over a year. You're good at your job, but you go too far. Every time. That attitude could lose us our conviction. If I can't control you, you're no good to me.' He rubbed a hand over his face. 'Look, I'm not an idiot. I know that you're working wonders on this case. You're making it look like it's Pace, but I know it's you. I want you to work with us, but I can't let you in unless you toe our line, not your own.'

'If I come back on your team I need to know the truth about why your name is on the arrest record.'

He stared at a point behind my head for a few moments. I waited it out as he deliberated.

'Okay,' he said. 'You were half right. I owed Grant, so I looked into his sister's arrest. But that was the debt paid, as far as I'm concerned. Your little theory about me protecting Grant is way off. I just have a feeling that he's messed up in his sister's death. I don't know in what way, but I sense there's something there. Until I discover more, I have to tiptoe around him. You hounding him puts him on the alert.'

'So what do you suggest I do?'

'Come to me with your suspicions—and stay away from Grant Faber.'

'I don't have suspicions. I'm just a fingerprinter, remember.' I stood up. 'I'll come to you with what I find if you stay away from my case files.'

I walked out of his office and back down to the fingerprint lab.

When I returned to my floor, I'd been assigned a new job.

Within ten minutes I was on my way to dust a service station in Cheltenham that had just been robbed.

28

The job took an hour. On my way back to the office, I stopped in at Monash University in Clayton.

The Science Section was a group of red brick towers set on the outskirts of the university's northern side. I entered from the first high rise and saw a reception desk set behind waist to head sliding glass panels. A notice board next to reception listed staff room numbers. Janine Wood's room number was 314.

New universities seem designed to promote commerce. I walked past notices threatening debt collection of outstanding fees, display shelves with the prices of staff members' latest books, and order forms for university logo t-shirts pinned to notice boards. The reconditioned air, overly bright florescent lights and the lemon smell of wax on the white vinyl floor reminded me of a shopping mall.

Room 314 was a tiny room with a grill on the narrow window. I wondered who would be desperate enough to scale the third floor and crawl through a scientist's window. Against the walls were four desks, two on each side of the room. Two were occupied. At the desk closest to the door was a mountain of a man with an avalanche of overhanging flesh. His brown suit hung off his body like a galleon's sail on windless seas. He turned his neckless head to me and raised a questioning eyebrow.

'I'm looking for Janine Wood.'

Beside him, in the shadow of his enormous body, a slim hand waved in the air. I peered around him to see a tiny woman with shoulder-length brown hair sitting at the next desk.

'Come on in,' she said. She jumped to her feet, grabbed an extra chair and placed it beside her own.

I sat down on it and handed her my identification.

She glanced at the card. 'This is about Emma?'

'You've heard?'

'I read it in the paper. Can you believe it?' she shook her head slowly. 'I wanted to call her parents, you know, just to tell them I'm sorry, but I'd never met them. It seemed silly somehow.'

'I believe Emma wanted you to do a job for her.'

She glanced pointedly at the occupied desk next to her. 'Actually, I was just going to take a break. Let's walk.'

Janine led me down to a small lake about half the size of a tennis court. Brown ducks rushed into the green-tinged water as we approached the edge of the shore.

'She wanted me to test some water samples from an Aboriginal reserve on the banks of the Yarra,' she said. 'I can tell by examining the micro-organisms in the water whether the water is bay water or from an underground source.' She spread her rainproof jacket on the ground for us to sit on.

I settled down beside her. 'Did you know why she wanted it tested?'

'There's a construction site inland from the Yarra, down stream from the Docklands. What stands between it and the river is Aboriginal land. The construction site needs water to be able to extract the soil they want moved. To do this they need to run pipes over or under the aboriginal land to get to the river. They applied for a permit to do it, but the land owners had to decline it.'

'Why?'

Laughter rang out behind us. She waited until a group of students passed. 'It's sacred burial land. Under the land there's

151

a reservoir. This is why the original Aboriginals used the land.'

'Can't the construction company just run pipes through a different section of land?'

'Have you been to the site?'

I shook my head.

'To get around the Aboriginal land, the company had agreed to run an extra ten kilometres of pipe.'

'That's not that much.'

'No, but it's a lot of extra money spent. Even if they did divert the pipes, the waste wouldn't wash away. The currents are at a cross point where their pipe would meet the river. They could pump in but anything pumped out would just accumulate there in a hump like a sand bar. They'd have to ferry it out to sea. The Aboriginal land, however, has a strong current flow. Anything piped out of their coastline would wash out into the bay.' She picked up a small stone and skimmed it along the water. 'But the company hasn't done that yet. There are no pipes coming out at the cross current point.'

'So, what's the problem?'

'There has to be pipes somewhere because they need access to water. It could be that the pipes are hidden on the river floor or near enough to the coast so that the refuse seeps out naturally into the river. Or they could have tapped into the underground reservoirs beneath the Aboriginal land.'

'What will happen if they take the water from underground?' I asked.

'If they drain off the subterranean reservoir then the Aboriginal land could dry up. There would be changes in the chemistry of the soil, changes to the vegetation and maybe alterations in the rate of erosion. And of course there's the whole issue of the sacredness of the land.'

I turned to face her. 'Janine, how important are your results?'

'Not enough to kill for, if that's what you're getting at. What the construction company is doing is illegal, but they'll never be prosecuted for it.'

'Why?'

She shrugged. 'Because it happens everyday. Big developers are worth too much to mess with. If the government does ever reclaim the land, it'll just sell it to the same developers anyway. With river and ocean views like this, it doesn't matter what damage lies beneath. Developers will snap it up.'

'If the land is so valuable, why does the government keep it reserved as sacred land?'

'It's only now that this end of the river is being upgraded that the land value has jumped.

'If the government's not going to do anything to stop the construction companies, why are you and Emma bothering to prove it? You're not thinking of a civil suit?'

She skimmed another stone. 'Not at this stage. Emma and her group, and the owners of the land, just wanted to be sure. They needed to know so they could work out a way to preserve the land.'

'And who pays.'

'That too.'

'So when will your tests be complete?'

She looked at me in surprise. 'When I get the samples.'

'Emma didn't give them to you?'

'No. I suppose Charlie will now.'

'But Emma had already collected them. Her neighbour said they'd been removed from Emma's fridge. Charlie thought you had them.'

'I don't have them. Emma said she was going to drop them in on Friday, but she didn't show up.'

'Were you and Emma close friends?'

'No. Acquaintances, really.' She brushed her brown hair out of her eyes. 'We'd sit together in chemistry classes. She was minoring in it, I was majoring. I was working at the CSIRO while doing my degree, and I managed to get her some summer work the year before she graduated.'

'When did you last see her?' I asked.

'A few months ago. She called me last week to ask if I could test the samples.'

'Did she mention feeling threatened by anyone?'

'Not to me.' She absently poked a finger into the earth beside her as if testing its moisture. Professional habit, I assumed.

'She said nothing about being followed? Someone's attention making her nervous?' I asked.

'Jesus! You're not implying Charlie, are you?'

'What makes you say that? Did she hint at something?'

'No, no. I've met Charlie a few times. I liked him. He seemed good for her.'

'Did she ever talk about her brother?'

'I didn't know she had one,' she said.

'Did you meet any of her friends since she finished uni? Or Charlie's?'

She shook her head. 'I went down to the river with her once, though. She asked me to look at the land, to give my opinion on the soil. I went with her one morning, but no one else was there, except a geologist she knew.'

'What was his name?'

'I don't remember. He was Italian, I think—very dark hair, olive skin, nice looking.' She checked her watch. 'I'm sorry but I have to give a class in ten minutes.'

'Of course. Thank you for your time.'

We walked along a dusty path that traced the back of the science building. The sound of metal grinding and the hum of small engines seeped through the closed windows.

Janine rubbed at a brown stain on the back of her hand. 'It's such a shock when this happens to someone you know. It's like you realise you've been living in a cocoon all your life, thinking life is good, that people are good. And then this happens.'

I squeezed her shoulder. I didn't tell her that I'd give anything to move back into the cocoon, that I dealt with so much darkness that sometimes I forgot that people have light too.

The traffic on the city bound side of Princes Highway was heavy and slow moving. I wound down the window and let the chill of August tighten my skin. This far inland, on the flat planes of black tar and squat brick homes with barren lawns, there is no breeze. The only movements of air are the snaking trails of car exhaust. In these suburbs, the black fuel clouds never seem to rise. Like tumbleweed, they just roll from street to street.

As I drove, I thought about the test tubes of river water. They hardly posed a danger to the construction companies. Environmental issues affecting government land rarely seemed to get press, and if no law court supported the Aboriginal protests, why would the company feel threatened?

Perhaps Jane Frommer had been wrong—maybe the test tubes were empty. Or maybe their content was not from the river site. Emma could have just thrown the test tubes out herself. She might not even have taken the samples yet.

But Charlie seemed to think that she'd gathered the samples. Had he actually seen her take them?

Charlie's report on his last words with Emma suddenly came back to me: *Something about the river's edge...*

He'd assumed she was talking about the water samples. But she hadn't got the samples tested yet. She couldn't have discovered something in the results.

What else about the river's edge had she uncovered?

29

I parked the Ford in the squad parking lot on Albert Street between a white Commodore Station Wagon and a dark blue Mitsubishi. After removing my fingerprinting kit from the boot and locking all the doors, I left the car park and began the five minute walk around the building to the front door.

Another dark blue Mitsubishi sedan drove by slowly with its left indicator blinking.

I paused, then turned around. It decelerated to a near stop and rolled into the carpark I'd just emerged from.

I remembered the car that Charlie said had been parked outside his apartment block for two days. A dark blue Mitsubishi with the number plate FBQ 397. Turning on my heel, I walked back to the parking lot. In it I counted five dark blue Mitsubishis. Two spots from my car, a short young man emerged from the one that had just driven in. He placed a McDonald's take-away bag on the roof of the car and bent over the front seat to retrieve a briefcase from the back.

I pretended to be rifling through my hand bag for my keys while he passed me on the sidewalk. When he was five or so metres from me, I stepped back into the car park and checked the license plates of all the blue Mitsubishis.

I found FBQ 397 at the back of the lot, nose to the cream wall of Headquarters.

I wanted to shout for joy. The car that had been in the vicinity of Charlie Hunt's apartment block the night that Emma had been murdered was a police car. I hoped to God it had been on surveillance. That would mean that the driver would know if Charlie had been home all night as he claimed to be.

All I had to do was find the driver.

I contemplated pulling out my phone and dialling Alex's extension but changed my mind. To do a license plate check you had to give your reason and your details. He would have to say that he had visited Charlie's apartment block, and that someone had given him new information or called in an anonymous tip.

Once again he would have to lie for me.

It would be better if I did it myself.

Of course, my method would be more complicated than just making a phone call.

I set my case down in front of the car, in the narrow space between the brick wall and the car's bonnet. I removed a squirrel haired brush, white powder, adhesive tape and my Polaroid camera.

When I was sure the carpark was empty, I dusted the driver's side door handle with white powder. The powder rose in a vanilla fairy floss cloud, then was whisked away by the breeze. The powder formed thick arcs and elegant swirls on the door handle, clinging to the residues of past touch. Finger marks tracked across the small surface like footprints on a crowded beach.

I could not give each touch an age. The force of a winter downpour can erase a ten minute old print but leave undamaged the split second contact of two fingers from six months ago. The newest impression may not leave the boldest lines, and the oldest needn't decay first. Newspaper ink on wood can outlive the fingertip that stained it. A hot wind can suck a print from a window before the finger has left the glass. Add ninhydrin to the hieroglyphs on Egyptian papyrus scrolls and the loops and lakes of 3000-year-old fingerprints appear.

The handle had so many layers of prints that it seemed alive with cross hatched lines and swirls.

I looked for a thumbprint. The ulnar leaning lines

characteristic of thumb tips always stood out from the confusion of lines and papillary fragments. The driver's door was on the right side of the car, so the driver would most likely use his right hand to lift the handle. The thumb would act as a brace while the pinkie, ring and index lifted the handle from beneath.

The same print was repeated at least four times across the narrow handle. The same person had opened the car door a few times. This, of course, didn't mean that the owner of the thumbprint was the person who had used the car on Emma's night. Each department of the St Kilda Road Complex was allotted a pool of cars that they alone would use. With one name, I would know which department had been watching Charlie's apartment block.

I photographed the door handle and then smoothed a strip of adhesive tape over the print. With the quick snap that parents use to rip a bandaid from a child's knee, I removed the tape from the surface. On the sticky side of the tape were the powder formations of the ridge patterns on the door handle.

I laid the tape sticky side down on a fingerprint card designed for single latents and ran my own finger along the back of the strip. Slowly this time, I peeled the tape from the cardboard. On the paper was a perfect replication of the print on the door.

With a baby wipe I cleaned the car door of white powder. As I began packing my case, I heard the crunch of tyres behind me. I kicked the case into the narrow space between the bonnet and the wall and squeezed in behind it.

A silver Mitsubishi Mirage spun across the gravel in a cloud of putty coloured dust and slid into a vacant spot in the middle of the lot.

I squatted down as a brown-haired woman in a light blue trouser suit emerged from the car and lifted a large cardboard storage box from the back seat. Hoisting it onto her shoulder, she crossed the gravel to the footpath and headed towards the St Kilda Road exit.

I waited until I could no longer hear the clicking of her

heels on the concrete pavement before I emerged.

The computer showed the print as belonging to Sergeant Domenic Roche of the Drug Squad. He was ten loops, nine of which rose and fell in unremarkable lines, the tenth a left thumb with a self contained oval which leaned to the ulnar. No unique scars.

I looked past the ordinariness of his patterns to the grace of the lines.

The ridges were a uniform thinness, elegant threads that gently echoed the curve of the fingertip as if embroidered by an Italian tailor. The black outlines showed elongated digits, without traces of fleshy spill or excessive pulp. In my mother's days they would be called musician's fingers—flexible enough to vibrate catgut with a caress, slim enough to slip between strings, but muscled enough to strike a forte.

Except this man's fingerprints bore no signs of contact with an instrument. The tip of the pointer and the index gave slightly lighter impressions, as if the ridges were pressed flat, offering less friction than the other fingers.

Paper shuffler's hands.

I pictured a tall man who wore his even temperament on the long lines of his face.

The picture from his identification badge confirmed that I'd read his fingers correctly.

A wide line of baldness that spared only the tufts above his ears seemed to add height to his face. His eyebrows were smooth lines set above the eyelids at such a distance that they seemed quizzical or surprised. The eyes were broadly spaced and intelligent, black in the stark tones of the computer screen. His nose was long and thin, lips like pencils. His chin was parallel to his windpipe and almost as long.

Statistics confirmed his height at 180 centimetres, and his weight at 70 kilograms. Eyes brown, distinguishing mark was an oval birthmark on his right thigh. He had joined the police force in 1981 at the age of twenty-six.

I printed a copy and phoned the drug squad.

Someone answered and connected me to Roche's extension.

He answered on the second ring with a voice like a cello.

'I've been watching that place for two weeks,' he told me. 'We're waiting for a well-known heroin dealer to make contact with someone in one of the apartments. It's been a small-scale operation, but after we shake our guy down he may give us bigger fish. How did you find out we were there?'

'The residents spotted you.'

He inhaled in surprise. 'No way.'

'They got the rego off one of your dark blue Mitsubishis.'

'But we're always swapping cars.'

I read him the license number. 'That's the one they were suspicious of. They're not sure that you're cops yet but they suspect it. Do you keep a log of who goes in and out?'

'Of course. We don't have everyone identified, but we've taken enough photos to be able to ID everyone later.'

'Charlie Hunt?'

'No. Which apartment is he?'

'10 D. Top floor, second last from the end of the balcony.'

I heard his fingers tapping on the desk as he thought. 'Oh yeah. Quiet guy, doesn't stay in much. Has a girlfriend. Blonde.' There was the scratch of pen on paper. 'His name is Charlie Hunt?'

'Yes.'

'That name sounds familiar.'

'His girlfriend was Emma Faber, the girl they found murdered at Williamstown beach.'

'Christ!' He took a few seconds to recover. 'Boyfriend a suspect?'

'He's upstairs in the lockup. Can you just confirm with me if you recorded his movements on Friday the 17th?'

'Give me a minute.' I could hear paper shuffling. 'July 17th? Surveillant Six, which is your Charlie Hunt, entered his apartment at 4 pm and didn't leave until the next morning.'

'Are you sure that he didn't leave?'

'There's only one way out of there, and that's the same way in.'

'The girl was killed between seven and ten pm. Were you guys on active surveillance the whole time?'

'Oh yeah, unfortunately.'

I couldn't help smiling.

Charlie Hunt was innocent.

30

I called Alex on his mobile. 'Anything new?'

'No. I'm upstairs.'

'Have you still got Charlie Hunt there?' I asked.

'For another two hours.'

'I'm sorry, Alex. He didn't kill Emma. Drug squad was doing a surveillance on the house and logged that he didn't leave the unit all night.'

'How do you know that?'

I explained everything, then added: 'Just call Domenic Roche and report that you've spoken to one of Charlie's neighbours. And take a photo of Charlie up to him, just to check he's been logging the right guy.'

'Peterson's gonna crack it. He was keen on Charlie as the perp.'

'Don't worry. I've got another one for him.'

'Who?'

'I don't know his name yet. And what about Emma's brother, Grant Faber? Have you run a check on him yet? He's ex-cop, now a P.I. He admitted working with Peterson at Green Heights.'

'Wasn't Green Heights where Peterson was when he got dragged into that kick back inquiry about glaziers?'

'Yep.'

'How did you know that Faber worked with Peterson?'

Silence fell between us.

'Sarah, don't tell me you visited Grant Faber?'

'He was going to let me print him.'

'No! You've got no grounds to print him!'

'I didn't think he'd know that. That was before I discovered he was a cop.'

'You said the tattooist thought he was a cop—you should have known better.'

'And you said the tattooist had to be wrong.'

'Don't blame me. You said Faber was going to let you print him. I take it something went wrong.'

'He had a change of heart.' I didn't tell him that Faber had called his lawyer. 'I looked at his hands. He didn't have any marking on his fingers. And he seemed genuinely surprised that we'd picked up Charlie. He warmed to the idea pretty quickly though.'

'Where was he that night?'

'At home alone. And he volunteered that piece of information, by the way.'

'How convenient.'

'And he's pointed the finger at someone.'

'Who?'

'Some old homeless guy.'

'How original.'

'I'm going into the city to check around for him.'

'Sarah...' I could read the exasperation in his voice.

'What?' My voice was sharper than I meant it to be.

He sighed. 'Nothing. Just be careful.'

Before I left I made two calls. The first was to my mother. The phone was unanswered. I felt the echo of each ring in my stomach. I let the phone ring until the line cut out.

The second call was to Peterson.

'I'm checking for fingerprints in a spot frequented by someone implicated by Grant Faber,' I said.

He sounded surprised. 'Who?'

'An old homeless man. It's just routine.'

'Do you need assistance?'

'No, it's a public spot by the river.'

'I'll send a cruiser to accompany you.'

'No, it's fine. There's a group of geologists working on that part of the river. I'll get them to guide me to the spot and wait with me.'

'I want everything by the book, you hear me?'

'Of course.'

'Good. And thanks for coming to me with this.'

Now, I thought, we'll see whose side Peterson is really on.

31

It was getting dark by the time I set out for the river. The mid-month moon was so bright there was no need for streetlights. Todd Road took me under the Westgate Bridge. Shipping yards kept the river hidden, but every building I passed had been built to service it. I turned into Lorimer Street and suddenly there it was—wide and brown, slipping past me silently. To my right were the skeletal masts of the dry dock, and across the water from this, the coal coloured bows of the yachts gently nodding on the new marina. Condo height apartments looked down from the opposite shore. A kilometre upriver the city squatted at the tide's edge, the water a mirror to the high rises and turn-of-the-century custom houses. Even the river's odour was secretive, the air only Vegemite and cheese from the food factory that stood on the land between the Westgate Freeway and the Yarra.

I turned the car left and followed the river downstream until its banks became open hinterland. The land swelled uphill as it backed away from the bank. The peaks of yellow cranes formed a tundra above the gum tree tops.

Movement down on the river caught my eye. White spotlights cut across the brown flow and combed through the tiny peaks that pushed past. I parked the car on the gravel shoulder of the blacktop and skittled down the shrubbed embankment.

I smelt the river suddenly. Dead fish, motor oil and the scent of a city's waste. As I looked across it, I realised I was on the wrong side of the shore. The Aboriginal land was across the water. I didn't know where a bridge crossed to it.

A man in a bright yellow slicker stood on my side of the red mud plain that separated the water from the bank. He swung the beam of a drum spotlight across the surface of the water.

A small skip with an outboard motor was anchored a few metres offshore. Another yellow slickered man was bending over the edge of the boat, fishing through the water with a skimming net.

'Hi,' I called to the man on the shore. I stepped onto the muddy earth.

He looked up in surprise and quickly raised his hand as a signal to stop. 'Careful. Stay on the bank. The grounds slippery there.'

I ignored him and carefully stepped further out onto the muddy plateau. I introduced myself as Sarah Arden from the Victoria Police.

He stepped away from the spotlight, letting its beam rest on the boat. The occupant let out an annoyed 'hey!'.

As the man repositioned the spotlight, I took a good look at him. He was short and barrel round in navy blue bib overalls and black rubber gumboots. Beneath the foggy overspill of light from the beam, his skin was a puff of cloud, his flesh spilling over the collar of his t-shirt like a seepage from a baking cake.

In contrast, the man in the boat was thin with movements as quick as the river that slipped around him. Legs like oars, open yellow slicker a sail against the slap of the wind, long brown pony tail swishing across his back to the rhythm of the current. I didn't need to see his hands to know the fingers would be riddled with splinters.

These, I assumed, were the geologists.

'I'm Carl Longford from the Geological Services Department,' the man with the spotlight announced. 'The permits are in the car.' He nodded toward the road above us.

I shook my head. 'I don't care about the permits. I'm looking for an old guy who's supposed to live down here.'

Carl rolled his hands down the front of his overalls. Long

166

brown streaks covered the area between his upper thigh and knees. 'The old guy lives on the other side,' he said.

'How do I get over there?'

He pointed to his companion on the river. 'That boat.'

I took another look at the boat. Small waves occasionally splashed over the side and onto its floor. 'I'd rather drive.'

'No bridge except that one.' He nodded toward the Westgate Bridge.

'I have to go back up to the freeway?'

'And get off at Williamstown Road, then drive down to Yarraville. Take you fifteen minutes.'

I stared at the silver skip again. Its metal side dripped brown with river mud.

Carl yelled over to his companion. 'Bring her in. We've got a passenger.'

My skipper introduced himself as Dario. 'What do you want the old man for?' he asked.

'He was an acquaintance of a murder victim.'

'The blonde girl they found at Williamstown?'

I nodded.

'She used to come down here sometimes and camp with the Aboriginal crowd upstream. I remember her playing a violin. The old man would sit with them. Sometimes he'd even play the violin. You don't think he had anything to do with her death?'

'I'm not accusing him. I'm just trying to find out who he is.'

'Can't help you there. I heard you picked up the boyfriend, Charlie. That's a surprise.'

'What makes you say that?' I asked.

'That boy seemed really keen on her. They've been coming down here nearly a year now, and I never saw him even raise his voice at her.'

'What about the old man?'

'I saw her talking to him, but I always felt he was harmless. He handles the boat sometimes when Carl can't make it down. Been boating before, that's for sure. Knows his tides and rips.'

As we glided across the water, the river whisked old cigarette packs and beer cans past us. Wrapped in the water, I could see it wasn't as brown as it looked from the shore, but more a tan colour. Its surface, though, shone with slick pools of oil. The putter of the small motor cut through the growl of the cars travelling above us.

'You've never asked him his name?'

'He's hard to communicate with. Doesn't speak much English. He's smart though. He knows something about this river's not right.' He shifted the skip up a gear. 'Hold on now, the breeze off the heads is pretty strong, even down here.'

The wind hit me like a tornado, whipping my hair into a stranglehold around my neck. The boat's bow dipped so low that water sloshed over the sides and into my shoes.

'Won't get much worse than this.'

I felt my dinner starting to rise.

Dario must have seen it coming. 'Keep your eyes up,' he said. 'Just watch the shore.'

I swallowed. The sides of my throat were as dry as dead leaves.

'What do you mean something's wrong with the river?' I croaked.

'This section of the river had no outward flow. We're trying to find where the waters diverting to. There must be an underground channel that empties into the bay.'

I remembered Alex told me the river was flowing oddly. 'Is this where the cross currents are?'

'No, they're further around the bend, near the construction site.'

'So this is the Aboriginal waterfront?'

'Just about.' He pointed a little further down the river, away from the ocean. 'A few metres down there. The underground channel is probably connected to their land. They've got a lot of water activity underneath them.'

'Has it always been like this?'

'Only for about a year now. The shipping that passes through here from the river to the bay reported a strong rough spot here. Leisure craft skippers from the marina started whispering amongst themselves that the bay was backing up. It sounded so outrageous that no one took it seriously.'

'How did you find out?'

'By chance. I have a boat moored at Williamstown. The river flow story had become something of a sailor's myth so I thought I'd debunk it once and for all.' He laughed. 'I tell you, I was surprised as hell when I saw it myself.'

Dario cut the skip's engine half a metre from the shore and let the wake push us into the mud plateau.

'Did the old man show any interest in Aboriginal culture?'

He shrugged. 'Not that I noticed.'

The boat slowed to a stop as the mud rose up around the hull.

'About three metres upstream,' he pointed back to the city, 'the bank runs up to a small bluff. Follow the trail through the shrub and you'll find a bunch of lavender bushes. Behind those is a small opening in the bluff. That's his cave.' He stepped over the side. The mud swallowed his leg up to the knee.

He offered me both hands. 'I'll grab you by the waist and swing you over to solid ground.

I stared at his skinny arms.

'Hey, if I can hold this tincan straight against a rip then I can toss you to shore with one hand.'

I took his hand and inhaled sharply as he swooped me into the air and across the mud plains like a father giving his child a whirly spin.

My feet hit solid ground and he let my hands slip from his grip.

I smoothed down my jacket while he swung a leg back over the side of the boat.

'Just give me a yell when you want to be ferried back. We're here for a few more hours. Here.' He tossed me a flash light. 'You'll need this.' He pushed off the shore with the handle of his net and the motor started with a cough.

32

I followed the shore upriver until the shrub line began to ascend.

Above the bank I could see the lights of the top floors of the city buildings. The river's bank would run under the bridge at the base of Flinders Street, then sweep away from the city towards South Yarra. The water, of course, ran the other way.

I climbed the ridge. The wind brought me the lavender before I could see it. The three bushes of long, thin flowers were like waving paths ahead of me. The moonlight turned the green of the foliage silver and the deep purple of the bloom was black against the mouth of the cave.

I squatted behind the lavender bushes and called into the cave. 'Hello? Are you in there?'

My voice bounced off the rocks inside the cave and leapt back at me.

'Hello?' I called again.

I stepped inside the narrow mouth of the cave and flicked on my flashlight. I could smell the odour of damp limestone. The walls of rock stayed narrow for a few steps, then broadened suddenly into a wide cavern. The air was cold and tight, like stepping into a wine cellar.

The sight of the walls made me gasp.

Seaweed hung along the rock face in a neat line.

Just like on my mother's porch.

I knew what it was for. When rain was coming, the seaweed would swell in size. When it hung limp, expect a dry spell.

Dead fish lay in rows three deep and three across. They were still scaled and not yet starting to smell.

They were long, thin and silver like the one that had appeared on my doorstep the morning after Emma died. I felt sick suddenly, that spinning dizziness of the belly that panic brings. Had this man been to my house? I swallowed down the taste of my stomach and forced myself to keep looking around the cave.

A small raft made from wood and bark rested against the back wall. This must be how he crossed the river.

In one corner stood a violin on a music stand, bow resting horizontally across the two prongs that held the body of the instrument.

I quickly crossed the dirt and lifted the violin from its stand.

The wood was warm against the nervous sweat on my hands, the slickness of my fear turning the grain from mahogany to tan bark brown and making the wood waxy beneath my fingers. I tried to hold it in places no one would touch. The instrument was old, grime caught in the turn of the cornice spirals, the varnish of the chin rest worn by decades of skin's caress. Half moon indentations of uncut fingernails followed the strings down the fretboard.

There was nothing about this violin that indicated that it was Emma's instrument, yet I knew it was. I placed the violin carefully back on its stand. My hands held its odour. Just as sealed wood holds fingerprints, so it holds scent. I lifted my palm to my nose and inhaled. My skin held the musty scent of old dust and airless rooms. Beneath this there was a hint of another odour. I searched for memory for a few seconds before it came to me: sandalwood. Emma's scent.

A bed made from sponge rubber off-cuts and a blue and brown chequered picnic blanket had been spread out in the corner. A big plastic bag was propped between the makeshift bed and the stone wall.

'Hello?' I called again.

A hurricane lantern had been placed by the bed. I lifted it and checked the level of fuel. It was nearly full.

171

My beam caught the edge of the carry bag again. I peered inside, then used the bow of the violin to shift its contents.

Inside was a heavy silver compass, the shipping lists from that day's newspapers, a small metal box filled with five and ten-dollar notes, and a black t-shirt that stank of sweat and mould.

Beneath the t-shirt was a small white pharmaceutical bottle.

I took it from the bag. The label identifying contents had been removed. I opened the bottle. Inside were white pills.

I wondered what Zaparin looked like.

I tipped out a few pills and put them in my pocket.

I shone my light around the rest of the cave. In a far corner there was a small bundle of blue material. I walked over and lifted the material with my flashlight.

A gun fell out.

Footsteps echoed against the stone floor of the narrow entry passage.

I spun around.

The man paused at the edge of the tunnel and peered into the cave. Our eyes met. For slow seconds he stared at me. Brown hair hung past his cheeks like rope and snaked down to his chest. A beard like a matt of hessian twine, woven coarse as a monk's horsehair vest, covered his face. What was left of the skin on his face looked like chicken wire, each section the texture of a different disease.

I held up my hands in surrender. 'It's okay. I just want to talk to you.'

The hair swung like a python and he disappeared back into the tunnel.

'Hey,' I yelled, taking off after him.

By the time I crossed the floor and stepped from the tunnel into the open night he was gone.

My eyes searched the foliage for movement and for any hint of a possible path—for that swish of lavender stalk knocked aside; or the rustle of branches closing behind a body.

But the shrubs seemed to have swallowed him.

I hurried back into the cave. Once inside, I pulled a tissue from my pocket and removed the compass from the bag. The tissue would keep the fingerprints on the compass in place. I made a makeshift sling from the blue rag that had covered the gun. Using the black t-shirt as a glove, I carefully piled the violin and gun into the sling and carried it out.

I left the cave and saw Dario walking past the lavender to me. 'I saw the old man go into the cave and then come running out again,' he said. 'I thought I'd check everything was okay.'

'I scared him off.'

'Probably better that way. You shouldn't go around cornering people.' He stepped into the water and waded halfway to out to the boat. He turned back to me with his arms outstretched.

'I didn't corner him. I just wanted to talk.'

'I told you, he doesn't talk.'

I brushed his hands aside and stepped unhesitatingly into the mud. The river slime enveloped my feet up to the ankle. I ignored it and waded further into the water. It wrapped around me, slippery yet dense against my movements. 'If he doesn't talk then how do you and he communicate?'

'We just use broken English and gestures.'

'And what about Emma? How did he communicate with her?'

'She spoke normally to him, just a bit slower.'

'So he understands but doesn't speak?'

'Yeah.'

I thought of the shipping lists he's ripped from the newspaper. 'He must be able to read.'

'I don't know.'

'Does anyone else come down here?'

'There are always cars up on the road above. You know, driving past, slowing down, young people looking for a quiet spot to be together. No one comes down here though.'

I tried to lift my leg above the water to climb into the boat. The river gripped it like a vacuum for a few seconds, then let go with a sucking sound and a tiny splash. Dario followed me into the boat. When I turned to look back at the patch of water we had just left, the surface was all knife-edge ripples.

33

I returned home to feed and check on Bess. As I watched her eat, I rubbed lanoline into my dry fingertips. The cold river air had tightened the skin and made the scars sting. When I went out again tonight I'd have to wear gloves.

It had taken a few years until I'd found gloves of perfect texture. I could never bear the scratch of wool. Alpaca is the warmest yarn but is too harsh against the puckered edges of my scars. It's leather that feels most comfortable against my fingers, as if it were merely a membrane between an object and my touch. With leather, I still feel the burn and chill of any surface. Perhaps this is because it, too, was once skin.

The night watchman waved me through the security gate of the St Kilda Road Complex. It was 9.30 pm. He recognised me as a frequent after-dark visitor and no longer requested my I.D.

Once in the elevator, I called Peterson's mobile and told him what I'd found.

'Print the compass,' he said, 'and make sure you log the gun into evidence. Oh, and get one of the Macleod biology people over here right now to test the gun for DNA. Grant Faber has a lot of friends still on the force. If he's involved, evidence could go missing.'

So Peterson was on our side.

I turned the gun over to the evidence storage department. I

wouldn't get to print it until the other branches of legal science had examined it. Advances in analysis meant that the biologists from the Macleod forensic centre could lift DNA from a fingerprint. They would need to take a sample before I started dusting and spraying. I was next in line after them, then it would be handed over to ballistics. The gun's rim would be examined to see how long ago it was fired, then the gun would be used in a soft range to see if the markings on the bullet matched the ones on the bullet that was pulled from Emma's chest. The gun would go through many hands before it could be matched to its owner.

As I entered my floor, I received a call on my mobile from Charlie Hunt.

'I've got you to thank for getting out,' he said. 'I was beginning to think I'd still be here in twenty years time.'

'Lucky you were under surveillance.'

'Yeah. Look, my lawyer's got some shit going down and I'm not supposed to talk to you, but I just wanted to ask you not to give up on Emma, no matter what happens.'

'What do you mean?'

'Just promise me you'll do what it takes to find out who killed her.'

'I can't promise anything. I'm not a detective. There are limits to what I can do.'

'You'll find ways around that. You found me before the other cops did, and you were the one who cleared my name.'

'That was chance.'

'No, you seemed to know from the start that I didn't kill her. How?'

I was silent. He was right. I had sensed he was innocent. Yet I couldn't tell him what had led me to that conclusion. 'I don't know how,' I finally answered.

'I think Emma's guiding you,' he said.

I tried to protest but he'd already hung up.

I pushed Charlie's words out of my head and started work on

the compass. I placed it on the workbench and prepared a batch of black powder. A light brushing with a squirrel-haired brush revealed the impression of the side of a thumb, a full pinkie, and slices of a fourth and index. This was typical of gripping a small object. I knew if I tested the bumpy back of the compass, I'd find a palm print.

I photographed the print, then durexed it onto a clean card.

Up close, his prints were astounding for their complexity.

A standard pattern grouping usually consisted of no more than two of the four generic fingerprint categories. The loop in its many varieties was usually the most common, followed by the arch and then the whirl.

Most of us have loops on all or nearly all of our fingers, and perhaps an arch or whirl on the fourth finger.

This man had a different print on each finger. Four fingers, four different ridge classifications.

An impression of his pointer was absent, so I assumed that would be a repeat of one of the four already represented.

I put on an eye piece and examined the thumb in magnification.

I was looking for the same mark that Emma and the wearer of the glove had on their fingertip. Logic told me I wouldn't find it. What did I expect? That they were all members of some cult that burned a brand into their thumbs?

I removed the eyepiece and blinked a few times to let my eye muscles relax. This man's thumb had no mark.

After a few seconds, I put the eyepiece on again and looked at the rest of his lines. His patterns were identifiable, but his ridge lines were broad. The white spaces between were far narrower then normal. I had seen this tendency before. It meant ridges so flat they looked as if they'd been drawn on with a fat marker. Through the pulpy centre of his index was a thick black band of disrupted pattern, small lines cross hatched across the surface.

I pictured what this would look like on the living fingertip. A swell of white cutting vertically across the skin, the imprint of something that left tiny fibres scars.

I examined the edges of the mark. They disappeared gradually—not at all like the abrupt and crisp borders of a scar.

These edges had the uneven texture of a burn, but the fibre marks in the centre of the mark were too distinct to be a burn. Burns mutilate the edges, swelling them in one section, shrivelling them to half their length in others. The ridge lines on this image had not been achieved in size, but simply stretched to their full elasticity.

Rubbed.

I had seen this pattern in some old men of manual occupations. The constant friction of a material or object pulled backwards and forwards against the fingertip.

A lifetime of yanking thickly twined cord.

Rope burn.

I set these prints aside and dusted the violin bow's handle with a gentle puff of white powder.

The prints that emerged were so terrainless that I had to dust them again.

They were the old man's.

I picked up the violin and dusted along the fretboard. It was like dusting the walls of a madhouse. Trenches dug by nails pitted the wood. Prints were engraved at all angles, running across the board from fret to fret as if in terror. Some prints were whole, some partial, most piled upon each other until they looked like a single disfigured mulatto of a whole. Crazed loops turned ulnar, radial and then ulnar again. Some overlapped the frets, as if unable to decide whether to escape left or right. I ripped off my eyepiece and took a deep breath.

After a few moments, I reapplied the eyepiece and increased its magnification. I focused on each furrow instead of running my eye over their trail.

At this magnification, the mad lines were less frantic, almost civil. The marks became the music that they had created. I could read the lines as if they were notes on a stave. A flicker of lines as light as leaves falling on the shoulder as you pass under a tree. Half moon scratches so shallow they could be mistaken for the wood's grain. These were the signs of quick and light contact: the quarter note and the semiquaver. The weight of the four beat note could be seen in prints on the base end of the neck, pores of the finger pad almost countable, each furrow as clear as the lines a fork makes through butter. On the thin end of the neck the prints were still frantic, but now they looked as if they'd danced a tarantella instead of scratched a wall.

These deepened into tango pairs pacing around middle C.

Then from the mahogany grain emerged a perfectly twinned loop.

Emma's hand.

Emma's violin.

34

I knew I should wait until morning to call the Faber household. Even if they were willing to talk to me this late, they would probably be too incoherent with sleep to answer my questions.

The violin was heavy in my hands as I carried it over to the lumalight desk and then turned it onto its front. I switched of the lights and ran each frequency in the invisible spectrum of light over the back of the violin, tracing the curlicue of the handle as it wound out of spiral slowly and became the instrument's neck, then its spine.

The lumalight picked up a trail of fingerprints layered like varnish over the wood. Some I recognised as the ones I'd lifted off the silver compass, the others fainter and smaller. On this side of the violin there was none of the madness I'd seen on the fretboard.

After photographing the violin, I collated the old man's prints. So far I estimated that I had the thumb, pointer, index and pinkie of the right hand and all the fingers of the left hand.

Impatient to do something, I ran the old man's prints through the database and fixed myself an ash strong coffee. The prints could take up to ten hours to return a hit.

I waited until 6 am to call the Fabers. Elizabeth Faber answered the phone on the second ring.

She grew hostile the moment I announced who I was. 'There's nothing more we can tell you. If you insist then you'll have to call at an appropriate hour.'

I apologised for waking her.

'My daughter is dead. Do you think I sleep?'

'Mrs Faber, I think I've found something.'

'Yes?' Her voice was cautious.

'I found a man who lives in a cave by the river. He had a violin with Emma's fingerprints on it.'

'You found Emma's violin?'

'So you knew it was missing?'

'I couldn't find it in her apartment.'

'How can I tell if it's hers?'

'It was an antique. I brought it for her in Vienna.'

'What colour was it?'

'A deep brown. The tuning nuts were mother of pearl. I've got detailed photographs of it for insurance purposes.'

'Great. I'll need to take a look at that. We have to hold the violin in evidence. I'll make sure it's looked after.'

'Who is this man who had it? He lives in a cave?'

'Yes, in a cave. To be honest, that's all I know. But now that we've got identification on the violin we'll send someone out to pick him up.'

'You didn't arrest him?'

'No. I had no grounds.'

'You had no grounds to come into my home and interrogate my husband and me, but legalities didn't seem to bother you then.'

'Hang on a minute, I was just doing my job by speaking to you.'

'Not according to your boss you weren't.'

I hoped to God she didn't mean Peterson. But of course, I knew she did.

'I'm a technician, Mrs Faber. I'm not allowed to arrest people.' Before she could accuse me further I shifted subject. 'While I've got you on the phone, I think it fair to tell you I spoke to your son yesterday.'

Silence fell between us. I waited it out.

When she realised I expected a response, she cleared her throat sharply. 'Why would you need to tell me that?'

'You said you had a falling out.'

'Yes.'

'Did you fall out with Emma too?'

'No. It's Grant that regularly falls out with everyone. My son is that type of person.'

'What type, exactly?'

'Argumentative.'

'Violent?'

She drew a sharp intake of breath. 'Why are you asking me this?'

'He was supposed to have met Emma the night she died. We only have his word that he didn't.'

She was silent. This was not surprising, given that I had just implied that her son may have killed her daughter.

'Look Mrs Faber, this is just a routine line of inquiry.'

'I haven't spoken to my son in nearly a year. He was never a violent person and I don't believe he's changed. Now, I've got a case before a magistrate this morning and I need to finalise my preparations.'

'Of course. Thank you for talking to me.'

'I'll get that photo of the violin couriered over to you as soon as I get to the office.'

She hung up.

How, I wondered, was it that she couldn't sleep but could still trial a case in court?

35

I headed home to grab a few hours sleep, shower and change clothes.

The road's blacktop was still slick from the early morning rain. I parked the car on the street outside my house and climbed out. Rainbow puddles of oil sat on the black pavers of the driveway of the house across the street. Gauze curtains had been hung from all the windows, but I could still see the outline of furniture in the half of the room closest to the windows.

A movement at their front window caught my eye. Through the curtain I could see a boy with obsidian coloured hair cut short and spiky. He was Jaiden, sixteen-year-old son of my neighbours. He was sitting at a piano, side on to the window.

With a start I realised he was watching me too. I waved and he waved back, then he rose and stepped up to the window. He pulled the curtains aside and beckoned me over.

We met by his front gate. He stood in between puddles on the black bricks, me on the white concrete footpath. His baggy jeans hung low beneath an oversized black shirt. A black strip of leather was tied around his neck and a brown leather one around his wrist.

'I saw someone in your backyard last night. Just there,' he pointed to the two metre gap between my house and the side fence that led into my backyard. His side of the street was higher than mine and he could see over my fence from his piano room and into my back yard.

'At first I thought it was just your dog 'cause all I saw was something move in the darkness, but then I heard the dog bark all muffled and distant so I knew she was inside.'

I felt sick suddenly, a surge of unsettled stomach that flooded upwards through my chest and clogged in the base of my throat. Had the caveman come after me? 'Did you see what he looked like?'

'No, it was just a shadow. I grabbed the torch and came over to check.'

'Oh God, you didn't!'

'Of course. But I couldn't see anything. Either he was gone or he was squatting in the bushes.'

'Don't ever check again, please. Just call the police.'

He laughed and patted me on the arm. 'It's all right. I had Roxy with me.' He nodded towards the iron fence that separated the driveway from the rear yard. His five-year-old Rottweiler lay with its snout lodged between the fence palings.

I laughed. 'Maybe I need one of those.'

He smiled. 'I think your Bess would be a little upset to hear that.'

'True. What time did you see this guy?'

'About two a.m.'

'What were you doing up at that time?'

'Surfing the net. Researching, I mean. I had an assignment I had to finish by today on internet security. You wouldn't believe what I had access to.'

'The day you start altering bank balances, do me a favour and move to another street.'

'Anyone who did that would be locked up within the day. Looking is easy, but fiddling with it leaves a trail.'

'You can look into someone's account details?'

'Sort of. You give me a name, I'll give you a dossier. There are dozens of databank scanning programs free on the web.'

'Whoa, is this legal?'

'Most of it. Come in for a coffee and I'll do yours.'

'Will your parents mind having someone in so early?'

'Naa, their bedroom's at the back of the house.'

We settled in front of the computer, its screen as black and flat as a Bang & Olufsen television. He'd given me a cup of coffee in a dark brown pottery mug. It was like holding a piece of earth in my palm.

'What's your full name?' he asked.

'It's not on me.'

He looked up at me in surprise. 'Wow, like a suspect's or something?'

'Not a suspect, just someone I'm curious about…'

I gave him Michael Faber's name.

I don't know how he did it and I don't think I ever want to know. But within a half an hour I had a dossier listing Michael Faber's personal holdings, credit purchases tagged by a customer loyalty program, his mortgage repayment schedule and statements from his private cheque account.

'You were able to access his bank statements?'

'Don't ask.'

I rolled my eyes. 'I'd better look at these at home.' I followed him to the front door. 'So you don't remember anything about the guy in my yard?'

'He was wearing dark clothes.'

'Do you think he was an old man, about fifty?'

'Could be. I think he had a lot of hair. Like a long beard and long hair. Or else he was standing in the middle of a bush.'

'No idea of his height?'

'Well, from my study window, I could see his head well above your side fence. Up to his waist, I think,'

'So he'd have been tall?'

'It depends on how far back in your yard he was standing. The closer to your back fence, the taller he'd seem.'

'Hmm. Okay, thanks.'

'Leave Bess outside, Sarah. It's the simplest way to keep people out.'

When I opened the front door I saw a floral suitcase sitting on the floor in the loungeroom.

I covered my eyes with my hands in dismay. 'Mum!'

I charged into the kitchen. A dirty tea cup had been left in the sink.

As I neared the spare bedroom I could hear little snores and snorts. I stood in the doorway and watched her sleep. A bottle of sleeping pills and a glass of water sat on the bedside table. Bess wagged her tail at me from the floor at the foot of the bed.

'Come on, you rat,' I waved Bess out of the room. She heaved herself to her paws and lumbered past me. I followed her to the back door and let her out.

She paused at the bottom step and made sniffing noises. I grabbed her collar and pulled her back.

Another dead fish lay on the concrete just beyond the step.

I dragged Bess back inside and threw the fish in the bin.

36

I spread the pages of what we'd gathered about Michael Faber's life across my kitchen table and made coffee. The house was cold. A draught ruffled the curtains and made the stained glass cabinet doors rattle softly. This cold air kept the skin of my scars stretched tight and chilled the floorboards. It brought in the smells from my neighbourhood: the smell of cigarettes from covert smokers in the lane, the bacon and eggs from the house next door.

Births, deaths and marriages listed Michael Faber as entering the world on January 7, 1944 and marrying Elizabeth Faber in 1965. A public business database cited him as CEO of Faber Constructions. The company was attributed with an annual turnover of more than 5 million in the last financial year. I rifled through a list of completed projects and current tenders until I found bank records that covered last year's transactions.

I scanned through them for a large amount accessed as two withdrawals—the classic before and after fee for a hit. There were no payouts over fifteen thousand dollars. The most common transactions were amounts between one and five thousand dollars made to a company called 'Federation Renovations'. This, I assumed, covered the maintenance of the Faber house.

Two lots of ten thousand dollars had been withdrawn in cash six months apart. Too small for a hit fee and with too much time in between. There were few other monthly cash withdrawals of a thousand or two. Summarised at the top of the account were customer details. The account was jointly in his wife's name.

I flicked through the remaining paperwork. Local council data told me he had a seven-year-old female German shepherd named Sheba that had been neutered. The Faber's had applied for and been granted a building permit to extend their back veranda into a sunroom. I gathered the printouts into a manila folder and put them in my briefcase.

The sheets on my bed were cold, but I was too tired to bother heating them with the iron. I set my alarm for five hours later and fell asleep. My sleep was deep and black.

If I dreamed, I didn't remember.

When I got up, Mum was in the kitchen going through my pantry. Her hair hung loose to the middle of her back. I didn't remember that it was so grey. 'What do you eat?' She scolded. 'There's nothing but pasta and dog food in here.'

I sat down at the table and rubbed my eyes. 'There's muffins in the freezer,' I said wearily. This was not going to be easy.

'Muffins?' She wrapped her pink quilted robe more tightly around her body. 'That's what you eat? Muffins?'

I braced myself for a fight. 'Mum, I told you that I couldn't spend time with you right now. I'm working on a heavy case.'

'You said you couldn't come up to see me. You didn't say I couldn't come down.'

'You didn't ask!'

'I had a dream—'

'No!' I held up my hand as a signal to stop. 'Don't go there. No dreams, no excuses, no charms. You have to go home.'

She stiffened. 'You have a man, is that it? Staying out all night, leaving your dog alone for so long when she'll give birth any second.'

I rolled my eyes. 'I was working—and I came home to feed her. What time did you get here?'

'Eleven last night. No one was there to pick me up so I had to catch a taxi from the city train station.' She shook her head as if I'd disappointed her. 'At my age.'

I slammed my hands down on the table. 'Of course no one was there to pick you up! You didn't tell me you were coming!'

'There's no need to raise your voice at me.'

I took a deep breath. 'Look, it's not safe for you here.'

'What do you mean?'

'Did you hear anything last night?'

She looked worried. 'Hear what?'

'You know, noises, Bess barking?'

'No. I took a sleeping tablet so I was out like a light. What happened?'

'The boy across the street saw a man in my back yard.'

'A man in the yard?' Her hand fluttered to her chest. 'Good Lord!'

'It's alright, I think he's harmless,' I said. There was no way I was going to tell her that I regarded him as a murder suspect.

'He must be the one in the dream.'

I held my hand up again. 'I told you, I don't want to hear it.'

'Before I left you were in my dream with a man. He was walking behind you but you didn't see him. I couldn't see his face, but he seemed wet, like he'd been caught in the rain. Sarah, I don't want to scare you but it wasn't a good dream. I felt like I had to call you when I woke up.'

I ignored her comments about the dream. 'I don't want you here while this is happening.'

'What about you?'

'I'm okay.'

She shook her head. 'I'm not leaving you alone.'

'I'm not alone. I'm not even here that often. In fact, I was thinking of taking Bess and staying over at a friend's house.' It was a lie but if it pacified her it was worth it.

Her eyes narrowed. 'I don't believe you.'

I changed tact. 'Alright, sit down.' I placed my hands on her shoulders and pressed her down into the chair. 'I'll tell you.

There is a man. He's a detective. I'll stay with him. How more safe could I be?'

'Not that detective you were seeing before your breakdown?'

I lifted my hands from her shoulders with a quick snatching movement. 'It wasn't a breakdown.'

'Call it what you like. It's not that married man?'

'Argh! I can't handle this! I'm booking you a ticket back this afternoon.'

'Sarah, you can't.'

'Oh, yes I can.'

'No. I mean I can't go back there.'

I waved my hand dismissively. 'Don't even try.'

'They painted words on my house. All over the outside. Witch. Satan lover. Rude words too.'

'Not again. Did you call the police?'

'Yes, but it never does any good. The constable just tells me to get a dog. His mother used to come to me for fidelity herbs before she left his father. He remembers that.'

'Can't you stay with one of your friends? What about Elsie?'

'She's got the kids down from Sydney for two weeks.'

I folded my arms across my chest and gave her my 'no-negotiation' glare. 'I'll drop you at a hotel on my way to work.'

She chewed on her lip, distracted. 'What did the man in your yard look like?'

'I don't know.'

She took a deep breath. 'Maybe it was your father.'

I sat down next to her with a thud. 'What? Last dream he was dead.'

'Well, we don't know for sure,' she said nervously.

'The man in my yard was not him.'

'How do you know? Did you get your father's fingerprints off the letter?'

'No. He was just an old homeless man, okay?'

She pulled something from her pocket. 'Here, I made you this after the dream.' It was a little bundle of leaves tied together with brown ribbon. 'Keep it on you.'

Six hours later the cave man's fingerprints identified him as Guillaume Perez of no fixed address. He was born on the 1st of March, 1940. I pulled his record from the computer archives. Arrested twice for petty theft. First for a bagful of fruit and then for twenty dollars worth of food from a Seven-Eleven. I assumed that if he was charged over a bag of fruit, then he'd obviously done it so many times before that the shopkeeper had lost patience with warnings. Vagrancy had been another favourite crime, with four arrests in the two years from 1996 to 1998. His record had been clean since the thefts in 1999.

I requested a printout of his patterns and called Alex's mobile while the computer was processing. The call was switched straight to voice mail. I remembered his night shift finished at 5 am.

I dialled his home number. The phone rang out so long I was just about to hang up when he answered. The growl in his voice as he said hello suggested he'd been asleep.

I explained what I'd found in Perez's cave.

The growl was replaced by caution. 'You got the gun?'

'A gun, maybe not the gun.'

'Has it got a serial number?'

'It's been scratched out.'

'The lab might be able to bring it back up,' he said.

'Are you going to send anyone out to the cave to pick him up?'

'The gun is grounds enough. Except that you taking it without a warrant could cause problems.'

'I don't see any problems. It was in a cave.'

'I still don't think -'

'Look, as a fingerprinter, I have the right to dust for prints in the same way you can seize property.'

'Sure, but only with paperwork to back it up.'

'Peterson let me go in.'

'You told Peterson you were looking for Perez? That was risky.'

191

'It was the only way I could work out if he was still fixing things for Grant Faber. Peterson offered me an escort while I checked out the cave. I don't think he's gone bad.'

Alex was silent.

'Okay,' I said. 'What's really going on here?'

'Nothing is going on.'

'Bullshit. You should at least be straight with me.'

I could hear the scratch of his bristle against the phone. I imagined him running a hand over his chin, feeling the roughness of morning stubble as he considered how much I should know. 'Hunt is suing.'

So that was why Charlie was not supposed to talk to me. 'Suing who?'

'Who do you think? The department. Peterson.'

'You?'

'No. It was Peterson he wanted. I imagine he'd rather kiss me and you than sue us.'

'Does anyone know I visited him? That it was me who got him off?'

'Hunt seems to be keeping quiet about that.'

I thought for a moment. 'So everyone thinks you found Roche?'

'Yeah, but I gave the information to Peterson. He held Hunt for another five hours while he claimed to be double checking it.'

'Five hours!'

'Hunt's lawyer says he should have been released immediately and that we should have known what our other arms were doing,' Alex said.

'He has a point.'

'Of course he has a point. In theory. But what police force in the world works like that? Anyway, Hunt's lawyer had been making noise about suing from the moment Hunt was brought in. We just gave him the opportunity he was looking for.'

'So that's why Peterson wanted to know every step I was going to take.'

Peterson must have sensed from the beginning that Hunt was looking to sue. He needed me on his side, and on my best behaviour, in case it did end up in court. 'So he won't pick up Perez?'

'Not yet. He'll probably tail him first. That's what I'd do.'

'But we've got enough to bring him in.'

'Not if he gets a lawyer like Hunt's.'

'Come on, we've got a gun, Emma's violin, and the brother said Emma felt threatened by him. I even found pills in his bag that could be Zaparin. This guy is looking more suspicious than Charlie Hunt ever did.'

'Get the tablets analysed. If they're Zaparin, we'll have a stronger case for picking him up.'

'By the time the result come back he may already have fled for good.'

Alex sighed. 'Fine, I know you, I see where you're heading with this. I'll go down and talk to him, just like we would with any other suspect.'

'Great, swing by the Complex and pick me up.'

'I think you should stay out of this.'

Charlie Hunt had insisted that I not abandon the investigation. I knew he was right. 'Forget it. I'm coming. You'll never find the cave without me—and there's something else you need to know.'

'What now?' he said, exasperated.

'I think he's mute and maybe even deaf.'

'A mute and deaf murderer?' He groaned, 'This is crazy.'

37

We parked on the rise above the cave, the car's front end to a hole in the cyclone fence. The road we'd just turned off traced the banks until about half a kilometre from the container park where I'd lost the old man. As we scuttled down the bank, the warm scent of lavender wrapped around us like a lover's arms.

The sun was low ahead of us, not yet strong enough to pick out the peaks of the river's waves. Halfway down the bank I pointed out the lavender clumps that concealed the mouth of the cave. As Alex moved past me and took the lead, the wind knocked against him and carried his smell back to me. It was there for hardly two seconds, a flicker between the layers of lavender. Still, I had smelt it.

Gun oil.

I grabbed his jacket at the elbow and tugged. He stopped and looked over his shoulder at me.

'Why did you bring your gun?' I whispered.

'Don't look so surprised. You've already frightened him once. He'll be on his guard now.'

Having grown up in the country, I was not afraid of guns. It was the idea of Alex and guns together that made me feel sick. 'I thought we were just going to ask a few questions.'

'He might not see it that way.'

He gave me his back again and changed direction from down to across. We waded diagonally through clumps of shrub until we were at the side of the cave's opening.

Alex called out, but got no answer. Tentatively, he stepped into the entrance of the tunnel. I grabbed his arm and whispered that Perez's bed was against the wall near the junction of the left and back rock faces.

As we neared the end of the tunnel, Perez's odour hit us. It was that mix of sweat and urine that unbathed people carry. Alex winced against the smell and then stepped into the open space of the cave.

Perez was asleep on his pile of foam rubber, still clothed in the rags of last night, facing the ceiling.

'You stay here,' I whispered. I crept across the space of the cave and stood above Perez. With my hands held palm out in front of me as a sign of peace, I nudged his calf with the toe of my shoe.

Perez's legs shifted, but he kept sleeping. I nudged him harder, then harder again until he woke with a small jump.

It took a second or two for his eyes to adjust to the light.

When he realised I was there, he let out a gasp and backed up against the wall.

'It's okay,' I said, nodding slowly and making a show of my empty hands.

His eyes rested on my hands, then darted to my waist.

I opened the flaps of my jacket and held them wide so he could see I had no weapon. His gaze darted past me to the exit of the cave.

He saw Alex standing there and drew his knees up against his body.

'We're police,' I said. 'Don't be scared.' I slowly pulled a newspaper picture of Emma from my back pocket and held it up so he could see the image.

He inhaled so sharply I could feel the edges of the clipping move between my fingers.

I knelt down so we were face to face. For a second I had a flash of recognition. His shadowed face through my laundry window, hair matted into long serpents. I dropped the photo in surprise. 'It *was* you in my backyard.' I had been sure before I'd come here, but seeing him up close confirmed it. The

195

turbulence returned to my belly in sharp jabs. He had been the one leaving fish on my doorstep. And he had returned my driver's license. 'Why?'

With his right foot he kicked the photo away. His lips parted and he began to mutter in a low voice. His front teeth were worn low, probably broken. Their bases were as black and slick as old engine oil.

I tried to understand what he was mumbling, but could only make out sharp sounds.

'What?' I said.

'Ez dut ulertzen. Lasai.'

His words sounded German. I looked at Alex in surprise. This was going to be easier than I thought. All we needed was a German translator.

'Look out!' Alex cried, gaze shifting over my shoulder. The alarm on his face made me scramble backwards away from Perez.

I felt the air inside the cave shift, a thin breeze tingling cool against the skin on my cheeks. Perez's stink grew suddenly overwhelming, the acrid spicy sweat almost on top of me.

His hands pushed flat against my collar bone and propelled me backwards. I hit the stone floor hard on my back and skittled across the ground for a metre before slamming my shoulder first into the rockface that was the left wall.

Perez ran towards Alex, hair twitching around his head like whips.

Alex yelled stop, but Perez kept running straight at him.

I jumped to my feet, ignoring the stabbing pain that seemed to be hacking my arm from its shoulder. 'No!' I called as Alex drew his gun and pointed it at Perez's approaching chest.

He wouldn't fire, I assured myself. He couldn't. Yet still I yelled.

Perez's pace didn't slow.

They collided in the narrow neck of the tunnel. Perez ploughed into Alex's chest and knocked him aside like a tyre bouncing over a gutter. Alex's gun hit the floor and bounced twice against the limestone slab, the sound two cracks as sharp of spring thunder.

Alex scrambled across the floor to retrieve it.

Perez disappeared into the tunnel. I barrelled after him and heard Alex's steps close behind me.

Despite the daylight, Perez was gone when we emerged from the tunnel. Still running, I followed last night's tracks and headed up the embankment in the direction of the container park.

'Forget it,' Alex panted behind me. 'He's gone.'

'He can't be that far ahead of us.'

Alex's thrashing against the lavender grew faint. I held my arms in front of me to ward off the shrubs and ploughed onwards. I hit the flat plane running. The snakelike movement of Perez's hair caught my eye. He was trying to squeeze around our car and through the hole in the fence.

I called Alex and heard his body separate the wall of lavender again.

Perez saw me coming and kicked against the fence, trying to create enough room to slip through. The fence sprung back and hit the side of the car. He disappeared suddenly, as if he'd ducked to the ground and I worried that he was trying to raise the bottom edge of the fence and crawl under it.

I dropped to the ground myself and saw him flat on his stomach, pushing against the fence with the palms of his hands.

Alex caught up to me and scooped me from the ground with both hands. 'Circle around the front of the car. I'll take the back,' he ordered. By the time I crossed the bitumen road, Perez had risen to his feet again and was trying to push his worn boot soles up the bonnet's slippery gradient.

I reached the car as Perez rose onto the roof. He tried to get a foot hold on the tightly woven mesh of the fence. His left foot secured a grip and his body rose onto the fence, right shoe desperately clawing flat against the wire.

I jumped onto the bonnet and threw myself against his body, then slipped my hands around his outstretched arms. I pulled him down, back first. The weight of my body jerked him backwards and broke his grip.

We fell backfirst onto the roof of the car and rolled off.

He broke my fall with a groan. Alex grabbed my elbow and ripped me off him. I screamed as my upper arm flexed out behind me and forced my shoulder to absorb the velocity of Alex's movement.

As I squirmed on the floor crying, Perez rolled over and tried to get up.

Alex leapt onto Perez's back, knees pinning Perez to the dirt at the base of the spine. Alex pressed the gun hard against the old man's nest of hair.

Nursing my shoulder, I retrieved a set of handcuffs from Alex's bag on the floor of the car, and then snapped them around Perez's wrists.

38

'Fleeing an interrogation?' Peterson said as he stared at the arrest report in his hands. His gaze snapped to Alex's face. 'Interrogation about what?'

I stared past Peterson and out the window behind him. I counted the seconds until he was going to throw me out of his office.

Alex folded his arms across his chest. 'He was known to be harassing Emma Faber in the days before she died.'

Peterson's eyes dropped back to the report. 'He lives in a cave? Tell me this is a joke.'

'It's government land,' I said. 'He's squatting.'

'It's all perfectly legal.' Alex said. 'He's not being held on suspicion. I just escorted him in for an interview.'

'Escorted? That's colourful.' He threw the report down on the desk. 'Why didn't you check with me before you brought him in? Pace, you know Hunt's lawyers are circling. We need to be extra careful.'

'He fled. We had to go after him.'

Peterson nodded curtly at me. 'Leave us alone.'

As I walked away from his office, I could hear Peterson's voice override Alex's bass tones.

I picked up the phone on the closest vacant desk and called special services. I ordered a translator.

'What language?'

'That's the problem. The guy's words sounded German but his name is Perez.'

'That's Spanish, yeah?'

'Maybe. But his first name, Guillaume, is definitely French.'

'We've got a translator who's listed as fluent in Spanish, French, German and Italian. Actually, he's in the building now for a meeting.'

'Send him up to homicide.'

My next call was to security. 'Can you send an armed guard up to homicide? And make it a male. We've got a guest up here who needs a shower and a clean set of clothes.'

I left the Homicide floor and hurried down to fingerprints.

'Sarah!' Paul called as soon as I pushed open the glass doors. He was sitting at his desk filling in a report form.

'Can't talk, gotta grab something and run upstairs to homicide.'

'Where the hell have you been? Rory's steaming. We've been filling in for you all morning.'

'I got caught up in an arrest.'

'Not the Faber case? For your sake I hope its not.'

I slowed my pace and stopped by his desk. 'What do you mean?'

'Rory hit the roof over you spending so much time on that. You're a pinkie away from freelancing.'

Why didn't that panic me. 'Is he here?'

'No, he's out covering one of your jobs.'

'What jobs? I've been keeping up. I've even been doing everyone else's drudge work here in the office.'

'That's what we told him, but I think he's getting pressure from above.'

I crossed the floor to my desk and took Perez's compass from my locked drawer. On my desk blotter was a yellow sticky note filled with Rory's neat script. It read: Call me the minute you see this. R.L.'

I ripped it off the blotter and then had second thoughts. If

I left it stuck there, maybe Rory would think I hadn't seen it. I blushed the moment the thought entered my head.

I thrust the compass into my pocket. Why was I suddenly acting like a deceitful child? I stripped the sticky note from the desk and stuck it into my pocket with the compass.

I'd hold Rory off for another half hour.

In the elevator I ran my fingers over the ornate back shell of the compass and then the thick glass of its face. I realised I had not actually looked at the markings beneath the glass, only those that seemed like fingerprints on the casing. I held it in the chub of my palms, a few centimetres from my face.

The needle was a standard compass arrow, the directional markings ornately drawn letters. A border of tiny wind roses circled the narrow space between the markings and the casing.

Weren't wind roses used in early maps drawn by sailors? I remembered the geologist saying Perez handled the small outboard skip expertly. He had tried to disappear into the shipping yards when confronted. His cave was by the river.

I got out at homicide and went straight for the phone on Alex's desk. 'Seafarer's Association, please.'

Ten minutes later, Alex emerged from Peterson's office, shoulders high up his neck, straight as a window ledge. His jaw was as tight as a trip tooth trap.

'He's switching me to another case while he works out what chapters of the book to throw at me. And you too,' he said.

I perched on the edge of his desk. 'What's Peterson doing now?'

'Filling out complaint forms against me.'

'How long will that take?'

'Judging by the number of them, a while.'

'Good. I've requested a translator for Perez. He should be here any minute.'

'Sarah, haven't you listened to anything I've said?'

'Peterson pulled me of this the night they found the body, but I'm still here.'

201

'Not for long.'

'That's exactly why we need to get to Perez now. We've come too far to give up so easily.'

I heard the elevator bell chime from behind the glass doors.

'Come on,' I grabbed Alex by the sleeve.

39

The translator was as short and round as a keg of beer. He wore a brown checked sports coat, dark grey slacks so tight around the waist that I could see his stomach spill over and under the button hole. He paused outside the elevator and patted a tubby hand on the comb tracks of his slicked back black hair.

I pushed open the glass doors and beckoned him in.

He moved out of the foyer with an old man's hobble and offered me a hand. 'Mario Verde.'

His fingers were pulpy as they griped mine. I introduced myself and Alex and then led him down the corridor to the holding rooms. I heard Peterson's voice call out across the offices for Alex.

We swapped glances. Another voice bellowed back. 'He's gone.'

A door slammed: Peterson retreating into his office.

We entered the holding rooms. Perez was lying on the bottom bunk, separated from us by a wire gate. He watched, unmoving. Alex dragged a vinyl table into the centre of the room. I arranged two chairs on opposite sides of it.

I unfolded two collapsible chairs and lined them up against the wall to the right of Perez. From here we would be able to see both Perez and Verde.

Alex unlocked the holding cell gate and beckoned Perez out.

Perez swung his legs over the edge of the bunk and stood up. His hands were still secured by cuffs but the brown shirt he'd worn had been replaced by a black pullover. Its V neck hung too far down his chest, and I could see the curve of his pectoral muscles. He, or someone, had folded the cuffs up to just above his wrists. The pullover's extra size seemed to remove some of his height, its waist band ending mid way down his thighs. His trousers were just as loose over his thin legs, but ended a centimetre or so above his ankles. He was sockless and shoeless.

Alex guided him to the card table and then placed a thick folder on the table. He stood behind Perez as Perez sat down.

Verde took the chair opposite then turned to me. 'I'll try to establish which language he speaks.'

'Try Spanish first,' I said.

Alex spoke, 'I thought you said the words sounded German?'

'I'm not sure now.'

Verde introduced himself in Spanish.

Perez placed his shackled hands on the top of the table and simply stared at Verde.

Verde said a few more words.

Perez looked down at the table top and began rubbing at a stain on the surface of the table.

Verde tried again in Italian.

Still Perez's finger worked at the stain.

French next, then German, then a language I couldn't recognise.

Perez sat back in his chair, eyes still on the table.

Verde met my eyes. 'Are you sure he can hear?'

'I don't know,' I said.

Alex clapped his hand above Perez's right ear. Perez flinched.

'Guess he's just obstinate,' Alex said.

I pulled out the compass I'd taken from Perez's bag and placed it on the table in front of him.

He stared at it in surprise, then picked it up with both

hands. He awkwardly shuffled it around in his fingers until its back was in his right palm. He rubbed at the glass with his left pointer.

'What if you write instead of speaking?' Alex suggested.

I jumped up and pulled foolscap-sized pad from the filing cabinet by the door. I fished my pen from my pocket and laid them both on the table. 'Tell him I can help him get home under a Flag of Convenience.'

Alex stared at me. 'What?'

I nodded to Verde. 'Write it.'

'In what language?' Verde asked.

'All of them.'

Alex circled the table and grabbed the notepad from the translator's hands. 'Whoa! What are you promising him?'

'I called the Seafarer's Association,' I said. 'He used to be a shipman on cargo ships. He's even worked on replicas of the old armadas.'

Alex lowered his voice. 'Outside,' he breathed at me. I followed him into the corridor.

'What's the story here?'

'I think he's waiting by the port so he can get work and then get home. We can use that as a bargaining chip to get information out of him.'

'Sarah, he's a suspect. We can't get him a ticket home until we know what his involvement is!'

'I know, but right now we need all the bargaining tools we can. I think he was working on a ship that flew a Flag of Convenience. That's a ship deliberately registered to a country that has lax labour and tax laws. It takes on any sailors of all nationalities. Working conditions are shocking but sailors work on them when they're desperate or need to get home.'

'If he was on the ship, why's he here?'

'Maybe the ship was going somewhere else and he just wanted to get home. So he jumped ship here and was waiting for a ship leading to Europe. Or maybe the shipping company dumped him here. Either way, he's an illegal immigrant. If he's even slightly deaf, that would add to his problems. Or maybe he doesn't speak English well enough to go through the application process.'

'Or maybe he just doesn't want to go back to sea.'

'Maybe he doesn't, but then why live on the river among sea transport companies and keep shipping lists.'

'Because it's all that he knows.'

'Look, maybe he's sick of sea life, but I'd bet he'd do anything for the chance to go home again, to get out of here.'

'You're fishing,' he said.

'Yes, but we've got nothing to lose and no time left.'

'Okay, but I want to try something first,' Alex said.

We stepped back into the room. Alex removed a photograph from the file on the desk and placed it on the desk in front of Perez. Perez glanced at the photograph and then looked back up at Alex quizzically.

I leaned forward and looked at the picture. It was the mortuary post that had been left at Emma's feet on the beach.

Alex stared at Perez, hoping for some hint of recognition: a tightening of the mouth, sweat on the brow, a nervous gesture.

Instead, Perez yawned.

'He doesn't know what it is,' I said.

Alex snatched the photo off the desk and put it back in the file. He sat down behind Verde as a signal that he had surrendered the floor to me.

I nodded to the translator. 'Tell him in Spanish that I can help him get his seaman's registration back.'

Verde scribbled on the notepad and read it aloud as he slid it across the table to Perez.

The minute the sentence was out of Verde's mouth I saw the reaction in Perez. His eyes lifted from the table and flashed from Verde's face to mine.

'Wait!' I leapt forward and grabbed the notepad before Perez could see it. 'He understood. Tell him again, ask him if that's what he wants.'

Verde spoke. Perez's eyes were fixed on his face.

When Verde finished, Perez looked down at the table again, but this time his jaw worked, teeth so outlined against his cheek I could almost count them. His brows clenched low over his eyes like warnings of a gathering storm.

Then, eyes still lowered to the table, he spoke.

His voice was low and his syllables were as guttural as a growl. He spoke for nearly two minutes in sounds unintelligible to me.

Verde stared at Perez, shock easily read on his face.

'What?' Alex urged when Perez was finished.

Verde couldn't seem to lift his gaze from Perez.

'Mr Verde?' I prompted. Verde's face held an unfocussed expression that I read as confusion.

'Mr Verde?' I said more loudly.

He shook his head in amazement.

Alex shifted form one foot to another impatiently. 'What? What?'

Verde's eyes shifted to my face. 'His language.'

'It's not Spanish or French?' I asked.

'French yes and Spanish yes. But...'

Alex jumped to his feet impatiently. 'Then what's the problem?'

'It's old French. And Basque. Mixed together with...well, mixed together with Iberian and some romance languages.'

I shrugged my shoulders as a question mark. 'Old French?'

Verde took a deep breath and laid his hands flat on the table, fingers spread. 'It's like old English.'

'Like Shakespearean?' Alex asked.'

'More like Chaucer,' Verde said.

'Uh huh...' Alex beckoned for more with a roll of his right hand.

'That language has been dead for over three hundred years. There are rumours that some small villages in the French alps, kind of like Amish communities, still speak it. He must be from there.'

'But he must be able to speak some modern language. How else would he have worked on ships?' I dragged my chair up to the table so that I was positioned between Perez and Verde. 'Do you understand it?'

'Some of it, but—'

'So what did he say?' Alex asked.

'It's not that simple,' Verde said as he shifted his gaze back to Perez.

Alex threw up his hands. 'For god's sake. I thought you were a qualified translator.'

Verde's back stiffened. 'It's taken me forty years to master five languages. This man just spoke seven in the space of three minutes, including a language that no one's suppsed to have spoken for three centuries.'

'Then pick one!' Alex demanded.

'I can't! He speaks all languages yet, yet...' he threw up his hands and shrugged his shoulders, 'yet he speaks none.'

I left Verde to pick, word by word, through Perez's speech and went back downstairs to report to Rory. He answered his mobile with a grunt.

'Is it too much to ask you to work?' he growled.

'Sorry, it's the Faber case.'

'Maybe my memory is running low, but didn't Peterson ban you from working that case?'

'Well, he mentioned something like that a few times, then changed his mind. But hey, no formal paperwork's been put through so guess that means I'm still on the job.'

'That makes it alright to just charge ahead?'

'It's not like that. I keep stumbling across things, Rory. Peterson should be kissing my ass.'

'You should be kissing his. The guy does you a favour by not marking your record with a formal complaint, but you still keep pissing on his leg.'

'Come on, it's Peterson we're talking about. He's not doing anyone a favour.'

'Sarah, you're a good printer, probably my most talented, but you've got a problem with authority. And that's one thing you can't have in this job. You're no good to Emma Faber if you're suspended. So I'm going to let you in on something. Peterson called me up to his office yesterday and told me that he'll keep you on the case on one condition.'

'That I report every breath I take to him. And I've been doing that.'

'Then do it more.'

'I already am. I've just come from Peterson's office.'

'Good. Now, you can take the rest of the jobs that come in today. We've carried you enough for the last two days.' He hung up and I wandered over to check the duty board and the fax machine's printouts.

Written under my name were the initials R.L—Rory had attended them.

I ripped the line of faxes from the machine and cut them into a sheet per job. In all there were 4 new jobs: an armed hold up at a Tullamarine freight factory, recovery of a knife suspected to be the murder weapon in the stabbing of a drug dealer in Collingwood, another break and enter at a house in outer Toorak and the discovery of a body in a car near the creek that ran along La Trobe University's southern boundary.

I grabbed the marker from the conference table and scribbled the La Trobe body beneath my name.

The state's main forensic lab was in Macleod, the suburb adjoining La Trobe University.

I took a deep breath and called Peterson's office. His answering machine took the call.

'This is Sarah Arden,' I said, 'I want to run some toxicology tests on something we found in the cave. Give me a call on my mobile when you get this message.'

Next I called Alex. 'Can you draw me up a testing request for the pills I got from Perez?'

'I thought we decided we'd get these done off the record.'

'Surely we've got cause now. And I just called Peterson to ask, but he's not in.'

'How convenient for you.'

'You don't need Peterson's signature.'

'I've just about been suspended, or have you already forgotten that?'

'Then you've got nothing to lose. But I think we should

come clean to Peterson. Sneaking around has left you with a suspension hanging over your head. I think Peterson will lift it if we're open with him.'

He was silent as he weighed up my words.

'Alex?'

'I thought you didn't trust him. His name is coming up in the wrong places.'

'I know, but we'll just make sure we go above his head. Maybe even to Borg.'

'Ok. My reassignment will kick in as soon as Borg processes the forms. I'll sign the testing order now and fax it to the lab.'

'Thank you. What did the translator say?'

'Apparently, you were right. Perez was waiting for a ship home. He refused to say anything about Emma though. Except that he knew her, that's all. I got Verde to ask about the violin. Perez indicated that Emma had lent it to him. I checked Perez's story out with Charlie, well, I mean Charlie's lawyer. He confirms that she lent it to somebody. He wasn't surprised it was Perez.'

'He thinks it normal that she lends a homeless man an antique violin?'

'He refuses to believe Perez would hurt Emma. He says that the fact that she lent him the violin means she trusted him.'

'Does Perez realise he's the main suspect?'

'Yes, but he's not saying anything more. Verde says he asked for a lawyer.'

'For his sake it had better not be Elizabeth Faber.'

40

The body at La Trobe University was still in the old brown Kingswood when I arrived. The car was parked nose to a thick oak tree in a densely wooded alcove known as a lover's spot for the local students.

The police had thrown open the vehicle's doors. As I neared, my nose told me why. A black hose had been taped over the exhaust pipe and snaked around the rear left tyre. Its other end coiled loosely on the thin grass by the back driver's side door.

Slumped over the wheel was a thick-set man in his early forties. He was wearing a dark blue pinstriped suit, jacket, trousers and a white shirt. His hair was deep brown but grey at the temples with a hint of pink scalp on the back of his head. A red and black striped tie sat on the passenger seat, knot still intact, simply loosened to create a loop large enough to slip over his head.

My eyes searched for his hands. The left hand I could see clearly, the right obscured on the other side of his body.

I was no expert in calculating the time of death, but his skin was simple to read. It's elasticity had gone, the space between fingertips and wrist elongated like stretched chewing gum. In hot seasons, this could occur within two days, but winter took its time. I was thankful they had left his face resting on the steering wheel. I knew his cheeks and the skin beneath his chin would be the same melted sinew.

I circled the car and checked the other hand. This one was resting on his knee, immune to the drag of gravity.

I explained what I would have to do in hushed tones to Detective Jamieson, the scene coordinator, and he laid plastic sheeting over the front passenger seat. The knot of the suicide's tie was sharp under my knee as I crawled into the car.

His arm was loose and light, lifting easily. The hand's skin stretched easily but held shape. I slipped the chopping board beneath his hand and on his thigh. The print rolled out easily.

Suicides were not a scene I attended often. Whenever I could, I swapped with the other fingerprinters. The air at murder sites was thick with anger and fear, but places of suicide were rank with pain and sometimes even hate. Murderers were angry at one thing at the moment of their crimes: their victims. But suicides often hated everything: the world, themselves, their family, their frailties. Their emotions spread through you like poison.

'It's strange he's got no I.D. on him,' I called over my shoulder to the coordinator. Suicides who create their scene usually take care to lay out something that tells who they are.

He leaned into the car casually. 'No note either. We think he barely had any gas in the tank. The car probably only ran for forty minutes.'

I wasn't surprised that he hadn't left a note. Few did. 'If he drove here without a driver's licence then it probably wasn't on impulse, yet if he'd planned it you'd think he'd top up the fuel tank, just in case. I guess suicide's not a logical thing.'

He flicked a fallen leaf from the arm of his jacket. 'Actually, suicides are usually incredibly organised and logical. I had a guy who deliberately overdosed on smack last week. He cleans his room, does his laundry, leaves a note ordering his mother to share his possession out between his siblings. Except his twin sister. He hates the sister's guts with a passion and instructed the only thing she was to get was the suicide note.'

'Did he say why he did it?'

'Oh yeah, the note calmly spelled out that his sister had

always made sure she got better grades than him, more attention from the family, that it was her idea that they try their first smack hit together. She got wise and gave up but he got a habit. So he killed himself to make sure someone would blame her for a change.'

'Suicide as revenge?'

'More common than you think.'

I crawled out of the car and packed up my things. 'I'll run his prints as soon as I get back to the office.'

The Forensic Centre was so close I could have walked there. The toxicologist on duty was Dr Sally Copal, a tall thin thirty something brunette with henna-streaked hair gathered loosely into a pony tail at the nape of her neck. She met me at the security desk, still dressed in a loose white labcoat. She offered a hand and I suddenly felt short and broad against her lithe grace.

'Let's have a look,' she said.

'Don't you want to go up to the lab first?'

'Zaparin has an unmistakable odour in pill form. I'll test it for you anyway, but I can give you an initial ID on the spot.'

I handed her the plastic sample container.

'Looks the right colour,' She flipped the lid and sniffed the mouth of the container.

Wincing, she nodded. 'That's it alright.' She screwed the lid on the container again. 'I'll run it through an infrared spectrometer just to fulfil procedure. Give me a call at about two-ish.'

She rolled a continuity label on the jar, signed it and then slipped the jar into her lab coat pocket. 'Looks like you've got your guy.'

I called Alex the moment I walked out of the Centre.

'Michael Faber is here,' Alex announced.

'Why?'

'He claims a journalist called him and told him that we'd arrested Perez.'

'A journalist?'

'Our department has no secrets.'

'More like journalists pay well and cops don't get paid enough.'

'That too. He wants to talk to Perez.'

'Tell him good luck.'

'I did. He didn't believe that Perez spoke no English. The translator's doing okay, by the way.'

'Good. So am I. I've just left the Forensic Centre at MacLeod. One of the scientists is doing a thorough test now, but she says it's certain the drug is Zaparin.'

'It's about time things got easy.'

I told him I'd be back at the office in forty minutes.

Alex was waiting at my desk. 'I need to talk to you privately.'

I looked around. The floor was empty except for Paul sitting at his desk, buried under visa forms.

'I think we're in the clear here,' I said.

He shook his head. 'Come into the kitchen.'

I followed him into our small lunch room and made a cup of coffee.

'Michael Faber wants to buy Perez a lawyer.'

'He wants to what?' I dropped my coffee mug into the sink.

'I don't get it either. Why pay money to defend the man charged with killing your daughter? Normally, the answer would be obvious—he hired Perez to do it, and paid for a lawyer as part of the deal.'

'Except that Perez can't seem to communicate.'

'We're trying to get details on Perez's finances now. If there are any large deposits then we'll find them. Checking Michael Faber's accounts will be more complicated.'

I kept quiet on that one. 'Why would Michael Faber want his daughter dead?' I asked.

'The tubes that were missing from Emma's fridge were river water from near the new construction site, right?'

'We think so.'

'Michael Faber is involved in property finance. We did a

routine check but didn't find the River View site mentioned. But you know what property finance is like. Everyone has a piece of the pie through subsidiary companies. He could be an investor. We'll just have to follow the trail harder,' Alex said.

'Or maybe it has nothing to do with business. And I have another scenario for you: Michael Faber thinks he can hire the lawyer and rig it so that Perez loses.'

'I hadn't thought of that.'

'And if he did hire Perez, it might not show up in bank account deposits. Perez's lack of language would make spending the dough a problem. Maybe Faber promised Perez something else.'

'Perez is homeless and Faber is in property. Maybe permanent accommodation was the reward.'

'Is Faber still upstairs?' I asked.

'Oh yeah. He's sworn he won't leave until he's spoken to Perez himself. And he's ordered his own translator.'

'His own translator? Legally he can't even go near Perez unless you release him. And why isn't Faber himself a suspect?'

'Whoa! One fish at a time. Let us deal with the one we've just reeled in. And I wouldn't advise taking Michael Faber on unless you had some hard evidence. This man has a lot of connections. And he has an abili.'

Alex's mobile phone rang. He pulled it from his pocket and moved into the corner of the room. He sat in an old armchair.

I poked my head around the door and scanned the department floor. Paul was still the only one there.

I heard Alex rise and cross the room to me.

'Faber wants to talk to you.'

I drew in a sharp breath. 'Me? That's a change.'

'You found Perez. He wants to thank you.'

'Has anyone told him Perez is just a suspect?'

Alex laughed. 'You can be the one if you want.' He grew serious. 'Be careful what you say to him.'

I hoped Michael Faber wouldn't be careful with what he had to tell me.

41

Faber was alone. He was sitting at a conference table in the homicide meeting room. His posture was tense—body upright, hands clasped together in a steepled point. He glanced nervously up as I entered the room.

'How are you keeping?' I asked.

He stood and cleared his throat. 'I just wanted to apologise for the other day.'

I held up my hands, palms out, in a gesture to halt. 'Don't, please. I understand this is an impossible time for you.' I pulled out one of the brown vinyl chairs and sat at the table opposite him. 'What's this I hear about you wanting to pay for Perez's defence?'

Faber shuffled uncomfortably in his seat and loosened his tie. 'Not his defence. I just want the guy to have a lawyer, that's all.'

'He will have a lawyer.'

'Not one of these Legal Aid appointees who'll only look at his case the night before. I mean a real lawyer.'

'This man may have killed your daughter. Surely you see how absurd this looks,' I said.

'I don't have to offer you reasons. But let me tell you, my wife is on the fundraising committee for Legal Aid. I've seen how inadequate the conditions are for state appointed lawyers.'

'You're telling me you want this man to get off?'

'All I'm telling you is that I believe in anyone's right to decent legal representation. My devastation over my daughter hasn't blinded me to my beliefs,' he said.

'How does your wife feel about this?'

He looked down at the table. 'Losing a child makes a person lose themselves. She's not coping well.'

'That I understand. You, I don't.'

He shrugged. 'I don't care what you think.'

'I'm not even sure what you're doing is legal.'

'You can talk to my wife about that. Apparently she'll be here soon.'

Suddenly my perspective shifted. It was like the wind had spun me around and I was suddenly facing a new direction, seeing things for the first time. 'You don't think Perez is the one who killed Emma. That's why you want to get him a lawyer.'

'I just want to be sure we get the right person, that's all.'

'Tell me what you know.'

He rubbed his hands over his face. 'I don't know anything.'

'Then tell me what you suspect.'

'I don't suspect anything. I'm just as confused as you are over why a man who lives in a cave and can't communicate would do these things to my daughter.'

A sharp knocked on the door was followed by a male voice calling my name.

Michael Faber stiffened. 'My wife is here.'

Elizabeth Faber stormed into the conference room. 'I think you'd better come home,' she said to her husband.

Michael Faber placed both hands flat on the table. 'At least think about it, Liz.'

Elizabeth Faber turned to me. 'My husband and I need a moment alone.'

I nodded and stepped out of the room, closing the door behind me. As I moved down the corridor, Elizabeth Faber's voice spilt out from under the door. 'There's a fund for this, Michael, I will not let you commit our money to help this man.'

I found Alex on the computer. 'I think you need to look harder at Michael Faber's records.'

'No one will disagree with you after this,' he nodded at the screen.

'What?' I positioned myself behind him and stared over his shoulder at the screen. It was a credit rating report on Guillaume Perez.'

'How did you get this?'

'It cost me twenty dollars. I just used the standard application form and quoted my badge number. Not that I needed my badge number. For five dollars you can check your own credit rating, for twenty dollars you can check anyone else's.'

The listing had only one entry: application and granting of a community housing voucher in Melbourne in 1989.

'What's your point?' I asked him. 'There's nothing outstanding here.'

'No, but there is on the bottom of the page.' He tapped the screen. 'See under section marked 'Previous Enquiries.''

'Leo Mantel and Sons. Sounds like a real estate agent or lawyers.' I noticed the date of the enquiry. 'This was made today!'

He handed me a yellow manila folder. 'This is the asset check we did on Michael Faber. Check out who his solicitors are.'

'Leo Mansell and Sons?' I said without opening the file.

'Bingo.'

'So Faber's solicitors checked Perez's credit rating. For the same reason we have, I assume.'

'Quickest way to check a financial status. One small time loan, no purchases on credit, no change in financial details.'

'No pattern to indicate receipt of large sums of money.' I paused to catch a thought. 'Have you investigated Faber's bank withdrawals? His checking account?'

'We'd never get permission for that unless he's a suspect. Even then it's tricky,' Alex said.

'Don't ask me how I know this, okay, but he's made large, regular payments from his cheque account. But as cash withdrawals.'

'How large?'

'Five thousand dollars,' I said.

'That's not large enough to pay for a hit.'

'That's what I think too. And if it was a hit paid for by Michael Faber and Perez was the gunman, Faber wouldn't be checking him out,' I said. 'But what if Faber was being blackmailed? Isn't that the way his accounts would look. And wouldn't you start checking out the spending habits of people around you if you didn't know who was blackmailing you?'

Alex scratched his chin, deep in thought. 'Or maybe he just checked Perez's finances out of thoroughness, like we did. He could be wondering if Perez is the killer, just the same as we are. I think Faber's clean.'

'So he's paying for Perez's defence just because Perez's finances indicated he wasn't paid to wipe out Emma? Still makes no sense. Perez could have whacked her of his own initiative. And just because Faber's lawyers checked out Perez doesn't mean they've passed it on to him. Faber's been sitting around here since 11 am, right?'

'Yeah.'

I closed the folder. 'Faber acting like this makes me look at Perez differently. Perez is too easy to blame, too easy to set up. If he was going to kill someone, he wouldn't go to all the trouble to arranging the body like that. And what would he know about Aboriginal artefacts? I reckon that Faber smelled something's not right as well.'

'That would explain why he's been checking on Perez's finances and why he wants to get him a defence. I'm going to check out your blackmail theory though. Those withdrawals do look odd.'

'I wonder if his wife can shed any light on this?' I passed Alex back the folder and returned to the conference room. I paused by the door and heard Elizabeth Faber's voice, low and soft.

I knocked on the door and entered.

Elizabeth rose and straightened her skirt. 'I'm sorry for wasting your time. My husband wants to withdraw his offer.'

I shifted my gaze to her husband. He sat staring silently at the table like a chastised child.

'Mr Faber?' I asked.

'My husband is also my client. As his lawyer I've advised him to stop any action which unintentionally interferes with your case and Mr Perez's defence.'

'You're officially acting as Michael's lawyer?'

'That's correct.'

I sat down next to Michael. 'You've had someone examine Perez's financial details. Why?' I asked him. 'Do you think that someone paid Perez to kill Emma?'

He stared at me, confusion compressing his features.

'Or is it that you think he's blackmailing someone? It's a crime not to report blackmail, Mr Faber.'

Elizabeth Faber slammed a hand down on the table. Both her husband and I jumped in surprise. 'This is insane.' She pointed at Michael. 'Get up. Let's go.'

'Can I speak to you alone, Mrs Faber?' I asked.

'That won't be necessary.'

'Please. Just for a second or two.'

She turned to her husband. He rose and trudged past us and into the hall. I closed the door behind him.

'I was under the impression that Leo Mantel looked after your husband's legal affairs,' I said.

'Financial details. I handle all other matters.'

'Forgive my forwardness, but I couldn't help overhearing you tell Michael that he couldn't use 'our' money on Perez. You're a co-signatory on all accounts?'

'That is a forward question. I'll be equally forward: what's it to you?'

'Leo Mantel and Sons made a request for Perez's credit record today.'

Her face registered neither surprise nor recognition. 'Oh?'

'Do you find that as curious as I do?'

She turned and walked to the window. 'Since Michael had this idea in his head of paying for Perez's defence, I suppose he wanted to check that Perez was really as broke as he seemed. What does this matter?'

'I just need to know why your husband wants to pay for Perez's defence.'

'My husband is that sort of man.'

'Or is it that he's looking for evidence that someone paid Perez to kill your daughter? Maybe looking for evidence that Perez has been receiving large payments for something? As a lawyer yourself, isn't that where'd you'd look if you had that suspicion?'

'If my husband suspects this, he's said nothing to me.'

'If I were you, I'd ask him.'

She stepped past me. 'Oh, I will.'

42

Alex was on the phone when I re-entered Homicide's offices, so I returned to my own floor. There was a message on my voice mail from Dr Sally Copal. I called her back. As I waited for her to answer I flicked through a copy of the Police Journal that someone had left two desks down from mine. On one of the pages was an ad with three small photos—a dirty creek, a dam and a serene blue ocean. I tore the picture of the ocean from the text.

Dr Copal picked up the line.

'I've got a result on the tablets you gave me,' she announced when I identified myself. 'You were right, they are Zaparin.'

'Can you fax or email me a copy of that.'

'You'll have it by this afternoon.'

I went back upstairs to homicide and slipped into the holding room. Guillaume Perez was sitting with his back towards me, staring at the wall. I walked straight up to the fence and rattled it.

'Guillaume. Hey! Look at me.'

He did not turn.

I unlocked the cell and stepped inside.

He turned his head slightly towards me, keeping his eyes on me but offering no other movement. Even after the shower and clean clothes, he still stank of stale sweat and moist earth.

I paced straight past him and stuck the picture of the open sea on the wall that he had been staring at. I stepped back out of the cell and locked it.

'Who did you see by the river?'

He turned his head back to the wall.

I waited.

He leaned forward and touched the photograph.

'You will never smell the sea again unless you help us. Don't you understand? They'll put you in jail forever.'

His hand dropped back into his lap.

'I don't think that you killed Emma. Neither does Emma's father. I think someone is trying to make it look like you did. Do you know who?'

Silence.

'At first, Emma's father thought that someone paid you to kill her. If someone did, things will be easier for you if you tell us. You'll be home sooner.'

More silence.

I slammed my hand against the fence. He jumped and turned his head back to me. 'Why walk all that way to my house and leave me the fish if you're not going to tell me? I think the river water is part of why she was killed but I need to know more.'

He rose then walked to the fence. He stopped a few centimetres from the wire so that we were not face on face.

'No,' he said, touching his lips and then closing his fingers into a fist.

'Why? Are you afraid?'

'No.' He touched his eyes and then made a fist again.

'You don't know who killed Emma? Is that what you're saying?'

'Don't know,' he repeated as if he were trying out the words for the first time. 'Don't know,' he said again, nodding his head.

'So why leave me the fish?'

His expression went blank.

'The fish.' I wiggled my hand to imitate a fish swimming through water.

He shook his head.

'Look.' I pulled out my little notebook and pen and drew a house, then a fish at the bottom. 'You,' I pointed at him, 'left me a fish.' I held up the drawing.

'Poisson.'

I struggled to remember my high school French lessons. 'Pourquoi?'

'Water bad.'

'The water is bad?'

He nodded.

'Emma knew the water was bad. That's why she was killed?'

He shrugged.

I sketched the outline of a family: tall father, shorter mother in a dress, young boy and small girl. I held it up. 'Emma,' I said, pointing at the young girl. I held the notepad in my teeth and mimicked playing the violin. 'Emma.'

He nodded in understanding.

I held up the drawing again and pointed at the taller child. 'Brother. Frere. Grant Faber.'

'Bad.'

'Grant is bad.'

He nodded and pointed at the image of the father. 'Bad.'

'They're both bad?'

'Bad.' He pointed back at Emma. 'Emma good.'

Was he telling me Grant and Michael had killed Emma?

I pointed at Grant and Michael. 'Did they kill Emma?' I tried to think of the French word. 'Mort Emma?' I mimicked firing a gun with my thumb and first finger.

He held his hands up in alarm, shaking his head.

'You don't know.'

He nodded rapidly. 'Don't know.'

I rushed back upstairs to Alex. He was at his desk filling in a report form. 'Hey,' he called when he saw me crossing the floor, 'we've got news on the bullet that killed Emma. It was fired from Perez's gun.'

'That'll make Peterson happy.'

'There's more. The gun's serial number is scratched out, but the lab managed to make it visible. It was confiscated in an arrest a few years ago. In Green Heights.'

'Grant Faber and Peterson's old beat!'

'Exactly.' He laid down his pen and checked his watch. 'Hey, I've got to go down to Flemington for target practice.' He collected his files, then drained his coffee from the blue mug on his desk. He placed it next to the phone. 'Peterson won't like the Grant Faber implication. He's keen on Perez as the perp.'

'I can see why. Perez has no job, he's squatting on government land, is witnessed as making threats against Emma, had the gun and her violin in his possession,' I said.

I watched him pack his briefcase and activate his voice mail.

'But I'm still not convinced he's the one,' I continued. 'There's no motive that seems to fit. And Perez hasn't lifted a finger against anyone since he's been here. I've seen grandmothers more aggressive than him.'

Alex walked past me, heading for the lockers in the foyer. I followed him out of the room.

'I seem to remember you bouncing off a few cave walls,' he said. 'And he shoved me out of the way so hard you could lift his fingerprints off my chest.'

'Come on,' I leaned against the locker next to his as he inserted the long silver key. The room had the smell of old metal and cheap alloy, then beneath that the stink of forgotten sweatshirts and muddy runners. 'We scared the shit out of him. Anyone else would have put a .35 though our chests.'

'You're running on a feeling here. That I don't like.' He opened the locker. The air that slipped out smelled like mechanic's hands, svelte and dense with oil residue. He removed his gun from a shelf and put his briefcase in. The room rattled as he slammed his locker door and twisted the key. He ran a hand through his hair, pulling it up and back from his forehead, then letting it float back into position.

'Come over tonight, sevenish. I'll cook something.'

'My mother's here.'

'Send her to the movies for the night.'

'She's staying at a hotel.'

'A hotel? Why?'

'I need some space. You know what mothers are like.' Now was not the time to tell him that Perez and possibly someone else had been prowling around my yard.

'So you'll come?'

I nodded, feeling the horizontal vents of the locker I was leaning against sharp under my shoulder blades.

'Call me if anything comes up.' He slipped the gun into the holster under his arm, then hurried out of the locker room.

I stood still for a moment as the breeze from his exit settled. The deep notes of his cologne reminded me of burning wood on cold afternoons: smoky and sweet. I stepped sideways so that it was his locker that pressed into my back. Through my blouse I could feel the metal vents were still warm from where he'd laid his hand on them.

I walked back into the homicide carrels and stood over his desk. After wrapping his mug in an A4 sheet of notepaper, I took it down to fingerprints.

The lab was empty.

The white powder clung to his prints like a lover. His curves circled the rim like an embrace, the papillary ridges so wide I'd call them inflamed. They were as visible as the thick inked lines of a linocut.

My heart fluttered.

These were the marks of intense emotion.

43

I'd been fuming visa slips with ninhydrin for two hours when a headache came on. I grabbed an orange juice from the cafe across the road and stood with the smokers on the steps outside.

'Hi,' said a male voice behind me.

I turned to find David McKenzie from Fraud dragging on a cigarette. I had sprayed a ransom note on one of David's cases only a month or two ago. A television celebrity's dog had been abducted with a fee of ten thousand set as a guarantee of return. The fingerprints on the note had matched her boyfriend's, just as David had said they would. The boyfriend had been a mixture of swirls and loops, with an arch on the right thumb. He had been a football player whose fingertips were as toughened as the red ball that had made him famous. It took two printings to get defined lines without the black patches that is the characteristic of hardened skin.

'How's the Faber case going?' he asked as he pressed his cigarette into the ground with the toe of his shoe. I noticed the shoes were steel capped Doc Martins. They were typical David. He was one of the younger breed of cops who eschewed the navy suit and burgundy tie formality of the old days in favour of red shirts and this season's trousers. He ran a hand through his razor cut spikes as he waited for me to reply.

'Slowly. What are you working on?'

'Blackmail of a bigwig lawyer. Been going on for a year but he's only reported it now that the demands have threatened violence.'

'Yeah? We suspect there's blackmail involved in a case I'm working, but we're not sure. How can you tell if someone is being blackmailed if the victim is keeping it a secret?

He looked at me in surprise. 'What's this got to do with fingerprints?'

I thought quickly. 'We need to know what the big picture is before I work out who and how to fingerprint.'

This seemed to satisfy him. 'Bank records, and behaviour. Your mark will be suspicious, his friends will complain he's gotten paranoid, moody and unsociable. Is he married?'

'Yes.'

He pulled out another cigarette and lit it. 'The wife will suspect something.'

'The wife's a lawyer.'

'Perfect. Do they share assets?'

'She's mentions 'their' money a lot.'

'Forget him. Aim at her. Ask her if she's noticed him syphoning off money from their accounts, cutting down on expenses. Tell her to check any cash hoards they have hidden away.'

'I should tell her my suspicions?'

'Definitely. It'll put him under even more pressure. Hopefully he'll crack and come clean.'

'Hmmm. It sounds like it might work.'

We chatted for a few minutes about the sentencing of the dog blackmail case and then I went back inside.

I took a deep breath and called up Elizabeth Faber at her city office.

The receptionist kept me on hold for a few minutes then transferred my call to Elizabeth's office.

'Ms Arden,' Elizabeth's voice was clipped and business like. 'I'm busy at the moment. You can call me at home tonight to discuss any matter regarding my family or my husband's representation.'

'I think it's better if I talk to you when your husband is not around. I need to ask you something as his wife, not his lawyer. Can you meet me today?'

'I'm afraid not.'

'We're going to apply for a court order to look through your husband's bank records.'

'You're wasting your time. No judge will grant you that just because Michael wanted to pay for Perez's defence. If you think he paid to kill her, charge him.'

'I don't think he paid to kill her. I think he's being blackmailed.'

There was silence. I waited it out. After a few moments she cleared her throat. 'And what would fingerprinting Michael's bank records prove? Only Michael touches them so unless you think he's blackmailing himself, you've got nothing.'

'I'm not interested in fingerprinting them. Please just meet me this afternoon.'

'This is absurd. I'm putting in a complaint of harassment. Why is a fingerprinter coming to me with this?'

'This could help your husband.'

'Do the detectives know about this?'

'Only one, but it hasn't been made an official part of the investigation yet because we have no proof. If this has nothing to do with Emma's death, then it's of no interest to us. I think it only fair that we find out before we make things more complicated for your husband.'

'What could blackmail have to do with Emma's death?'

'Maybe nothing, maybe everything.'

She paused. I could hear her fingernails tapping on the edge of her desk. 'Okay, come up to my office in about an hour.'

I took down her address, thanked her, and hung up.

Elizabeth Faber's office was on the twelfth floor of a gothic style building near the corner of Collins and Queens Street. A century of grime had turned the mason colonnades dull and blackened the edges of the small windows that ran across every storey of the facade. I guessed that this, like many of the other Melbourne buildings of this style, had once been a bank.

The entrance was a narrow corridor that led into a broad parlour. I could smell the mushroomy odour of old moisture behind the walls. I stopped in front of a high marble desk. Plush burgundy carpet and red and brown vertically striped wallpaper made it clear that the businesses here were as conservative as the building itself.

Elizabeth Faber kept me waiting in the foyer, flipping though Business Review Weekly, for twenty minutes. Finally, she appeared in a grey wool skirt with matching jacket, her hair scooped up into a tight chignon.

'Sorry to keep you,' she offered a hand and gave mine a quick, business-like squeeze. 'Come up.' She escorted me to the elevator and up to the twelfth floor in silence. The room she'd chosen was barely large enough for its six seater boardroom table and four chairs. I could smell the woody musk of old books from the office next door.

She glanced pointedly at her watch. 'You've got twenty minutes.'

'Your husband has a personal cheque account?'

'Yes.'

'We think he's paying the blackmailer out of that. By cash withdrawal.'

'I've yet to understand how you've concluded he's being blackmailed.'

'Let's just say an inside source has given us some information.'

'What information?'

'About his money flow.'

'You mean his investment banker? That's impossible. He's bound by the banker's code of ethics and privacy laws. He can't reveal that type of detail.'

'I didn't say it was his banker.'

'Oh, come on, who else could it be?'

'You'd be surprised. but how we found out doesn't matter. I assume you're a signatory to that account.'

'I can use it, yes.'

'Then I suggest you get a hold on the statements and ask your husband some hard questions.'

'My husband's financial details are his, not mine.'

'Put it this way. If my husband were secretly paying out large sums of money, I'd want to know why and to whom.'

'It may not be what you think.'

'And,' I continued, 'while his bank account may be under his name, I'd say his assets weren't his alone.'

'What's your point?'

'What happens when he empties that account? How do you know he won't start raiding other accounts? Joint accounts? Selling assets you never keep an eye on.'

'That's impossible.'

'Blackmail never stops. As a criminal lawyer, you should know that.'

'What do you want from me?'

'I want you to put pressure on your husband to come clean with this. We can't help him unless he comes to us.'

She rose. 'I think you're stabbing in the dark.'

'Ask him or look at the statements yourself.'

'This is absurd.'

She pushed her chair under the table and opened the door. 'You can find your own way out.' She stepped into the corridor and firmly shut the door, leaving me alone in the room. Her perfume, a spicy oriental, hung in the air over the table.

I completed the rest of the jobs on Rory's list and met my mother at her hotel at 4pm. Her bags were packed and sitting inside the entrance of her room.

'What's with these?' I nodded at the bags.

'I heard on the radio that the police arrested someone for that girl's murder. I can come back to your place now.'

'Not yet. I'm not sure it's safe.'

'But I came down to Melbourne to stay with you.'

'No you didn't. You came down to get away from the town, remember? Sorry Mum, but my place is off limits.'

'Then can't you stay here with me?'

'Mum, you need to go back home and face this.'

She grabbed the closest bag and threw it on the bed. 'Fine. I'll stay here.' She opened the latch and began removing her clothes. 'You just go off making the world safe for people who are already dead while I rot away here.'

I clenched my teeth to keep the angry words in.

She stormed into the bathroom and slammed the door behind her.

I sat on the bed and picked up one of the dresses she'd packed. It was the pink floral one she used to wear when she caught the train into the regional shopping centre. It still smelled like the Riverina: the Christmas smell of nettles from pinetrees, the lavender washing powder she bought at the Sunday market, her own perfume of roses. The scents drew me back and I remembered her waiting under the pines by the school gate for me so that the other kids couldn't pick on me as I walked home.

'Okay,' I called out. 'You can stay with me. But I have to go out tonight so I'm asking a friend to keep you company for a while until I come back.'

The bathroom door swung open and she appeared in the doorway. 'I don't need a baby sitter.'

'I'm not getting you one. I'm introducing you to someone you'll like. Someone that I think can help you find Dad.'

Surprise and then hope lit up her face. 'You're helping me look?'

'No, he is.' I carried her bags out to the car and rang my sixteen-year old neighbour Jaiden.

44

On the way home my mother wanted to stop at a pharmacy for sleeping tablets. As I waited in the car outside the shop, I wondered if anyone had asked Emma's doctor if she took Zaparin.

I phoned Peterson and asked.

'Her doctor claimed he had never prescribed it,' he said.

'What about Elizabeth or Michael Faber?'

His tone was businesslike. If he was harbouring a grudge against me, he'd buried it under professionalism. 'We checked that as a matter of routine. There's no record of a prescription in their name.'

I decided to test Peterson's trust a little more. 'Have you heard that the gun we recovered from Perez's cave had been logged in at Green Heights?'

'Yes, I'm working on that now.'

'You'll tell me if you find out any more?'

'Of course. And thank you for the call, Sarah.'

I echoed his formal tone. 'Thank you.'

As I hung up, I hoped once again that we were on the same side.

Elizabeth Faber called me at home at 5.30 pm that night. Mum was safely installed at Jaiden's house, watching him check through open databases for all the names my father used.

'You're right,' Elizabeth announced. 'I think he is being blackmailed.'

'You asked him?'

'No, he's not here. I've just fished out his bank records.'

'You need to confront him.'

Her voice was hesitant. 'I don't know.'

'Don't make us get a court order to go through his records.'

'You'll never get one.'

'Then it's up to you.'

She whispered something.

'What was that?' I asked.

'I said I'm afraid.'

'Knowing what he's got to hide is easier than guessing.'

'No, you don't get it. I'm afraid of him.'

Somehow I couldn't picture Elizabeth Faber afraid of anyone. I drew a cautious breath.

'In what way?' I asked.

'He can get...,' she took a shaky breath, 'He can get worked up. He's not the easiest person to deal with when he's angry.' Her words hung in the air, an unsealed road whose surface was shifting under my feet.

'Do you feel threatened?' I asked.

'I don't want to talk about me.'

'Yes you do or you wouldn't have called me. Has he hurt you?'

'He could.'

'But has he? In the past?' As I waited for her to answer I remembered the first time I'd seen them together. He was physically gentle, but quick to admonish her. She had shrunk from his touch.

'Yes,' she whispered.

'Did you report it to the police?' I knew there was no record of violence committed by Michael Faber.

'No, no. He's too influential, too important. It would ruin him. It blew over and he was sorry.'

'It only happened once?'

'Yes. Well, no, only once that badly. The other times he

didn't hurt me like that. He just threw things at me.'

'The neighbours never called the police?'

'No. I always assumed they never heard.'

'You can't remain your husband's lawyer.'

'I know.'

'Do you think he killed Emma?'

'I, I...' her voice collapsed. 'I don't know,' she sobbed. 'He threatened to once. That's why Grant left. Michael threatened to hurt him too.'

45

Alex lived in a narrow, one-way, side-street in Richmond. Terraced cottages built at the turn of the century for factory workers squatted above cobblestoned gutters. Behind the houses were one person-wide alleys that wove through the four main streets that surrounded his block like a grid. I left my car on Victoria Street and walked up the alley to his back gate.

The lane smelled of vinegar fish and clove cigarettes. It rang with the sing-song tones of Asian languages. Like all inner-city lanes, occasional syringes lay in-between the curves of the cobblestones like weeds. Alex's house had been broken into five times in the past four years that he'd lived here. Last year, he'd installed an alarm system and brought a German shepherd he named Wolfgang. Razor wire stretched taunt above the line of his brown palling fence. I pulled out my phone and let him know I was here.

Wolfgang's deep snarls became excited whimpers as Alex opened the gate. Alex was fresh from the shower, curls loose against his head, a strand flopping over his eye like a pup's errant ear. A thick black wool jumper hung low across his neck and his green cargo pants looked freshly washed. His black hiking boots, however, had peeling toes. I stepped past him and held out a palm of introduction to Wolfgang. His nose was damp heat against the coldness of my skin. His long snout opened and he dropped a soggy tennis ball at my feet.

'Quite the killer, hey?' I said.

Alex kicked the ball into the centre of the yard. Wolfgang bounded after it.

'I had a word with him before you arrived,' Alex said.

'Ahhh,' I followed him along the terracotta-coloured pathway and up into the house. Like every other terrace in Richmond, the backroom was a lean-to laundry that led into a kitchen. My cheeks burned with the warmth of the room. Something on the stove smelled of oregano, basil, olives and tomato.

He grabbed a bottle of Shiraz from the larder, uncorked it, and then filled two glasses. 'I've been called in to do nightshift tonight. I tried to get out of it but no one else was stupid enough to answer their phone.'

Relief washed over me. 'That works well. My mother is staying with me and I have to get back early. Hey, I got something new on Michael Faber today.'

He handed me a glass and took a sip of his own. 'Uh huh?'

'Elizabeth Faber claimed he gets violent.'

The glass froze on its way down from his lips. 'That puts a new spin on things.'

'And she thinks there's definitely something not right about the cash withdrawals he made.'

'If he's got a violent temper, he could have killed Emma himself and planted the gun in Perez's cave.'

'The blackmail started six months before Emma was killed. So it's not like someone saw him do her and is holding it over him.'

'Any witnesses to his short fuse?'

'The son. Elizabeth didn't report it to the police.'

'Too prominent a guy?'

'Exactly.'

'I've heard that excuse enough times before.' He placed the glass on a wooden dining table and stirred the olive and tomato sauce with a wooden spoon.

'What's happening with Perez?' I asked.

'Peterson's having him charged tomorrow morning.'

'His fingerprints aren't even on the gun.'

'Yeah, but he had the gun and he was making threats towards her. We've got more on him than anyone else.'

'But the gun was logged at Green Heights,' I said.

'Well, that definitely implicates Grant Faber.'

'Peterson said he'd speak to the head of the Green Heights Station and find out what happened to the gun.' I took a drink from my glass. 'But I'm still nervous about Peterson. He told me he wanted me to keep away from Grant Faber because he was investigating him for something else.'

Alex looked surprised. 'Something else? Like what?'

'I don't know.'

Alex shrugged. 'The evidence points to Perez.'

'I'm still not convinced.'

'He has no proof of where he was that night, Sarah.'

'What about the geologists? Has anyone checked if they saw Perez at the time of the murder?'

'You said you asked them.'

'But no one's asked them since? Maybe they remember better now. They weren't really clear on what night it was that they saw him leave.'

He let the spoon rest against the side of the metal pot and stepped over to me. He grabbed my hand and sat down at the table.

'Just stop for a minute,' he said.

He pulled on my hand to get me to sit. His fingers curled around the base of my thumb and met at the back of my hand. His middle and ring fingers lightly traced the vein that descended from my ring finger. 'You need to step back for a while.'

'But I'm clearing a path through this. You know I am.'

'I know, I know. I'm just nervous for you. I didn't bring you in on this so you could lose your job.'

I watched the sauce spit from the pot onto the stovetop. 'Remember that glove I found in Emma's bin? I still haven't identified the print on it.'

'I'm not sure it's worth pursuing.'

'It would be if it was Michael Faber's print.'

'We don't have his prints.'

'No.'

His hand slipped off mine. 'Here we go again,' he jumped up and walked to the stove. 'No more under the radar fingerprinting. It's getting too hard to explain away.'

'He may just give it to us.'

'Does he know about the glove?'

'No—and there's no prints on the gun.'

'Can you grab two plates from the cupboard behind you,' he asked me over his shoulder.

I selected two white pasta plates and let my eyes wander through the contents of his cupboard. He had two sets of dishes, one white with a watercolour blue rim, the other russet terracotta with a pattern of strokes impressed on the edge of the ceramic. I wondered if these had been bought by his wife. An assortment of plastic microwave containers huddled untidily on the bottom shelf, the lids scattered among them.

He warmed the plates on the microwave and then filled them with steaming ravioli squares. As he poured sauce over them, I refilled our glasses with red wine.

He sipped his wine and then replaced the glass in front of his plate. It stood between us, the red liquid magnifying his thumbprint on the glass. The loop of his thumb was a darker red than the wine, the curve doubled in size.

I moved the glass to the side of the table and took his hand. Turning it palm over, I let my nail dip and climb over the hills and valleys of his thumb's friction ridges. His skin was hot, tiny coins of sweat and olive oil smeared across the knoll of my nail. I ran my fingertip around the shape of his pointer.

He winced. 'I hurt that finger today.'

I turned it over.

'No, on the side, where you touched it.'

I shifted his hand sideways so I could examine the part where the finger curls inwards into the groove between the first joint and the curve of the tip.

The skin had been worn raw, rubbed away to the tender patchiness that precedes a graze.

'Firing practice again?'

'Yes. Friction from the trigger of my gun. That's what you get after three days of practice.'

'How did you go?'

'Passed for another two years, thank god. This sort of stuff is the last thing I want to worry about right now.'

We ate and chatted—rumours of promotion for Peterson, funding increases to the forensic centre, people we both knew who had left the force. When we'd finished, we cleared the table and carried our wine glasses into the lounge. The interior had changed little since I'd last seen it. Splintering coffee table with an old map of the world under glass, the dusty smell of an old wool rug, the scent of oregano as he pushed my hair back from my chin.

I took his hand and bit gently into the side of his right pointer. The thin skin split beneath my teeth. He jerked his hand back in surprise at the pain. I grabbed his hand again and placed it on my waist, then leaned forward. My hand beneath the fur of his jumper smoothed the creases of his chest, the other palm found the outward turn of his hip.

I kissed him.

His right hand moved down the line of my spine and the left felt the tilt of my jaw.

He kissed me back, his tongue olive bitter.

The imprint of his fingertips burned against my cheek, those swelling loops of desire that I wanted to measure and compare—and keep.

I tasted the rosemary scent of his hair, groaned at the sharp cut of his neck bristles on my tongue. His hands were suddenly at my nape then lost themselves in the slick stands of my hair.

'I'm thinking of sticking around this time,' I breathed.

'Good.'

I slipped him out of his jumper and lost my lips in the curve of his neck. He lifted my head to his and kissed me as he

240

removed my shirt. I took his right fingers and pressed them against the back of my hands, then spread them over my arms, shoulders and breasts, pushing his fingers into my muscles until the surrounding skin turned white. I wanted to wear his fingerprints like a brand. The loops of his thumbs gave my oriole petals. My skin greedily swallowed the points of his arches. On my thigh he was two lines with no peaks.

I wanted to strip the balance from his fingertips, to let new lines loose amongst those loops. Tonight I wanted him to lose himself to the influence of the curve.

I moved his hand over my thighs and then inside me. Despite the heat, my soft folds would keep his detail longer. Not that it mattered. When they faded I would let his fingers carve their patterns all over again.

Never, I decided, could I live another six months without this man.

46

When I woke he was gone. The clock beside the bed read 10.50 pm.

I wandered into the bathroom and slipped into his robe. The lapels that lay against the neck were still damp. The sliding shower door was open so I reached in and pulled out all the bottles sitting in the shower rack. Rosemary shampoo, a tab of white soap that smelled like vanilla, an unopened bottle of Lynx shower gel.

Curious for details about his life without me, I went through each cupboard and drawer in the bathroom, then rifled through the papers on the desk in his study. Much of the desk clutter was notebooks from work—piles of reports to be filled in, and an application for leave was dated late March of that year. A department stamp dated March 30 circled the word rejected. He'd applied for leave just after I'd left. I wondered if he was coming after me or taking time off to recover from us?

Suddenly I felt sneaky for poking around. I took a shower, dressed and wandered into the kitchen.

Our wine glasses from earlier in the night stood in the sink, my lipstick still on the rim, his thumbprint still spread broad and bulky across the rounded belly above the stem.

I washed my own glass and scrubbed our dishes. With a tissue, I picked up his glass, wrapped it in a clean tea towel and slipped it into my handbag.

Mum was still at Jaiden's when I got home. I chatted with his parents until he and Mum emerged from his study with a few sheets of printout.

'Find what you were looking for?' Jaiden's mother said.

'Sort of,' Jaiden answered. 'Sarah, your father sure liked changing names.'

I laughed. 'It was that or get arrested.' I slipped my arm through Mum's. 'Come on, we'd better let these people go to bed.'

Mum excitedly gave me a run down of what they'd found as we got ready for bed. As I'd expected, my father had no Internet presence. His generation were not comfortable using the Internet, and so he had no email or login details stored on the data-collection systems. What Jaiden had found were credit card applications under at least ten different names and a listing on the NSW fraud squad's site for wanted offenders. I'd instructed him not to check for bank accounts or conduct any search that verged on breach of privacy. My father's last known address was a transient's hotel in inner Sydney. That was dated over a year ago.

'I thought you decided he was dead,' I said as I drew the curtains in her room.

'You won't confirm it for me, so I can't be sure.'

'It's not up to me to confirm. The police in the area where the body was found will find out. And I ran the fingerprints on the guy that was in my yard. It's not him.'

'How do you know if you haven't got your father's prints?'

'I know.'

'You're not the only one who can test fingerprints, you know. That friend of yours that I spoke to in your office. She could test them for me.'

'She'd have to charge you for it. You couldn't afford it.' She placed a fresh bowl of water on the floor beside her bed and dragged Bess's bed next to it. 'Have you laid out Bess's birthing spot?'

'She has to do that. She'll burrow away in a place where she feels alone and safe. Listen, I'll get the prints from the police where the body was found. Our search engine is more comprehensive than theirs. I still may be able to I.D. his body. But it could take a while.'

'Not if you test the letter and take it up there.'

'Mum! I've got a job here. I can't just jump on a train and trek across the country. I've made my offer to you. Take it or leave it. I'm going to bed.'

The following morning I sent her off on a discount shopping bus tour and went into work. As soon as I arrived at the office, I checked the duty board. Under my name, someone had written 'Treasury Gardens Suicide.' The login time on the file was 7.45. It was already 8.15. I read the notes in the file. The body of a 26-year-old male had been found hanging from a tree in a wooded area behind a small rookery waterfall. A driver's license had been found on him, but I still had to take his prints to establish it was actually him. I called CIB Operations and arranged to print the body at the Morgue that afternoon.

Amir stepped from the lab. The acrid sting of stale ninhydrin pushed past him and wrapped around me like a cloak. His white labcoat had a caricature of him drawn on the breast with a black marker. The artist had sketched enormous safety goggles the shape of milk crates over his eyes. His thick legs had been exaggerated into bulges the shape of broadbeans.

'That's it for this morning,' he nodded up at the whiteboard. I scanned everyone else's jobs. Paul was off sick, Catherine had been on overnight call and had gone home for the morning. She was due to return at 1pm for the afternoon shift. Mark was out at a robbery in Werribee. Amir was on housekeeping.

'How long have you been here?' I asked.

'Since 7.30 am, waiting for you to come in so I could run across the road for a real coffee. I'll be back in fifteen.'

'Sure.' I settled into my desk and made a show of unpacking my brief case. The moment he left, I grabbed the phone and called Michael Faber's office. A bright voiced secretary informed me he'd just arrived. She transferred my call to his office.

Faber's hello was distracted. I could hear the thump of something being placed on his desk.

'Mr Faber, it's Sarah Arden from the fingerprint branch.'

All movement at the other end of the line seemed to cease.

'Hello?' I said. 'Are you there?'

'Yes.' His voice was weary.

'I'm sorry to disrupt you again.'

'Has my lawyer authorised this contact?'

'Your lawyer? Would that be Mrs Faber?'

'No.'

'Well, I'll be happy to talk to your lawyer if you insist, but I don't think we need to bother. I just need to take a copy of your fingerprints.'

A pause, and then a sigh. 'When do you need to do it?'

'Whenever you're free. I can come up to your office if that suits you.'

'Fine. I don't care. Get this over with.' His voice was toneless, almost bored.

I was surprised he'd not put up a fight. The Michael Faber I had first encountered at the Brighton mansion would have his lawyer on the phone the second I hung up.

'Half an hour?'

'Yes.'

I checked his address. 'First floor, Albany Road?'

'That's it.'

I packed my briefcase with my eye on the phone, but it didn't ring. By the time Amir returned, there was still no word from Faber's lawyer.

Why, I wondered, was Michael Faber so resigned?

47

The building was the opposite of his wife's. Stark glass planes and steel buttresses instead of ornate cornices and colonnaded ledges. I stepped through the automatic sliding doors and walked up to a high reception desk made of a black shiny stone. Dwarfed by the desk, a young dark-haired woman sat tapping at a keyboard. I announced myself and watched as she spoke to Michael Faber on the phone.

'Go on in,' she said when she'd hung up. 'He'll be with you in a minute.'

When I entered his office, it was empty.

Michael's voice slipped under the door of the ensuite. 'I'll only be a few seconds.'

I took the opportunity to look around. His desk was weighted on each side by neat piles of paperwork. The chair faced the window, its back to me. Along his side of the desk were a line of yellow sticky notes with names and phone numbers, dates and instructions. All were marked urgent. I stepped around the desk and glanced at the dates printed neatly on each yellow right hand corner. Some were a week old. Two were marked with '2nd call.'

I looked around the room with fresh eyes. The coffee percolator on the bookshelf was empty and clean. A blue bin by his desk was empty. On the bookshelf beside the desk stood a tumbler a quarter full of reddish brown liquid. I guessed it was whisky. Here was a man who was not spending much time working.

I walked to the window and checked out the view. It looked out over the slow crawl of the river, overgrown Heron Island and the edge of St Kilda Road. Cars and vans emerged from the dark mouth of the Burnley tunnel. Through the leaves of the Domain I could see the fume of the South Eastern Arterial motorway, jammed to gridlock even this late in the morning.

The city below was a mime. Hands made rude gestures from open car windows and mouths shaped obscenities. Hawkers ran after shoplifters mutely. Trucks bounced over ditches without a sound.

I needed windows like these. From my lounge at home I could hear every screech of brake on Beach Road.

When Michael Faber finally appeared I fought the urge to gasp. The skin on his face was the light grey of old fish scales, shiny with the sweat of ill health. The weight of his skin looked so heavy, it seemed to melt into a line of folds beneath his jaw line.

'Are you alright?' I asked.

His eyes on me were distant, the pupils tiny black dots in a maze of bloodshot veins. Even the whiteness between the branches of vein were discoloured conjunctivitis pink.

'You wanted my fingerprints?'

I began unpacking my kit. 'It will only take a few minutes.'

He held his hand out absently.

I cleared my throat. 'You just hang on to that for a bit longer. I need to set up first.'

He placed his hand flat on the desk.

'You've got a bit of work banked up here,' I said as I laid the strip and index card along the desk.

'Yeah, I'll be here this weekend, I think.'

I prepared the strip and gestured for his hand. Its pressure was an iron in my palm. I rolled each of the fingers on his right hand and then his left. I eyed each impression as I lifted the finger off the white card. None showed the distinctive mark I'd found on the rubber glove.

I offered him a pre-packaged tissue sachet with industrial strength soap and watched as he wiped his long fingertips clean.

'I'm going to ask you a frank question, Mr Faber. You're being blackmailed, aren't you?'

He stiffened. The tissue disappeared into his fist as his fingers tightened.

'Mr Faber?'

He looked at a point somewhere above my head. 'I don't know what you're talking about.'

If it were not true, the Michael I'd first met would have shot me a withering gaze and thrown me out of his office. If it were true, the old Michael Faber would have looked me in the eye and lied smoothly. This Michael Faber could barely concentrate long enough to create a sentence with the subject, verb and noun in the right places.

'You're not being blackmailed?' I persisted.

'No,' he said.

'You're not curious about why I'm asking?'

'Not really.'

'It's only a matter of time until we find out for sure. If you're not going to come to us with the blackmail, then you should get psychological help to cope with all this,' I said as I packed my case.

'I'm not the one who's losing their mind,' he tossed the tissue into the wastebasket by his feet. 'Even my wife thinks I killed my daughter. My own wife! Can you imagine that?'

'This is what happens when people are murdered.'

'Not my own wife, for Christ's sake!'

'She's grieving. Nothing makes sense to her anymore.'

'Well it sure as hell doesn't to me.' His phone rang. He let it go. It stopped after six rings. There was a knock at the door.

I rose as the dark-haired secretary entered. Without the camouflage of the desk, she was tall and elegant. Her brown pinstriped suit made her seem more business-like than her boss. 'It's Mark Angelino from Accounting,' she said. 'He's been trying to get you for two days.'

Michael nodded in resignation. 'Put him through.'

I followed the secretary out of the office and waited by her desk as she transferred the call.

'He needs help,' I said when she replaced the receiver.

She shrugged. 'I've told him that. He's in here when I arrive at 7.30 and still here when I leave at 6.30. Yet nothing gets done. I've had to delegate as much as I can to his juniors. They're sympathetic but not experienced enough to run this place.' She lowered her voice. 'Sometimes I'm scared he's going to...'

'Kill himself,' I finished for her.

She nodded.

'Have you spoken to his wife?' I asked.

'She never calls here. I don't think I've ever met her.'

'How long have you worked here?'

'Three years. I've seen his son though. The policeman.'

'He's not a policeman.'

She looked surprised.

'He used to be,' I explained, 'but he's a P.I. now.'

'Oh, he had a gun so I thought he was a cop.'

'He had a gun?'

'In his bag. About a year ago he came in to see Michael and left the gym bag he was carrying on the floor there,' she pointed to a spot just under her desk, near her feet. 'I accidentally knocked the bag with my foot and a few things spilled out. The gun too. So I quickly kicked everything back in.'

'What type of gun was it?'

She looked apologetic. 'I don't know. That was the first time I'd ever seen a gun.'

I smiled. 'Of course. Did you notice the colour?'

'Black. All black.'

I stared at her. 'Are you sure? It didn't have a silver barrel or a brown rubber grip?'

'No. It was definitely all black. I remember because it looked so scary.'

'Okay, thanks.'

The gun we recovered from Perez's cave, the gun that had passed through Grant Faber's old post at Green Heights, had been all black. Was it a coincidence, or had the gun that killed Emma Faber once belonged to Grant Faber? If so, how did it end up in Perez's cave?

There seemed only one answer.

I sat in one of the plush armchairs.

'Are you okay?' the receptionist asked.

'I just need to check something.' I rifled through my bag until I found the small note book containing details of my interviews for the case. I flipped to the pages I'd dedicated to Grant Faber. It was, according to my notes, he who had first mentioned Guillaume Perez. Without Grant Faber guiding us to Perez, we'd have no suspect.

But why? Why would Grant Faber kill his own sister? Did he suspect she had been blackmailing their father? Yet he had not communicated with his parents for over a year. How would he know his father was being blackmailed?

I remembered Grant Faber's recent relocation to a grand office in the expensive part of town, his early dismissing of his receptionist, the quietness of the office. Business had been slow, the receptionist said, yet how could he afford such plush surrounds?

'I'll just be a second,' I called as I jumped up. I strode towards Michael Faber's office.

By the time the receptionist called out for me to wait, I was already through the door.

Michael looked up in surprise as I slipped into the seat in front of him. Not a paper had been moved on his desk since I'd left.

'Hard at it, huh?' I said.

'I thought you left.'

'I nearly did. I just need to ask you one more question.'

I interpreted his raised eyebrows as a cue to continue.

'When did you lose contact with Grant?' I asked.

'Eight months ago.'

'What did you fall out about?'

'You said only one question.' He exhaled wearily. 'We argued about money. His lifestyle was rather excessive.'

'He was in debt?'

'Always.'

'Have you heard how his business is going?'

'Things do get back to me. People we both know.'

'Of course. So how is he financially?'

'I heard that he owed $40,000. But he's stopped asking our friends for 'investment assistance' and the loan sharks don't bother us any more. I assumed he'd paid it all off somehow.'

'Thank you. That's all I needed to know.'

'What about me? Is there anything I need to know?'

'Not yet.'

I called Alex the moment I left the building.

'What if it was Grant who was blackmailing Michael?' I told him what Michael Faber had said about Grant's lifestyle.

'But blackmailing him over what? That's still unanswered.'

'I don't know,' I said.

'You think Emma found out the brother was blackmailing their father? She may have threatened to blow the whistle on Grant. Or maybe she wanted a cut.'

'Could be either.'

'Looks like we'd better have a word with Grant Faber.'

Adrenaline rushed through me like a shiver. 'Now?'

'I'll be finished here in about ten minutes. I'm in Richmond.'

'Okay, I'll meet you outside his office in half an hour.'

48

I arrived fifteen minutes before the appointed time. I decided to go upstairs and wait for Alex in the warmth of Grant Faber's lobby.

The receptionist was reading the employment section of the daily paper when I stepped out of the elevator. She quickly slipped the newspaper under a folder. 'Mr Faber's gone home early,' the receptionist said. 'When we're quiet, he prefers working at home.'

'How long ago did he leave?'

'This morning at about 11.00.'

I leaned against the desk. 'Do you mind if I ask how many clients he has?'

'That's confidential. Mr Faber would get upset if I answered that.'

'The last time I dropped in, you mentioned there wasn't much work. Does than mean under three clients? Under five?'

'Mr Faber does the billing himself so even if I was allowed to tell you, I couldn't.'

'In the market for a new job I see,' I nodded at the folder. 'I saw you slip it under there.'

She blushed. 'Just keeping my options open.'

'Not much to do around here, I guess. You answer the phone, schedule appointments, type documents?'

'That's about it.'

'Except that I've never heard the phone ring when I've been here and I don't see many documents lying around to be typed. And obviously Grant doesn't have too many appointments if he spends most of the day at home. Where can I find a job like this?' I chuckled.

'It does get a little dull,' she admitted. 'This week's highlight was when I went to the Laundromat to wash Mr Faber's handtowels. They were ink stained so I had to do two washes. I had time for three visits to Starbucks.'

'He had ink on his towels? Like from a pen?'

'No, he said it was some type of henna.'

'Henna?' My mind struggled to process what she was saying. 'Like a temporary dye?'

'I didn't ask any questions. I was just grateful to get outside for a bit.'

'Did the ink come out of the towels?'

'Mostly.'

It all seemed to logical now. A temporary tattoo would alter the ridges of a fingerprint for a few days and then wash away. The ridges would spring back to normal, leaving no trace of the mark that had been etched on the skin.

I had to get something that he'd touched when he had the tattoo. I thought quickly. 'Did Grant leave the photo with you?' I asked. Nothing like a little white lie.

'What photo?'

'He said he was going to leave a photo of his sister with you —the one that died.'

She looked confused. 'No, he didn't leave a photo with me.' She reached for the phone. 'Here, I'll give him a call and ask where he's left it.'

'Oh no, don't bother. It's probably on his desk or with him at home. I'll check on his desk.' I started towards his office door.

'Hang on, I'll check for you. He gets funny about letting people in his office.'

'So he should. Okay, let's look together.'

She stepped ahead of me and opened his door. She made a

bee-line for the desk. I stayed close behind her, my eyes quickly scanning the desk top.

It was nearly empty, save for a few pens and a silver letter opener standing handle up in a black plastic caddy. She fossicked through a black wire in-tray, her back to me.

I needed something insignificant enough not to be missed, but something only he had touched. An absorbent surface or something varnished or glossy. Not plastic because I'd have to superglue that and I wanted a quick result.

At the edge of his desk, behind the caddy, sat a wooden ruler. The down light above us picked up a glint of shine. A varnished wooden ruler.

I pulled a tissue from my pocket and snatched up the ruler. As she placed the pile of paperwork back in the tray, I slipped the ruler up my sleeve.

'The photo's not here,' she turned to face me. 'Are you sure you don't want me to give him a call?'

'Don't bother. I'll drop down to his place.' I moved back into the reception area. She followed me and pulled Faber's door shut behind her.

Within ten minutes of leaving Grant Faber's office my car became a make-shift lab. On the front passenger seat I spread a sheet of old newspaper I'd found in my boot. I dusted white powder over the wood with a squirrel hair brush and gently blew off the excess.

Grant Faber's ridges were as jagged as the edges of broken concrete. I grabbed a magnifier and held it to my eye. On the index was the star-like mark just as I'd found on the glove. It was so faint it was almost a shadow. The ridges were only slightly compressed, only marginally flattened. The skin had almost completely sloughed off the henna impressions to reclaim its landscape of line, dip, line.

I photographed the ruler roughly with a small fixed aperture camera I kept in the glove box and then packed everything away. I stored the ruler in a large PostPak cardboard tube and called Alex to tell him to meet me outside Grant Faber's house.

'I'm calling Peterson now,' he said.

'Ask him if he's checked out how much Grant owes.'

'Okay. Make sure you wait for me.'

'Of course,' I lied.

49

Grant Faber lived in a new, mock Victorian terrace in Windsor. The suburb was like a conservative nook between arty St Kilda and the high camp of Prahran.

His front yard smelled of jasmine. The two-way streets were the size of alleys and no house was larger than a suburban garage. On occasion we were called out to break-and-enters around here, but nothing much was ever stolen beyond the usual thief-on-foot goods of laptops, CD's and jewellery. No loot truck would ever make it through Windsor's roundabouts without collecting the front porches of the corner homes.

Even the prints found here were small.

The houses were so narrow the windows were only slightly wider than gun turrets. If they came in through the roof no more than two tiles were missing. When an arrest was made the perp was usually a child, teenager or a thin, short adult.

All with small hands.

I followed the driveway the two metres to the front door. The house was built over and around the garage, with a balcony lining its top edges.

I rang the bell set into the wall beside the security grill. Its echo chimed inside the house. I waited. There was no shuffle of movement from within. Maybe he'd gone out. I rang the bell again and stepped over to the garage to see if I could peer inside. There were no windows on the outside. I tried to lift the garage door.

It wouldn't budge.

I walked past the garage to the right hand perimeter of the property, hoping there would be a walkway between Faber's property and the identical brick terrace next door. But they were joined as one building.

Frustrated, I crossed the yard again and checked for the space between the left hand neighbour's building and Faber's.

Again there was no gap.

'You looking for Grant?' a male voice called.

I glanced up at the house next door. A squat, middle-aged man in a white shirt and brown tie leaned over the upstairs balcony with a bottle of Hahn's Premium beer in his hand.

'He's supposed to be home,' I yelled up at him.

'He is. His stereo has been thumping like a NASA launch since I got home two hours ago.'

'I can't hear it.'

'It's in the back room. It beats through my kitchen wall like a jackhammer.'

'Okay, I'll give him a call.' I waved a thanks and returned to my car. After fishing my mobile from my handbag, I called the phone directory and got his number. It rang five times when I called and then switched to his answering machine. I left a message.

Damn it, I thought. This gave me no choice. I drove my car into the street behind Grant Faber's house and parked it as close as I could to the house that backed onto his.

Grant's house was four properties from the nearest intersection. I counted four homes along and stopped out a ramshackle single-fronted terrace. The left side of the tin roof dipped south at a 45-degree angle. A grey blanket covered the front window. The exterior of the house was a peeling light green weatherboard with a patchy couch grass lawn covering the two metres between the front door and the fading white picket fence.

I knocked on the front door. The wood beneath my fist felt damp and weak. I knocked again. No one answered, so I darted around to the side of the house and kept going until I entered the small space used as a backyard.

Without hesitation I climbed the fence and checked out the house behind. I recognised the new terracotta bricks of the row of terraces that held Grant Faber's home.

I swung my legs over the fence, landed on the ground flat on my feet and hoped I wasn't about to be dog food. The garage extended out from the back of the house. A bare window looked over the yard from the side of the garage.

I peered in.

A red Honda Convertible with plates reading 'Grant F' sat between cardboard boxes.

I walked up to the back door of the house and beat against it with my knuckles.

'Grant? I called.

I could hear a Bruce Springsteen song playing loudly inside. I tried twice more and then checked the two sets of slide-up windows that faced the yard.

One was open.

I took a deep breath and pushed in the flyscreen, hoping Grant Faber wouldn't greet me with a gun. I climbed through the window into a tiny bedroom.

'Grant?' I called again.

I found him in the kitchen, lying on the floor on his side. His legs were bent at the knees, thighs close together.   My eyes raced around the room.

Gun on the edge of the table above him.

Blood on the wall and furniture to his left.

A chair pulled out.

A handwritten note on the table.

I squatted down and checked the pulse in his wrist. There wasn't one. I tried the cardioid vein in his neck but nothing moved under my fingers.

I rose to read the note. The handwriting was slanted so far to the right I had to lean sideways to decipher the words. The language was just as skewed.

'I love Emma but I had to do it. She was going to talk too much. She

258

knew about the money I was nailing Dad for. I never trusted her but I did love her. She made me kill her She wanted a cut or she'd tell Dad it was me. I went to her place but she wouldn't listen. So I had to drug her and take her to the beach and leave her and then go back to her place and take out everything that proved I'd been there. I put the gun in the old man's cave so people would think it was him and took off her finger skin and put the aboriginal thing at her feet so the police would think the old man was crazy and just killed her in some crazy ritual I can't live with myself anymore, sorry. Sorry, sorry.'

He'd killed Emma because she discovered he was blackmailing her father? Why, I wondered, didn't he just pay her off? Surely cutting your sister in was easier than killing her. And the reason for removing the fingerprints sounded dubious. Removing fingerprints would have been messy and time consuming. Why bother if it was just to suggest ritual?

I thought about the big picture. Michael Faber blackmailed by his own son. The question was still why? What did Grant have over his father?

I didn't feel the sense of relief that usually settled when the pieces of the puzzle interlocked. Grant Faber was a cop, a man who knew the boundaries of the law. We had nothing concrete to tie him to Emma's death. Blackmail, I'd have suspected him of. He'd been incriminated in illegal dealings before. It was an easy trap for a cop to fall into. But how did a blackmailer make the leap to killing his own sister, displaying her body on a beach and removing her fingerprints? The scene the killer had created was pure theatre, a stage too heavy with props to indicate the simple desire to remove someone who had complicated a plan.

I read the note again. The sentences ran into each other with little punctuation. The words and style clearly communicated emotional disintegration. Detective Jamieson had said suicide notes were usually logical and practical, not so repetitive. I thought back to the few suicide notes I had seen. The style of writing had always suggested sureness, not disintegration.

Perhaps this scene was pure theatre too.

259

I moved into his study and quickly ruffled through the paperwork on his desk. There were standard bills: electricity and water, and a case file in a blue manila envelope. I flicked it open. Handwritten pages of notes floated loosely inside. I pulled them out and carried them back into the kitchen. After laying them beside the suicide note, I compared the slopes and loops of the three pages. The letters on the suicide note held the same characteristics as the pages of notes: looped 'L's and 'G's, cursive 's's . The loops of the suicide note were looser and broader, the angles wider, slanted close to the baseline. It was hurried writing, certainly less legible. The hand under stress.

But definitely Grant's.

I flicked through the rest of the case file. The job was to locate a missing teenager, last seen six months ago. I closed the file and rifled through his desk drawers. They held stationery and an unused cheque book in the name of Faber Investigations.

I spent a few minutes going through the three drawers of the filing cabinet. There was little of use to me—just old case files dating back from when he'd left the police force. I cast an eye around the room for the brown leather briefcase I'd seen in Faber's office. It didn't seem to be there.

Where would he keep his briefcase?

Maybe his car.

His keys were on the kitchen bench by the telephone.

The sports car was immaculately clean with a leather dashboard that smelled like linseed. It was empty of all clutter except what was in the tiny glove compartment—an Eagles CD and two pens. I popped the boot. The briefcase was sitting on the top of the spare wheel.

The case's lock was unsecured. I lifted the flap and examined its contents. These were a black leather diary, a thin black portfolio with a black note pad and calculator, and a copy of a journal article. I pulled out the article and read the title page. "Discovery of seawater fish in the Mekong: a report from the British Institute of Environmental Science". A web address sat at the top of each page. He'd obviously downloaded this from the internet.

I examined the top of the report's pages. He'd seemed to have read only a quarter of the document. I slipped it back into his briefcase. Why would Grant Faber be reading an environmental study on seawater fish? My memory stirred. Didn't Emma have a book on fish by her bed?

I opened his dairy to the current day entry. It was blank. I flipped back a few pages. An appointment with his accountant had been pencilled in for yesterday. The address and phone number section was at the back. I ran my finger down the list of names, looking for something familiar.

Then I found it.

Ron Peterson. 9789 – 1854.

On a whim, I opened the dairy to the day that Emma was killed. It was blank. I returned everything to the car and examined the boot.

I went back inside the house and stood in his study again. On his desk was a small flip calendar. I flipped it back to the day before Emma was killed. There was nothing written in for that date. I slipped the entire calender in my pocket anyway. From the study I moved directly into the kitchen. On the wall beyond the table and his body were the sink and cupboards. I checked the sink for glasses or dishes. It was empty. I opened the bathroom cupboard. A bottle of Zaparin sat on the top shelf. The bottle and the gun would be tested for prints by the fingerprinter who'd be called in. I knew it wouldn't be me. The fact that I'd found the body would give Peterson a hernia. It was a safe bet that I'd be barred from the scene.

I left the house the way I'd come in—through the open window in the spare bedroom.

I called Alex from my mobile when I got back to my car. I assumed he was still in Shepparton.

'You're Grant Faber,' I said the moment he answered. 'You're blackmailing your father. Your sister finds out and threatens to blow the whistle. How do you deal with it?'

'I'd pay her off or bump her off.'

'How would Grant bump her off?'

'He's a cop so he'd take her somewhere quiet and out of sight and then pop her. Execution style. Minimum fuss.' 'That's what I thought too.'

His voice grew impatient. 'So what are you telling me here?'

'Grant Faber is dead.'

Guillaume Perez was released from police custody within the hour. I stood by the holding cell, waiting for one of Alex's colleagues to finish the release paperwork. Perez sat on a chair outside the cell, watching the two of us. I had arranged for a liaison from a men's shelter to collect Perez and install him in temporary accommodation. I knew there was little point to this, Perez would simply walk out and disappear back into his cave so that he could be near the shipping lanes.

The liaison officer would also help Perez regain his permit to work on cargo ships. The translator had explained all this to Perez as best he could.

As Perez scribbled the identifying mark that passed as his signature onto the paperwork, I stepped into the cell. The picture of the open sea was still stuck to the wall.

I plucked it off and placed it the table next to Perez.

He stared at it for a few seconds and then picked it up.

He met my eyes.

'Merci,' he said.

50

Peterson pulled Amir off lab duties and gave him the job of printing the Grant Faber scene. I was to continue his work on matching a short list of prints for other cases. I called his mobile and told him that I'd taken the page of Grant's desk diary. After I'd given a statement on how I found the body and entered the house, I returned to the lab and picked up Amir's trail through the dozens of prints the AFIS had shortlisted.

Peterson demanded I not leave the office until he returned from Grant's house. 'You're temporarily suspended until I get back. You contacted him again, didn't you?'

'I did not.'

'I knew Grant would do something drastic if he thought we were on to him.'

'I went to see him at his office, but he wasn't there. I haven't seen him since I first met him in his office.'

'But you went to his office.'

'I told you, he wasn't there.'

'You were supposed to speak to me before approaching any of the Fabers.'

'Look, if you thought Grant Faber was so psychologically unstable, why didn't you warn us or bring him in?'

There was an angry silence on the line for a few seconds before he finally spoke. 'I didn't have enough on him. I wasn't sure where he fitted in. I guess now I know.'

When I had finished Amir's work, I took the desk diary page into the lab. I applied ninhydrin's purple liquid in a fine shower and then left it to settle while I made myself a cup of coffee.

I passed Catherine on the way out of the lunchroom.

'Hey, I hear you're grounded.' She tossed her bag on an armchair. 'How are you holding it together? Apparently the body wasn't a pretty sight. I still get sick…you know…when I see them.'

I looked down into my coffee cup. 'I'm trying not to think about it.'

She squeezed my shoulder. 'Hey, whatever you've sprayed in the lab has come up. Take a look.'

I followed her into the lab. She was right. The ninhydrin had already stained the amino acids that Grant Faber's fingers had left as he flipped over the page of his desk calendar.

'The impression's light, though,' she said.

'He would only have touched the page for a few seconds.'

The loops and lines of his middle finger's arch glowed on the back of the page and the smudge of his thumb's edge spilled over the corner of the page, searching for grip.

'What's that?' Catherine asked, pointing at the oval mark on the arch of his middle finger's print.

'Exactly what I've been looking for. There's a disruption just like it on Emma's fingerprint, on the inside of the glove I found at the scene, and on the ruler I took from Grant's office.'

She grabbed a magnifier and examined the mark more closely. 'What is it? Not a scar. A burn, maybe?'

'The temporary tattoo.'

She looked up. 'Temporary? But they're just painted on. They wouldn't leave this degree of ridge damaged.'

'It must have penetrated the first layer of skin.'

I remembered that Grant had asked Roo if he did paint ons. Roo didn't, so obviously Grant found someone who did.

'This guy was a cop, right?' she asked.

'Yeah, used to be. What I don't get is why he left a glove with his print on it at his sister's apartment. He knew we'd treat the area as a crime scene. Surely he'd be careful not to leave evidence linking him to the crime scene somewhere where he knew we would look.'

'Maybe he wanted to get caught.'

'So killed himself when he didn't get caught?' I said. 'I don't think so.'

She shrugged. 'Then maybe he didn't leave the gloves there. Maybe he gave them to his sis and she wore them.'

'Her prints aren't on them.'

'Did you check everywhere on the glove? Maybe she handled them, not wore them. Or maybe someone planted them there to mislead us.'

'Let's take a look.' I carried the gloves from my filing cabinet into the lab.

Catherine turned on the scanning microscope and rotated to the lens's shortest focal length.

I slipped the cuff section of the glove, outside up, under the lens. If someone had handled the gloves after they'd been removed from Grant's hands, their print would be on the inside of the glove near the wrist or palm.

I looked through the eyepiece. Once magnified, the fibres of the latex were visible—a crosshatching of plastic and rubber that extreme heat had bonded. The fumes in the Perspex cube had polymerised other traces of sweat that I hadn't bothered looking for. I could see the semicircle of a palm print, the press of the muscle of the thumb. I hadn't sprayed these parts of the glove with gentian violet, but the glue had defined them enough to be detected by the naked eye.

Catherine mixed up a solution of gentian violet and sprayed it on the rest of the glove. As the glue stained pink, we could make out the long elegance of a partial loop in the part of the glove that covers the wrist. I turned the glove over and put it under the scope again.

'Look!' I stepped back from the table.

She positioned her eye over the microscope. 'Goddam. That's a thumb!'

'Whose are they?'

'Not Grant Faber's. His edges are worn to hell.'

'Let me see again.' These definitely too thin and elegant to be Grant's.

I photographed the prints and resealed the glove into a paper evidence bag. We did a quick point comparison between this loop and Grant's. There were no matching deltas or bifurcations.

'I don't want to break your heart,' she said, 'but these prints could belong to anyone involved in the manufacturing process of the glove. Or maybe Grant Faber got the gloves off someone he knew in a lab.'

I heard my mobile phone ring from the bag on my desk. I stripped off my own gloves, tossed them in the bin and hurried into the room of carrels.

It was Alex.

'I've just left Grant Faber's house,' he said.

'When did you get back from Shepparton?'

'A few hours ago. Grant's body is at the morgue. His parents have been informed.'

'What do you think?' I asked him.

'The doc thinks it's straightforward suicide.'

'And you?' I asked again.

'Well, the scene itself seems normal. Nothing disturbed. The powder marks on his head suggest a close range shooting. The angle of the wound and the splatter marks match up with what they'd be if he did it himself. The handwriting on the note seems to be his.'

'Fingerprints?

'None, except his.'

This still didn't feel right. 'He couldn't have killed Emma. His method is all wrong. And he was too cool and in control to kill himself.'

'Don't underestimate the power of guilt. Or maybe he lost

his nerve, realised that the way he killed her wasn't as foolproof as it seemed.'

'That's not what his note said,' I argued.

'Okay, so he felt remorse.'

I was still not convinced. 'Anyway, how are the parents?'

'Shattered, of course. They've lost both their children now.'

'I found another print on the glove,' I said. 'Two people have handled it.'

'Yeah?'

'Grant and someone else. Maybe it was planted in Emma's garbage after Grant had worn it.'

'Run the new print through the database, I guess.'

'You don't sound enthusiastic.'

'Unless something dramatic surfaces, Grant's death has tied this up in a bow.'

'But what did Grant have on his father?' I asked.

'I have a feeling we'll never know.'

We may not know, I thought, but I bet Elizabeth Faber will find out.

His voice grew low. 'I want to see you.'

'I'm in the lab. Catherine can man it for a while, but I need to see Elizabeth Faber.'

'Elizabeth Faber can wait. I'll pick you up from the carpark at the back of the building in ten minutes. '

We drove to a secluded spot by the beach.

In his arms, I surrendered the grief of finding Grant Faber dead.

I sobbed it out and let him hold me. He was the only one I could let see me like this. Catherine and I would drink it out together at a dark bar, but we cried separately. Seeing each other across the room every few hours seemed to put emotional distance between us. Other police are too hard. I knew they had to be, that they had to store their emotions in the clench of a fist, or they would grow brittle and break. Other people were too soft. They'd collapse under the weight of what I see.

Only Alex, with his balance of arches and curves, was strong enough to let himself be weak.

'Your fingers always smell strange,' he said as he kissed their tips. I listened to the waves roll across the bay. We were lying, curled together, on the same seat. The headrest touched the back seat.

'Ninhydrin. Talcum powder from the gloves,' I said.

'No, something else. Something fruity.'

I laughed. 'Probably cabbage! Thank my mother's recipes,' I said. 'She believed in an old myth. If you tied string around a wrist and an ankle with knots, you wouldn't get pregnant. If the knots get untied during sex, your child will be cursed with disfigurement. When she dressed the morning after being with my father, she discovered the knots had unravelled. She fell pregnant. I was born without fingerprints.'

'She thinks she caused it?'

I nodded. 'And she thinks she can cure it with anything that smells weird.' Talking about smells reminded me of the fish at my back door, the fear I felt knowing someone had been in my yard. 'I love her, but she needs to go home.'

'You mean you need her to go home.'

'No, that's not what I mean. It's not safe for her here. Things still feel unresolved. I feel vulnerable, like I should be checking over my shoulder.'

'Let her stay with me.'

I felt sick at the thought of my mother nosing through Alex's things, pumping him for information about me, him, us. 'Forget it. She'll drive you mad.'

'No more than you do.'

I laughed. 'Oh no, you've got no idea.'

He moved away from me. 'This isn't about her, is it?'

'What?'

'This is about you. You need to keep space around you. You can't handle the thought of the two people who know the most about you being under the same roof. What do you think we'll do? Sit around the fireplace trading Sarah stories?'

'Of course not.'

'Well?'

I stared out the window. I tried to shut out the image of his wife wearing his shirt as she answered his door.

He grabbed my hand. 'I want to be a big part of your life.'

'I want that too.'

'So start by letting me in.'

I rolled my eyes. 'Okay, I'll ask her. But I still think she should go home. She threatened to ask Catherine to test for my father's prints.'

'Sarah,' he whispered, 'give her closure. Don't you want to make peace with your past as well?'

51

'You've got to be joking.' The woman's bulk blocked Elizabeth and Michael Faber's doorway. 'You can wait a few days to talk to her.'

'It'll only take a few minutes,' I insisted.

'Forget it. I'll pass your name on and she'll call you later in the week.'

Elizabeth Faber appeared behind the woman. 'It's alright, June.'

June? This had to be June McNaughton, the friend who spent the night of Emma's death with Elizabeth.

Elizabeth's face was pale, the skin under her eyes black. Her hair was unstyled, the ends kicking out in all directions.

'Detective Pace said you're the one who found my son's body,' she said.

'Yes, I'm sorry.'

'So what do you want?'

'To ask one question.'

'Well, that's a change. Would that be the same one that the rest of the detectives have been asking me?'

I shrugged. 'Can I speak to you in private?'

With her right hand on June's shoulder, she guided the woman away from the door. 'Quickly then.' She unlocked the security door and held it open. 'My husband has gone to identify the body. He'll fall into a rage if he sees you here.'

I stepped around her and moved into the entrance hall. June grabbed Elizabeth's arm and they exchanged words in tones too low for me to hear.

'Come into the library,' Elizabeth said, and pointed to a corridor beyond the lounge.

June locked the security door again.

Elizabeth overtook me and led me through the lounge and into a room two doors down the corridor.

The room was lined with oak bookshelves. She settled into one of two facing Chesterfield sofas. I perched on the edge of the other and watched her as she stared out the French doors at the ferned terrace that led into the backyard.

'I'm sorry about your son,' I said.

'You've already said that. What was it you wanted to ask me?'

'What do you think your son was blackmailing your husband with?'

She shook her head in disgust. 'Remind me again what this had to do with fingerprints?'

'We need to secure any blackmail letters and check them for evidence. That will be final proof. We also need to check any of your husband's documents that your son might have come in contact with.'

'Check them for what type of evidence?'

'Fingerprints. To prove or disprove the blackmail claim.'

She looked confused. 'But he confessed. He's dead. What's the point?'

'It's just routine.'

'No, you just think my husband was being blackmailed because he did something illegal. And you won't rest until you've ruined his life even more.'

'I just need to tie up the loose ends so we can all move on.'

'My husband has done nothing wrong.'

'How can you be sure? Why else would he be being blackmailed?'

'I know my husband.'

'Elizabeth, the detectives must have pointed out that the

blackmail claim has to be treated as a whole new investigation.'

'Not if what he was being blackmailed for was an internal family matter.'

I paused. 'I see. The fraud squad may require you to prove that.'

'That's between my husband, myself and the detectives.'

'Do you believe Emma wanted a share of the money?'

'Isn't that what my son wrote in his letter?'

'Even though you were estranged from him, you believed him?'

'Why would he lie on a suicide note? What purpose would there be in smearing Emma's name? Why else would he have done what he did to her?' she asked.

'You believe your son was blackmailing your husband over something your husband was keeping from the rest of your family, even you, and that Emma found out and was killed because she threatened to blow the whistle?'

'That's what my son's note said.'

'But I'm asking if you believe it.'

She threw her arms in the air. 'For God's sake, what does it matter what I believe? I've lost my only two children and you're trying to push me into believing my son lied about why he did it.'

'Maybe what was written is unreliable. Suicide isn't always suicide.'

Every movement in her body seemed to stop. When she spoke, her lips barely opened. I had to lean forward to catch her words.

'Not suicide?' she whispered.

I wondered if I had gone too far. Telling a suicide's family that you suspect murder seems to give them hope. It eases guilt, explains the unexplainable. Those left behind want to think that their loved one cherished life, and the people in it, too much to deliberately end it. I should have waited until I had more evidence before giving Elizabeth that hope. My questions and comments should have kept more closely to the task of finding out what Grant had on his father.

'I'm sorry,' I said gently. 'I have no proof that he didn't take his own life. My words were just —'

She cut me off. 'You think he was murdered?' Her voice grew loud and shrill. 'Who the hell are you to tell me this?' She jumped to her feet and reared over me. 'Get out! Get out now before I do something I'm going to regret.'

I stared at her, confused. Whatever my words had given her, it was definitely not hope.

'What do you know that implies he was murdered?' she yelled. 'What?'

My hands rose in an attempt to pacify her. 'Calm down.'

Her voice dropped in volume. 'The only way I can feel calm is if you're no longer in my house. You'll not be satisfied until I go mad, will you? Whether it's suicide or murder, the result's the same. Changing the wording isn't going to bring my children back.' She crossed the room and swung the door open. 'June,' she called. 'See this woman out.'

June appeared in the doorway so quickly I figured she must have had her ear to the door. I let her usher me out. The library door slammed behind us.

I followed June through the house and paused behind her as she unlocked the front door. A gush of jonquil scent ruffled our clothes. Over June's shoulder I saw a man in a brown suit walking up the front path.

'Hi,' June smiled.

The man offered her a tight smile back. 'Is she okay?'

June nodded. 'She's in the library.' She stood aside to let the man pass. He nodded curtly to me.

I recognised him. The man Elizabeth Faber was lunching with at the Doberville.

I waited until he'd disappeared down the corridor before I spoke. 'Who was that?'

'My husband.'

'Oh. I saw him last week.'

She turned to me in surprise. 'You saw him?'

'Yeah, in Southbank. Eating lunch with Elizabeth at the Doberville.'

'Last week?'

'Yes.'

'Couldn't be. He was interstate last week.'

'He's very distinctive looking. I don't think I'd have mixed him up with anyone else.'

Doubt folded the skin at the bridge of her nose.

'Do you know the Doberville?' I asked her.

Her hand tightened on the door handle. 'It's a hotel.'

'Yes.' I saw it clearly then, and the whiteness of June's knuckles told me she knew it too. Elizabeth Faber and June's husband were having an affair.

I placed my left hand on her shoulder. 'I'm sorry.'

Her face was hard. 'Save your sympathy. My husband is not cheating on me. And neither is Elizabeth. Michael's the one with the roving eye.'

I froze. 'Michael had an affair?'

She bit her lip. 'Well, I'm not sure, but women do find him attractive.'

Could that be what Grant was blackmailing Michael with?

'Did his son know?' I asked.

'Look, I couldn't say. But I do know Elizabeth and I can tell you, she would not have an affair. She wouldn't risk being the one to blame. Divorce payouts are touchy enough. If you're a woman, you get virtually nothing if you're the cause. It's cruel, but that's the way it is.'

'She's a lawyer. Surely she makes enough money not to need a payout from him,' I said.

'Sure, she's a good earner, but nothing like what Michael makes. He's closing a big deal soon too. If that pulls through, he'll be worth millions more,' she said.

'June, I saw them together when he told you he was interstate. Use your logic.'

'If she was having an affair, it wasn't with my husband.'

'Who then?'

'Someone else. I don't know.'

'But how do you know it's not your husband?'

'Because he wasn't with her the night Emma died.'

I waited for her to explain. She stared out the front door.

'The night Emma died...?' I prompted.

'I called him at work. He wasn't with her.'

'I don't understand what you're saying. If Elizabeth was with you, why did you need to ring him to see if he was with her that night? Elizabeth would have been sitting right opposite you that night.'

She pushed me away and stepped back into the house.

The door slammed behind her.

52

As I drove home, I started putting the pieces together.

Maybe Michael Faber was about to pull off a sensitive deal when his son discovered something that could ruin Michael's marriage. An affair. If Elizabeth found out, she could sue for divorce and get half. Then Michael Faber would lose big money, maybe even half his company. The big deal he was about to close would collapse if his co-investors got cold feet. So he made the payments. All went smoothly until Emma found out. Maybe she saw her father with the woman, maybe she heard it through the grapevine. Either she wanted a cut of the blackmail money or wanted the world to know that her father was a cheat.

So wasn't it in Michael Faber's interest, as much as Grant's, to keep Emma quiet?

What if Grant and Michael agreed to kill Emma and Grant was the one who actually did it. But Michael didn't trust Grant, so he planted Grant's gloves in her bin.

But Grant was still greedy and kept up the blackmail, so Dad finished him off and made it look like suicide.

I pulled over to the side of the road and called Alex.

'Where's Michael Faber?' I demanded.

'How should I know?'

'He was going to the Morgue. Shouldn't you have someone on him?'

'What for?'

'At least until the autopsy is done. Until we're sure Grant Faber killed himself.'

'Forget it. Peterson's not spending a penny more. Go home, Sarah. It's over.'

I heard someone call his name in the background.

'I've gotta go,' he told me. 'I'll call you later tonight.'

He hung up.

Back home, I was restless. I cleaned the house and then unpacked and repacked my sets of brushes and powders. I rubbed one drop each of chamomile, juniper berry and geranium with two drops of almond oil into the skin on my hands. I pressed my palms to blotting paper and examined the results. All I saw were the little pebbles of my dysplasia. On anyone else, I could have measured heartrate.

Two hours later, I was still looking for things to do.

I fished out my father's letter and took it into the St Kilda Road Lab.

I ignored the words and searched for imprints.

It was my mother's loss that I read in the smear of loops and whorls. Lines so thick they overlapped. Ridges laid over ridges seconds and years apart. Residues blurred by sobs. Paper crumpled by anger and smoothed out again in regret.

On the back, the print of my mother's palm and five fingers. On the front, fibres of brown wool. She had held the letter against her heart.

I looked for unfamiliar fingerprints.

At the top of the page, the ulnar loop of a thumb. At the bottom, the turn of a whorl on the pointer, the peak of an arch on the index and another ulnar loop in the fourth. All from a right hand used to steady the paper as my father wrote. I counted the ridges and scanned the prints into the database.

I checked the lines for the pebbles of dysplasia. There were none.

My disease had not come from him.

I looked for impressions that were not fingerprints. I found big smears running across the page. This could only be marks left by the side of a hand as it followed words across the paper. With my magnifier I examined the ink of each letter. Their right sides were smudged. He was left handed.

I closed my eyes against science and looked for emotions.

His lines were strong, growing thicker as the ridges moved closer to the centre of the prints, narrowing to hairline width as they moved inward along the turn of a whirl. They were indistinguishable from the prints of people in love—dense with the sweat of a rapid pulse, suddenly thin as the heart missed a beat.

What had I expected? Lines patchy from lack of emotion? Prints starved of feeling? Signs of madness?

How could a sane man run from what he loved?

From my mother?

From me?

I thought of the way I had left Alex six months ago.

I realised I had inherited more than I imagined.

I sent the Riverina police an electronic copy of my father's prints.

They responded in forty minutes.

As I called my mother, I wondered if I was doing the right thing. Perhaps it was better that she suspected he was dead. At least that way she could get on with her life. If she knew he was alive, she would just continue calling churches, looking for him in the religious papers, trying to dream his return.

'The body in the river wasn't him,' I said gently.

She inhaled sharply. 'Are they sure?'

'They can do a DNA test, but it'll cost us. And the result will be the same.'

Silence.

'Mum?'

Her voice was frail. 'Just leave me alone for a while.'

I felt an ache in my chest. 'Do you want to go to Alex's? He said you could stay with him instead of at the hotel.'

'Alex? The man you're seeing?' Her voice brightened. I knew then that I was doing the right thing.

'Yes, the one who was married,' I said.

'Tell him to come and pick me up at the hotel.'

'You'll like him.'

'He can drop me at the train station.'

'The train station?'

'I'm going home.'

'Stay until the weekend. I'll drive you back home then.'

'No, you've got to give that dead girl peace. I know what you're like. You'll be thinking about the investigation the whole way. It'll be like driving with a corpse.'

I rolled my eyes. 'Don't say that.'

'You know, I was sure he was dead.' Her voice was so soft it reminded me of a baby's sigh. I wished I'd told her in person.

'I love you, Mum.'

'Then keep that charm I gave you in your pocket.'

I stood on the Port Melbourne side of the shore and watched the lights of the geologists on the river. The darkness hummed with the vibration of pistons from the refineries down stream. The air picked up the oil slick on the surface of the river and brought it to me as I breathed. My tongue felt coated and heavy. Wattle from the acacias scattered across the bank below me, hitting the couch grass and then getting snatched by the breeze and thrown high into the black sky above me.

Carl waved at me from the water's edge. Dario was out on the boat, his back to me. There was a figure beside him. I recognised the long whips of hair.

Guillaume Perez.

I climbed carefully down the bank until I reached the point where the greasy decline became a sandy plateau. Carl was bent over a cooler filled with test tubes, his long black overcoat billowing out from his legs like a windsock.

'Dario! Hey!' I called at the boat.

He looked over his shoulder, still bent low over the net.

'You again. You're a brave soul.'

Guillaume raised a hand in greeting and then turned back to the net.

'Stupid, more like it.' I yelled back. I turned to Carl. 'You've recruited Perez?'

'The extra hands are welcome.'

'What's with the nets?' I asked.

'We need a sample of fish. With the confusion in the river's flow, we need to check how the fish are coping.'

'What do you know about fish? I thought you were geologists?'

'Dario's a double major.'

I watched Dario roll the net.

'The girl that died, Emma, did she ever question you about fish?' I asked Carl.

He wiped his hands on the side of his overcoat. 'Sure.'

I pulled the notes I'd taken at Grant's house out of my pocket and looked down at the title of the report that I'd copied. 'Did she ever ask about freshwater fish turning into seawater fish?'

'About what?'

'There was a report written about it by a guy called Edmund Bowler. In the Royal British Institute of Environmental Studies journal.'

'Oh, Bowler. Yeah, I know his work. He wrote about the mutations of sealife in the Mekong.'

'That's the one. Emma's brother had a report on fresh water fish surviving in sea water.'

'She didn't ask me about it. She might have asked Dario.' He beckoned to the men in the boat.

Dario steered the boat onto the silt at the shoreline. He and Perez jumped ashore, then dragged the boat onto the bank.

'Perez has a thing for fish too,' Carl said to me.

'I noticed. What's that all about?'

Carl laughed. 'Food, probably.'

'Are you sure?'

'Hey Dario,' Carl called, 'Did Emma Faber ask you about

fresh water fish surviving in sea water?'

Dario pulled out a packet of cigarettes and a lighter. Bending low against the wind, he lit one. 'She asked me a lot of stuff—water tables, river currents. She did ask me a weird question about fish once, now that I think about it.'

'What exactly?'

'About the percentage of salt water that fresh water fish could breathe in. I remember because I don't think anyone's ever asked me that before. It's too technical a question for most people.'

'Did she say why she wanted to know?'

'No, actually, she didn't really ask me personally. She left a message on my voice mail at the CSIRO. That would have been a day or two before she died.'

Perez slipped two fish into a plastic bag and walked into the shrub towards his cave. So much for a men's shelter.

'Have you told the police this?' I asked.

'No, I just got my messages two days ago. Carl and I have been stationed here all night and we sleep during the day. As you can imagine I don't get much chance to check into the office. Our department secretary passes on the urgent messages to me on my home phone. Emma's wasn't deemed urgent, I guess.'

'So why would she be asking this?'

Dario pulled two old camper seats from his tent and set them up in the mouth between the canvas flaps. 'Okay, grab a pew.'

I sat in one and watched him pull out a deep red metal flask and two tin cups. Carl sat on the grass beside my stool. 'Your girl and her group were looking for evidence that the water table under their land was being raided, right?'

'Uh huh,' I said.

'Fish could provide that evidence. See, a water table is a reservoir that's filled by a small outlet stemming from the river, so it usually holds freshwater fish. If the water table has algae in it, then the fish from the water table will have that algae too. Now, the water in the river may have different algae in it. If you give me a fish, I should be able to pick if it's from the water table or the river.'

'So if you found a water table fish in the river, you'd know that the table either has an outlet back into the river or that someone has been pumping water from it back into river,' I asked.

'Exactly.' Carl took the tin cup of coffee that Dario offered him. 'With the ocean flooding into the mouth of the river, there's a stretch of water where the fish are exposed to both sea and fresh water. If the construction company have been digging into the banks of the river, they may have accidentally released an inlet of salt water.'

'That's what the report is about? Fish exposed to both sea and fresh water?' I asked.

'Yes, but Bowler wasn't looking at the immediate adaptation of fresh water fish to salt, but more of a slow multigenerational change. Emma would be thinking of a growing tolerance to different water within one fish's life time,' Carl said.

'So she was right?'

Carl looked surprised. 'Salt water fish in the Yarra? It's not something that would slip by unnoticed. If a fisherman casting a line off Victoria Dock found a tuna we'd have heard about it.'

'Hang on,' Dario wagged a finger in the air. 'Bowler did say that the Mekong fish lost a lot of their markings. Theoretically, the fisherman may not recognise what they were reeling in or throwing back.'

'You guys would notice, surely.'

Carl shook his head. 'We've been focussing on the river flow, not marine life. It's only tonight that we're looking at the fish.'

'What would happen if Emma found fresh water fish were breathing in salt water?'

'The government would have to re-assess the planning permit. Any construction on the river could be paused. There was a similar case in the Yarra Valley recently. It was thought that construction would interfere with a population of rare Macquarie perch. It was proved the fish would survive so the development went ahead. The construction company was lucky though.' Dario finished his coffee in a big gulp. 'Bad press means investment jitters. Construction is big business. If investors think their money is at risk, they'll just pull out,' he said.

I watched the choppy flow of the river lurch and slop a few metres in front of me. If what Emma had seemed to be researching was true, she had the power to collapse her father's river development. Maybe even his company.

Perez had known something in the river had changed and Grant had Bowler's report in his briefcase the day he died.

Could fish be the key to a terrible secret that had killed two people?

I jumped to my feet. 'Thanks guys. Tell me what you find.'

53

I stopped at a service station close to the Westgate Bridge. I pulled up to a petrol geyser and filled the car's tank.

As the pump hummed, I looked out over the Bridge. Traffic at this time of the night was light, with only two cars passing in the Western-bound lanes at a time.

An orange Torana pulled off the freeway and rolled into the service station. It's lights briefly picked out the shape of another car parked on the side of the road that ran beside the service station. I'm not sure why I noticed that parked vehicle or why I remembered it with such clarity. My eye's training, perhaps. It seemed to be a large white sedan with the streamlined shape of that year's model.

The Torana's headlights swept past and illuminated me. Blinded, I looked away. When I turned back, the parked sedan was gone.

I paid the attendant and drove my car back onto the road that ran under the Westgate Bridge. I slowed down through the residential twists and bends of Port Melbourne and picked up speed when I reached Beach Road.

Headlights moved out of a side street and swung in behind me.

Instinctively, I checked my speed. I was doing just under sixty. The car stayed tight on my tail. The lane ahead broke into two and I kept left, thinking the driver was impatient to overtake.

The next time I looked up, the car was so close I could no longer see the headlights.

Suddenly it swung into the lane on my right and sped up until it was level with the length of my car. I looked at the driver but could only see a red baseball cap. For an instant my mind focussed on the cap. Something tugged at my memory. The cap seemed important, maybe even familiar.

I took another look at the driver. The cap obscured his features and hair.

I flicked my eyes back to the road ahead. From the corner of my eye I watched the car stay level with my own vehicle. A movement by the driver made me glance over again. I caught a metallic glint of something through the other car's open passenger window.

A gun!

I slammed on the brakes just as the shot was fired.

The bullet caught the metal frame between my driver's side window and the windscreen. The driver's side windows shattered but didn't break.

Instinctively, I ducked my head and shoulders below the gunman's line of sight, all the while wrestling with the steering wheel to keep the skidding car under control. What was worse, I wondered, to die by gunshot or to smash my car through someone's loungeroom window?

My car finally stopped. I popped my head up to window level to check where the shooter's car was. It had surged ahead and was in my lane now, slowing down ahead of me. I started my car again and accelerated into the right lane, ready to swing into a U turn and race into oncoming traffic rather than pass him.

His brake lights went off and he accelerated suddenly.

He spun left into a wide street. I heard the engine roar as he sped away.

I sped up and drove with trembling hands to the nearby St Kilda Police Station on Chapel Street. I just sat for ten minutes, trying not to stare at the shattered windows or the twisted metal that had been my car's window frame.

Finally I called Alex.

'Go into the police station. Make a report. Stay there until I arrive,' he ordered. 'Did you see who it was?'

'He was wearing a red baseball cap.'

'That's it? That's all you saw? What about the car? What colour and make?'

His voice faded. With a start, I remembered where I'd seen the cap before—at the Faber house. When we first interviewed them, Michael Faber had entered the room in a red cap.

'Michael Faber had a cap like that.'

'Faber told me he was going to the morgue tonight to oversee the arrangements for Grant. I'll call to see if he's been there,' he said.

'I was going to see Michael Faber. I'm still going to see Michael Faber.'

'Are you nuts? Stay there. We don't know where Faber is.'

'So I hide out until you find him? If you find him. Forget it, I'm not going to let anyone scare me off.'

'I'm coming down,' he said.

'No!'

'Sarah!'

I hung up on him and dialled the Faber home. Elizabeth answered on the third ring.

'Mrs Faber, where's your husband?'

A pause. 'Who is this?'

'Sorry, it's Sarah Arden. Where's Michael?'

'At the Coroner's Office. He wanted to ask some questions about how Grant died.'

I started the car again and steered it out of the carpark and into Chapel Street.

'Okay, thanks.'

'Is anything wrong?'

'No, no. Thanks. Oh wait. Elizabeth?'

'Yes?'

'Does Michael have a white car?'

'He has a white Fairlane he uses for business.'

'Is that what he drove to the Morgue?'

'I don't know. I suppose.'

I hung up and sped over to the Morgue.

On the way my mobile phone rang. It was Dario calling from the river site. 'We've taken a deep river sample of fish,' he said.

'Already?'

'It's just a toss the net in and grab it type of thing. Nothing scientific. But we found something weird.'

'Uh huh?'

'A panther fish. It looks ordinary. But when we did an impromptu autopsy, the insides were all wrong.'

'Like how?'

'Like this fish should be out in the bay, not here in the river. Its gill mechanism is for sea water, not fresh water.'

'So Emma was right. The fish are mutating. Knowing that is what killed her.'

'You don't mind if we write this up? We'd credit the discovery to Emma. A discovery like this would make a difference to our funding.'

'Go right ahead.'

I hung up.

54

Michael Faber was sitting in the foyer of the Coroner's Office, his back to me when I walked in. I explained who I was to reception and checked his log in time. Every visitor had their name and arrive time recorded. He had entered the building an hour and a half ago.

'Did he leave at any time?' I asked the receptionist.

'Not that I saw.'

He must have snuck out.

I left the reception desk and walked up behind him. 'Michael.'

He swivelled towards me. I expected him to jump in surprise or react oddly. After all, he'd just tried to kill me.

Yet he simply looked up and nodded distractedly, as if my being there were perfectly natural.

I crossed the room and stood in front of him. Unsure of what to say, I kept it neutral. 'Your wife said you wanted to speak to the doctor about the autopsy report.'

He shrugged. 'There are some things that I need to know. Although I have a feeling they won't make sense of anything.'

'You don't know that.'

'Even if it did make sense, it doesn't matter now.' He looked past me and massaged his neck with his left hand. His movements were slow and sleepy. I could jab him with a pin and he wouldn't even twitch. This man was walking dead.

How could he have just tried to kill me?

'Did you suspect it was your son who was blackmailing you?'

'I'm not going to talk about this with you, not now.'

'I've been down to the river,' I said.

'The river?'

'The land you're going to build on.'

'Oh, right.' His flat gaze seemed to be reading the posters on the wall behind me.

'What would happen to your deal if something rare was found in the water?'

His attention swung back to me. 'Something rare? What do you mean?'

'Like a new breed of fish.'

His jaw slackened slightly. That was the sign I needed.

I leaned close to him. 'I know you killed your son and daughter over the real estate deal by the Yarra.'

He leapt to life, jumping to his feet. 'You're crazy. I've got no idea what you're talking about. Leave me alone.' He stormed past me and walked to the receptionist's desk.

'You knew,' I yelled at him, 'you knew what was happening in that water. That's what he had over you. That's why Emma died!'

He waved frantically to the receptionist. 'Excuse me! This woman is harassing me. I want her removed. Call security.'

I paced over to him. 'You knew that you'd be shut down if it got out that part of the river was a breeding ground for rare fish.'

'That's absurd.'

'You could lose the deal.'

'There's always the risk that a deal will fall through. That's part of the business.'

'Emma knew first and then told Grant. He wanted you to pay up or he'd release the news.'

'Money exchanged between Grant and me is none of your business.'

'I found a report in your son's briefcase about construction pollution altering the fish of the Mekong River.'

'I have no idea what you're talking about.' He slammed a hand down on the reception desk. 'Will you call security, please!'

The receptionist backed away from the counter.

'You know exactly what I'm talking about because I know you've seen that report. Your fingerprints were on it.' It was a lie but I guessed that Grant would have shown his father the report in order to prove he could shut the development down.

Michael stared at the reception desk in silence. The receptionist stared open mouthed at us both.

I continued. 'I know the river deal was worth millions to you. I know that if it goes bust, so do you.'

He kept his eyes on the reception desk.

'It's going to come out. Scientists are already examining samples of the fish in that section of the river. They've already found irregularities. There's no way the deal can go ahead.'

Finally he looked at me. 'I don't care if the deal falls through,' he said quietly. 'Emma was right, it was theft from the start.'

'Emma said what?'

He slumped into a chair. 'None of it matters anymore. You want to know it all? Fine. Elizabeth talked me into the deal and even put up half the collateral. When Emma confronted me about the environmental damage the deal could do, it was Elizabeth who said she would talk her into understanding how important the deal was. Liz even threatened to leave me and take half the business if the deal fell through.'

'And Emma told Grant?'

He looked away, 'Emma discovered it first, but didn't know what to do. She told Grant and promised him she wouldn't tell anyone else, not even her boyfriend, until they got proof.'

'But Grant started blackmailing you.'

'Don't call it that, he was my son so it was just money between family. Of course, I didn't know who it was at the start. But then Emma found out. She told me she was going to turn him in and make the discovery about the fish public.'

'So that's why Grant wrote that Emma wanted a cut of the blackmail money?'

'That's what makes no sense to me.'

'Is that why you're here?'

'I just wanted to look at the autopsy report.'

'But for what?'

'He's my son. I don't need a reason.'

'I'll give you a reason. Someone shot at me tonight as I was driving home.'

'Really? God!'

'Someone in a white Fairlane.'

Awareness sparked in his eyes. 'You don't think it was me? I've been here nearly all night.'

'Can you prove that?'

'I don't have to. I'm not the only one who drives a white Fairlane. I have another one in the garage at home. We use a fleet of them for work.'

I took that in but didn't let him notice. 'What are you looking for in your son's autopsy report?'

'Like I said, he's my son. That's reason enough.'

'Then why isn't your son's mother here?'

'She doesn't know I'm here. She was out when I left.'

'She told me you were here.'

'She knows I'm here?' He looked afraid suddenly, eyes wide, hands clenched.

It hit me then, the final click of comprehension as everything fell into place.

Elizabeth Faber.

He suspected his wife had killed his son. And probably his daughter. I thought of the fingerprint on the glass I'd found at Emma's and on the outside of the glove. It was like Emma's, but not Emma's.

Family members can have inherited fingerprint characteristics. Something as subtle as the turn of a loop can be born our mother's, then ours. A great grandfather may give only one of his great grandchildren his twinned loop, or it may appear in every child in each generation after. And then there

291

is the suck and swirl of the ambiotic fluids. Genetics may have decided you were to have your father's radial loops rather than your mother's tented arch, but the pressure of your mother's belly fluids creates whorls instead. The randomness of environment can also intrude. Your mother unknowingly ingests a chemical or loves a food that alters the composition of her water. What was to be a loop begins to change into an arch, but stalls in between. A strange mutation of both is the result.

Inherited patterns are not rare, but they are not common.

The print on the glass was so similar to Emma's, it could only be family.

The small distinction between rare and not common had blinded me.

I knew the print was not Grant's or Michael's. There was only one person left.

Elizabeth had claimed she'd not been to Emma's flat in weeks.

If only I'd matched her print with the one on the glass, her lie would've been noted. And her story unravelled.

But Elizabeth had an alibi. Her friend June verified Elizabeth had been with her the night Emma was killed.

I recalled the last conversation I'd had with June. June knew Elizabeth wasn't with June's husband 'that night' because June had called her husband at work.

June had not denied the liaison on the grounds that Elizabeth had been with her that night, but rather because she knew the exact whereabouts of her husband. And why had she checked her husband's whereabouts?

Because she didn't know where Elizabeth Faber was either.

But I was still only guessing.

Only June could prove it.

I turned my attention back to Michael Faber. His eyes were on mine.

'Elizabeth would have lost a lot of money if Emma had leaked what she'd discovered,' I said.

'Everyone would have lost a lot of money. You can't isolate

my wife.'

'You know she did it, don't you.'

'Know what? Did what? I can't believe what you're implying!'

'I think she did it. And you're afraid she'll get to you next. But you think you're safe if she doesn't know you suspect her.'

'That's absurd.'

'You're here to check the autopsy report for any indication she killed Grant. A drug, maybe, that she slipped him to make him more compliant. Like maybe the same sedative that she gave to Emma. Or proof that there was alcohol in his body. That would be suspicious given that Grant doesn't drink anymore.'

'I paid for his alcohol treatments. He hadn't touched alcohol in a year. He was clean.'

'But your wife didn't know.'

'No, she gave up on him.' He slumped against the counter, head low, running a hand through his hair again and again.

It could have been Elizabeth who tried to shoot me. She had access to the red cap. The Faber's had two white Fairlanes.

Yet she had answered the home phone when I rang.

'What happens if I ring your home phone when no one's home?' I asked him.

'It diverts to Liz's mobile.'

How does it feel to be married to a murderer? I wondered.

I patted him on the back of the hand and motioned for the receptionist. 'Go ahead and call security. Get a guard to sit with him until the police arrive.' To Michael I said: 'I'll call someone to take you somewhere safe. You can't go home right now.'

I left him sitting in the waiting room of the Coroner's Office and called Alex.

'Send someone to the Morgue and take Faber back to St Kilda Road.'

'I went down to Chapel Street to get you. The duty cop said no-one had been in. You didn't even file a report!'

293

'There was no time. Look, I think we've been looking in the wrong direction. We need to go to the Faber house and check that Elizabeth Faber is at home. If she's not, we need to find her.'

'Elizabeth Faber? What do you have on her?'

'Michael Faber thinks she did it—so do I.'

'But what evidence do you have? She's the one with strongest alibi.'

'I'm not so sure about that.'

'I spoke to June McNaughton myself.'

'I think she was lying.'

'I think you're still feeling traumatised from the shooting.'

'Please, Alex. Just confirm that Elizabeth's at home. Tell her it's for her own safety or whatever. I'll call you in a half hour or so.' I hung up before he could answer.

55

I knocked on June McNaughton's door. When she appeared, she was still dressed in day clothes despite the late hour.

'What do you want now?' she demanded. 'Haven't you done enough?'

'We know Elizabeth wasn't with you the night Emma died.'

Shock tightened her face. 'That's not true.'

'If you had to ring your husband to check if he was with Elizabeth, then she obviously wasn't with you.'

'I meant later, after she'd left.'

'Stop covering for her, June. Where did she tell you she was that night? Out with her imaginary lover? He had to be imaginary because the only person she was screwing was your husband.'

'That's a lie.'

'And now she's screwing you over, that's for sure. You'll go down with her if you keep lying.'

'I'm not lying. She was here.'

'Not at the time Emma was killed. The police are going out to her place now. You can expect them soon too.'

'I've done nothing wrong.'

'Where do you think she was that night? How naive are you? She killed both of them. Her own children.'

'You don't know that. You can't say that.'

'You know it too, June.' I said quietly. 'What time did she

leave?'

'I told you all this already.'

'She tried to kill me tonight. I work for the police and she tried to kill me. When is she going to come for you? If I were you I wouldn't be meeting her in any quiet places. If she killed her own children and tried to kill me, then she'll think nothing of rubbing you out.'

June pressed her hands against her ears. 'Stop it, just stop it.'

'What time did she leave here?'

Tears ran down June's face.

'She's already ruined your relationship with your husband. How stupid are you that you think you owe this woman something?'

'She gave me a job when no one else would. She lent me money to pay off my gambling debts. She made me get help. She was my friend when everyone else had abandoned me.'

'Some friend. She steals your husband and asks you to lie to the police. If that's your definition of a friend then you've got some weird dictionary. She's using you. She was probably using you all along. The only reason she solved your gambling problem was to get you in her pocket.'

'You can't say that!'

'If she's done nothing wrong then why does she want you to lie?'

'All right, all right. Ten minutes. She was here for ten minutes that night. She left at seven o'clock.'

'You need to tell the police this.'

Her hand covered her mouth and she began to sob.

I called Alex.

'Listen to this,' I told him. I handed the mobile to June. 'Tell him.'

In between sobs she repeated what she'd told me.

When she'd finished I hugged her and handed her a tissue.

'Is she still at home?' I asked Alex.

'I didn't want to tell you this, but it appears that she's left.'

'She's left?'

June's eyes grew wide. 'Oh my god! She could be coming here.'

'I guess you inadvertently warned her when you called,' Alex told me.

'Did you check her office building?' I asked him.

'Not yet. Maybe she just went out for a walk.'

'More likely she went out shooting. I'm dropping June at the police station.'

'I want you to stay there too.'

'Sure.' I hung up and called June a taxi. 'I'll wait with you until it arrives.'

As we waited, June gathered enough clothes for a few days stay away from home. I figured Elizabeth Faber was driving to the airport, boarding a plane out of this mess and into a new life.

But that took time to organise. Where would she lie low?

What if she didn't realise she was being looked for? As far as she knew, we were still gunning for Michael.

Something still nagged at me. Surely she'd know we didn't have enough evidence to arrest Michael. If we did, he'd be in custody already. Everything against Michael so far was circumstantial. We had nothing to place him at the crime scene physically. Had she planted something at the house to implicate him? But that could just as easily implicate her.

Unless she planted it somewhere else. Somewhere only he had access to. Like his office. But his office was organised and arranged by his secretary. If anything was there that he and his receptionist hadn't found, it would have to be hidden in an infrequently accessed spot.

What could be planted that implicated Michael? So far we had found the gun in Perez's cave and the Zaparin drugs in Grant Faber's bathroom. There had been no mention of the test tubes in Grant's suicide note. They'd been destroyed, I was sure of it. If the samples of river water had the power to bankrupt a company and take two lives, there was no way they'd just be hidden at the back of the killer's wardrobe.

So what other evidence had we not recovered?

Suddenly I felt sick.
Only one thing remained missing.
The skin of Emma's fingertips.

56

I parked my car right outside Michael Faber's office block and scanned the windows for lights. All seventeen floors were black.

The front doors were locked, so I followed the narrow lane that ran along the side of the building. The back entrance of the skyscraper was a metal fire door with a standard round lock. I had it open in five minutes. There was an alarm pad on a panel inside the door. My heart jumped. Of course there'd be an alarm. How could I have not thought of that? I swung to face the control panel. A LCD display read 'unarmed.'

I let out a sign of relief. A red light flashed in what was labelled as sector ten.

It stopped and then lit up again.

Someone else was in the building.

There was no indication which part of the building was sector ten.

I took the lift up to the eleventh floor.

The venetian blinds over Michael Faber's windows were drawn. I picked the lock on his office door and, once inside, kept the lights off.

I shone my flashlight around the room. His desk looked the same as when I first saw it. The blinds and the ensuite door were closed. The filing cabinet was locked.

I started with Michael Faber's desk, but found nothing

incriminating. I turned to his filing cabinets. The lock was old and I opened it with a paperclip. I found nothing unusual. I opened the large cupboard doors. Inside, the top shelf held a stack of storage boxes. I pulled the top one out and flipped off the lid.

It held old diaries and a small ornate wooden box. I lifted the wooden lid. Inside was a specimen jar with what looked like scraps of skin.

Emma's fingerprints.

The ensuite door opened open and a torch beam bounced into the room.

I squeezed my eyes shut against the sudden explosion of light as the beam hit my face.

The person holding the beam gave a feminine yelp of surprise. 'What are you doing here?'

It was Elizabeth Faber's voice.

I forced my eyes open. As my vision adjusted, I could make out her form in the doorway.

'Answer me,' she said.

Elizabeth Faber had already killed two people. There was no way I was going to admit that I was looking for her. 'The police are with Michael. I had a feeling I'd find something of Emma's here.'

She lowered the beam from my face. I could see her clearly now. She was wearing navy blue slacks and a black turtleneck. One hand held the flashlight, the other was empty.

'Something of Emma's?'

I waved the specimen jar in the air quickly. Her eyes followed the jar's flight through the air.

'Emma's fingerprints. It's better that you don't look. Michael kept her skin. But you obviously suspected something like that. Why else would you be here?'

She was silent.

'You need to come to the police with me.'

'I don't think so.'

'They'll want to talk to you. About Michael.'

'I'll meet you there.'

'No, we'd better go together.'

She stared at me and shrugged. 'Fine then.'

We left the office and exited out into the back alley, me first, she a few steps behind.

I stopped and stepped to the side quickly. It wasn't safe to have her behind me. I paused to let her pass. Suddenly I felt a gush of air ruffle the hair at the back of my head.. Something hit me across the skull with such force that I stumbled forward and fell to my knees. My vision fizzled, then blackened.

I could hear her moving around me.

When my vision returned she was standing over me with a fire extinguisher in her hands.

I sat up groggily.

'Why didn't you just leave us alone?' she mused.

'Let me go.' I stuttered. 'My department knows I'm here.'

'Of course they do. That's why you were lurching about with the lights off.'

'Just turn yourself in, Elizabeth. We know you killed Emma.'

She shook her head. 'You think I'm an abhorrence, I know. But they were useless, both of them. One a degenerate who joins the police force to be above the law, the other a moral crusader who would bring down her own father to save a piece of land for a race she doesn't even belong to. A daughter who tries to drive her father bankrupt, and a son who finds out and then tries to blackmail his own father. Who is the abhorration?'

'You killed Grant too.'

'I had to. He worked out that it was me who had stopped Emma.'

'Stopped Emma? You mean killed Emma.'

'Yes.'

'And you made the man who loves your daughter a suspect, then your own husband, then a poor homeless man who can't even communicate. Are you trying to destroy as many lives as you can?'

'They were all leeches,' she said.

'But why kill them? You could have turned Grant over to the police, you could have warned your husband about Emma's desire to save the land.'

'My children wanted me to lose everything. I'm a solicitor. I process the cases of their kind every day. I know where this would have ended up.'

'It could have ended up in a court, not a cemetery.'

'It would have been the end of me. It was my money that my husband was investing on the river development, my money that Grant was blackmailing him for, and my money that Emma was going to lose with her save-the-environment crusade. I gave them everything and they tried to destroy me. So I had to destroy them first.'

I inched backwards until my spine was against the wall. I felt a warm splash against my cheek. When I touched a hand to my face, I saw my fingers speckled with blood.

She set the extinguisher down by her feet. 'You think it's a crime against nature to kill your own children, yet as a mother I'm expected to give my life for them. They lived off me from their moment of conception, for another nine months after that, and then I was expected to risk my life to birth them. As if that's not enough, I had to nearly kill off my professional life to mother them.'

'It was your choice to have children. You can't blame them for their own conception!'

'I don't. I loved my children. I just didn't expect to have to suspend my existence for theirs for the rest of my life. I willingly let them consume me when they were young. I asked nothing in return, just to have my own life back when they became adults. But what happened? One is so greedy that he sucks our finances, my money, dry and the other is so ungrateful that she would send us to ruin for a species of fish and a piece of land. They wouldn't have stopped until I ended up in the gutter. So I had to stop them first.'

'That's insane.'

'What's insane is that they assumed I would let them be parasites all over again. That I would let them bleed me dry again.'

'You went to Emma's house and slipped her the drugs. You cleaned the place up and got rid of the test tubes. Why plant the gloves?'

'That wasn't planned. The day before Emma died I was at Grant's house. The gloves were in his bathroom bin. He'd had a tattoo of some kind done and had worn them around the house so the tattoo wouldn't get infected. Or maybe it was so the ink wouldn't run. It doesn't matter. I realised that I'd need gloves to wear when I was clearing up at Emma's house. So I just took them out of his bin.'

'After you drugged her, you took her down to the beach. You shot her there, on the sand, and arranged it all so that it looked ritualistic. Like something you thought the strange old man would do. Then you made June McNaughton lie so that you had an alibi. That morning you said you drove down to Emma's house. You didn't really go there, did you?'

'No. Grant called me to say that he'd read Emma was dead in the newspapers. He was distraught, out of control. He accused me of killing her. He said that he knew she was going to blow the whistle on their father's deal, that I was the only one who would have reason to kill her. I told him if he wasn't careful, the same thing might happen to him. I convinced Grant to lead the police to the old man.'

'But we settled on Charlie Hunt first.'

'Yes. Your homicide detective, Peterson, was pushing me to give information on Grant, but I couldn't let Grant be implicated. He would have just turned on me, so when Peterson mentioned Hunt, I went with it. You all seemed so happy with that.'

That explained why Grant Faber had seemed surprised that Charlie was our first suspect. He had been expecting Elizabeth to point to Perez. So when Hunt checked out, Grant readily pushed Perez's name forward.

'So if your plan eventually kicked in, why kill Grant?'

'I didn't realise he was blackmailing Michael. Once I knew, I realised there would be no stopping him. If he blackmailed his father over a business deal, imagine what he would try on me over a murder. There was no way out except to stop him permanently.'

'So you faked his suicide.'

'It wasn't hard. He thought that being a cop made him smarter than me. That made him let his guard down. He didn't know what hit him,' she said.

'How did you make him write the suicide note.'

'I put a gun to his head, of course.'

'His own gun?'

'Grant had always kept a gun in the hall cupboard. He hadn't changed.'

'And the gun you used to kill Emma was Grant's.'

'He stored his guns in our garage for a while. I had the key to the cabinet and to a chest he used to store the unregistered ones.'

'You just took one.'

'An unregistered one, of course. I hid it in our bedroom. Michael never noticed.' She nodded towards the doorway. 'Stand up and start walking.'

My eyes took in the extinguisher in her hands. It was too heavy to throw a long distance. The only way she could use it against me was to swing it at my head. Again.

I took a sidestep away from her.

She laughed. 'Oh no, you don't.' She dropped the extinguisher to the floor with a crash and pulled out a gun from her jacket pocket. 'This is another one of Grant's. It's registered, so I don't want to use it. But I will if I have to. Now, move.' She pointed it at me and flicked the barrel towards the door. 'Let's go.'

As I passed her she took a step backwards and fell in behind me.

Something hit me and I stumbled forward.

The back of my head felt like it had exploded. I heard her grunt and then her voice: 'Look what you've done, what you made me do'.

I was Emma, then me, then Emma again.

The lino floor was hard against my face. How did it get so high?

How could it be wrapping around me?

I heard the sound of my bones resisting gravity as the floor tried to absorb my fall. Where did my legs go? I felt my teeth shift in my gums, my jaw shoot sideways. My shoulder seemed to jolt out of its joint as I rolled against the floor. Every bone in my body seemed to move.

But I could not.

57

I could smell the river before I'd even opened my eyes.

My brain throbbed as if someone were prying each fissure of my skull apart with a chisel. With each beat of pain, nausea swilled around the base of my throat, trying to bubble to the root of my tongue and up into my thoughts.

When I finally opened my eyes, I was lying on the back seat of a car. My hands were tied together at my chest with blue material, my feet bound at the ankles with rope. The car was stationary. The door at my feet was open. Beyond my feet I could see the moonlight sparkle of the river as it pushed through the darkness.

The car rocked up and down. Through the rear window I could see the boot was open. I watched Elizabeth lift a blue tarp out of the boot and toss it to the ground.

I quickly closed my eyes as the boot slammed shut.

Playing dead seemed the wisest thing to do. If she knew I was awake, she'd be more cautious. This way I might have a chance to overpower her. The seat beneath my head felt sticky. I licked my lips. They tasted metallic.

The flavour of blood.

I heard her footsteps near the open door and sensed her standing at my feet. She grabbed my feet and pulled me roughly from the car.

I bit my tongue in pain as my back bounced against the

metal of the door frame and hit the ground. I managed to lift my head so that it hit the earth last and softly.

She spread the tarp out next to me and rolled me onto it. I felt a rough weight on my legs.

A rock.

Suddenly I got the picture. She was going to weigh me down and tip me into the river. I swallowed my panic. Once I was in the water, I'd be in trouble. There'd be no way I could get out of the plastic tomb with my arms and legs bound.

I heard her move away. I opened my eyes and saw her back to me, bent low to the ground. Looking for more rocks in the darkness.

I strained my hands against their ties. The material stretched a little. I lifted my wrists as high as I could and lowered my head. With my teeth I pulled at the material. It loosened enough for me to slip my hands out.

Quickly, I worked at the rope that bound my legs. The knots were tight.

Elizabeth's body turned towards me. I dropped onto my back and clutched my hands together as if they were still tied.

When I heard her move towards the water, I opened an eye.

She was fossicking around at the water's edge, her back to me.

I sat up and lifted the rock off my legs. I rolled off the tarp as quietly as I could, cringing when the plastic rustled. She didn't turn around.

I tried to undo the rope at my ankles again. Forget it, I thought, it's too tight.

With a burst, I threw myself upright and leaned backwards until my balance was squarely on the soles of my feet.

I was standing.

I bent over at the waist and picked up the rock, then tried to waddle up behind her. The bindings around my legs only let me take tiny steps. It would have been easier to jump, but I was afraid she'd hear the thump of my feet.

She moved backwards on her haunches, coming closer to me inch by inch, her hands still searching the ground at her feet for rocks.

It only took a few seconds to reach her. I raised the rock above my head.

Suddenly she turned towards me. Maybe she heard the rustling of my clothes or perhaps she sensed my shadow looming over her.

Her eyes widened in surprise.

I hesitated for a second, instinct holding me back. I didn't want to kill her. I couldn't. But it was her or me.

She took advantage of my pause. Surging forward, she rounded her shoulders and thrust herself at my chest. The blow knocked me backwards.

I lost control of the rock, feeling it sway above my head.

It slipped from my hands and tumbled downwards as I fell backwards.

Her face loomed over me, her body following me to the ground.

I saw the rock as if it were in slow motion, gravity pulling it towards my head.

We hit the ground together, her body pinning me.

The rock hit her at the point where her neck became her head. Her eyes bulged in shock. Her head slammed forwards and hit my chest hard enough to wind me.

She tried to raise herself off me. I felt her hands pushing and scratching my chest, trying to find leverage. Our arms were locked between our bodies. I rolled to the left quickly.

She slipped off and hit the river's sloping bank face down. The lower section of her head was a pulpy mess. Blood trickled from the corner of her mouth.

Her body rolled downwards towards the water.

I toppled away from her and turned on my stomach. I rose to my knees and then rocked backwards until I had enough momentum to jump to my feet.

I heard a splash. By the time I managed to turn around, the river had closed over her. She was a shadow beneath the murky waves, rushing away from me towards the mouth of the sea.

The river held her at its mouth, shifting her from left to right bank, rolling her like a log below the surface. The white of her hair flashed above the water like the flicker of a flame. Her head bobbed through the surface.

Her eyes opened.

She was still alive.

I hopped down to the shore and threw myself in. With my legs tied, I couldn't tread. Nevertheless I tried to steer through the water towards her. My own weight pulled me down and my lungs felt like they were trying to push past my bones and through my skin.

The blackness of the river circled me, then closed in.

Peterson's face creased into a relieved scowl as it loomed above me.

'You idiot!' he yelled. The force of his breath scattered the debris that the river had slicked to my hair.

I tried to yell back but all my lungs could expel was a gurgle of water.

'Shh,' Alex's faced appeared on the corner of my vision. He smoothed back my hair. His own hair was plastered to his face. His arm under my shoulders was wet.

'She's in the water,' I finally coughed out.

'We can't find her. She'd be out in the bay by now.'

'She was conscious. She could have swum to the shore just before the opening to the bay.'

'She's gone, Sarah. I saw her go under,' Alex said. 'Just lie still for a minute.'

I tried to sit up.

Peterson smiled. 'See, she still can't take orders.'

58

'I don't understand it,' Dario said.

Alex and I were standing on the west bank of Yarra, at the geologists' camp. Dario pulled the electronic float from the edge of the water, reset it, and then threw it back into the river.

The three of us watched it gently bob up and down in the same spot. The water slopped in slow, lazy troughs against the bank.

'Where's the cross point of the current?' Dario said. 'How can it just disappear?'

From the skip anchored in the centre of the river, Carl caught the float with a pole and dragged it through the water. 'Nothing!' he yelled at us.

'Try circles at starboard,' Dario called.

Carl manoeuvred the float around the skip. He shook his head.

'The flow from the underground source must have stopped,' Dario said.

I hugged my coat closer around my body. The wind off the bay was flaccid but still icy against the uncovered skin of my face. Alex unwound his scarf from his neck and curled it around mine. The wool felt warm through the bandage at the back of my head.

'You must have got enough data from the last few weeks,'

Alex said.

Dario shrugged. 'Not enough to explain what happened. All we can hope is that the cross flows suddenly come back. We'll have to keep monitoring them.'

I slapped him on the shoulder. 'At least you've got the fish abnormalities to write up!'

Environmental agencies had granted the geologists' six months worth of funding and a marine biology team to investigate the mutations in fish. The construction site had been blocked by government legislation. The river would no longer be ignored, but it would be left to decide its own course.

We left the geologists watching the currents for changes that would never occur again.

From that moment on, whenever I crossed the river I always hurried across.

Praise for
THE MEMORY OF MARBLE
Carolyn Beasley
The Collected Short Stories

'The Memory of Marble' is a collection of ten stories that examine the boundaries we create between passion and obsession. The people in the stories seek refuge from emotions by cocooning themselves in the worlds of books, pianos, art, and fingerprints.

"…has the quality of an exquisite mathematical equation"
Fiona Capp on the story 'Temperament'.

"An amazing story, really arouses the tactile responses of the reader. My fingertips tingled"

Ania Walwicz on the story 'Cocoon'

"…proposes complex inner states of human consciousness through simple objects and the conglomerates of everyday life…This is the kind of domestic drama that reaches the proportions of the unknowable universe."

Ania Walwicz on the story 'The Clock Collector'

"shows sensitive understanding…"
Colleen Geebel, Judge of the Sunshine Coast 7th Annual Short Story Competition

"Imaginative…and beautifully developed"
Lyn Hatherly Wilson, Judge of the Mount Isa Annual Literary Competition

Lighthouse

www.ingramcontent.com/pod-product-compliance
Lightning Source LLC
Chambersburg PA
CBHW032206030726
47494CB00020B/635